Raider

Book 2 in the

Combined Operations Series

By

Griff Hosker

Published by Sword Books Ltd 2015

Copyright © Griff Hosker First Edition

A CIP catalogue record for this title is available from the British
Library.

Cover by Design for Writers

Dedicated to my little sister, Barb, and in memory of my dad who served in Combine Operations from 1941-1945

Chapter 1

If we thought that when we returned from our raid in northern France that we would be afforded a leave then we were sadly mistaken. We were moved instead, to join the rest of Number 4 Commando at Weymouth. I suspect part of the reasoning behind the move was the problems caused by the Luftwaffe who had spread their bombing raids to the whole of the south east. Harwich was not safe any longer. We could not get out of the harbour as easily as we had.

We travelled by lorries to our new homes. It was a shame to be leaving the old one for we had learned many important skills there. Daddy shook his head when I complained about leaving our old home. "The way I see it, Tom, moving us around will help to improve our ability to fight. We have to learn to adapt to each new place. Besides the Germans guns, the bombers and even the ships shelling the land were causing more casualties than we could afford. And this new base, at Weymouth, will be dead handy for the Channel."

Sergeant Major Dean felt he owed Sergeant Daddy Grant and me a favour for the work we had done with the new section. It was now the best in the whole troop. He found four boarding houses close by each other along the sea front. There was little business for them and they were more than happy to accommodate the non-commissioned officers. It saved us a job. We were all close together and the landladies were delighted to have an income and be part of the war effort. Far from demoralising the British people the German raids had created community spirit in a way the Germans could never have predicted.

Gordy Baker grumbled, "Except we'll have longer at sea when we do cross the Channel. More chance for Jerry to jump us and more chance for us to be seasick."

Norm Ford said, "A right moaning Minnie you are!"

The bickering and bantering was a good sign. It showed that they were happy. Silence was always a worry. Luckily, they were rarely that.

"What do you think about the RAF, Corp?"

"What do you mean, Polly?"

Polly Poulson was a bit of a worrier and, I suspect, a thinker. "Well your old man is RAF brass, isn't he? Will they beat the Krauts? If we can't beat the Luftwaffe then they can just come over. They have these new paratroopers, don't they? They could land by air. Wouldn't even need to come by sea."

They all knew that my dad was a war hero and a Wing Commander. They didn't know that he was in the Middle East and knew as much about the battle over London as we did. "I am not certain what my dad would think. But I do know this; I grew up on RAF bases. We have the best fighter in the world in the Spitfire. Our pilots are the best and we are hitting them for six when they come over."

"Aye but they have started knocking London about a bit, haven't they?"

"They did that in the Great War too. The Germans were the ones who invented bombing civilian targets. My mum was in London in the war and she told me about it. It doesn't mean they will win."

Daddy threw his dog end out of the back of the lorry, "Corporal Harsker is right but I reckon the bombing is going to get worse before it gets better. That is why our little jaunt across the Channel was so important. We were hitting back at old Adolph and he won't like that believe me. This isn't over yet. We British are tough and it takes more than an Austrian house painter to beat us. You just do your job, Poulson, and everything will turn out fine."

I knew why Polly was worried. His family lived just north of London. The German bombers were a little indiscriminate in their targets and were causing widespread civilian damage. Some dropped their bombs early and some late. Daylight bombing guaranteed success. The Spitfires and Hurricanes had caused the Germans to change to night time raids. To many of the lads it seemed despicable and underhand that the Germans were hitting their families. That was not right. Most had joined up to fight and would be happy to take on any number of Germans. The ones who had volunteered for the Commandos were even more determined to fight back than most.

After we had found our digs and checked out our new operational base Daddy and I found a pub to have a quiet pint. We had not had a chance to talk about our new squad since we had returned from the raid. For both of us it had been our first experience at leading men under fire. Dad had always said that being a leader was easy; perhaps that was just him. Ted and Gordy, his comrades, said that he made it look easy. I was not so sure. Too many things could go wrong. When did you trust the lads to do jobs on their own without checking? My sudden promotion had caught me unawares.

As we sipped the indifferent beer Daddy said, "I think we have been lucky with our lads. They didn't panic under fire. I think that we should count our blessings. If we had handpicked them we couldn't have a better team."

I nodded, "The trouble is that we have made two raids and in both of them we encountered totally different problems. How do we prepare the lads for the unexpected?"

"The Corps has done that, Tom, giving us seemingly impossible tasks, like getting from Oswestry to Poole without money. Having to find our own digs, find our own food. You were in the regulars like I was. We were told when to eat and when to do spud bashing. Our lads have to think for themselves. It breeds the right spirit.

"I'll tell you what will make a difference; if they could speak a little of the local lingo. I mean it stands to reason that we will be operating where they don't speak English."

"Then teach 'em. You speak French and a bit of German."

"I'm no teacher."

"No, you are a corporal in the Commandos. You would be able to show them how to strip a Colt wouldn't you?"

"Yes but…"

"Then it is the same with French. Teach them what you know. I wouldn't mind learning a few words too. Consider it part of our training regime eh?"

"Well if you think it will do any good."

He grinned and downed the beer, "I reckon we are going to be behind enemy lines more than we are at home! It will help. Believe me."

The next day we were marched to a cinema in the town. It had been closed for the duration. Outside stood a dozen redcaps. We piled in, wondering what this was about. Sergeant Major Dean roared, "Attention!"

We all stood. It was not easy to do so for they were cinema seats. Officers marched in following what looked like a gamekeeper wearing a sweater and carrying a stick. He was both tall and lean; at his side stood a Scottish piper. It was bizarre. He said, "Sit down. Smoke if you wish." There was a ripple of noise as we sat down and I saw Sergeant Major Dean glaring at the one or two who whispered to their neighbours.

He folded his arms behind his back and rocked gently backwards and forwards as he spoke. "Number 4 Commando I am Lord Lovat and I am the chap who gives you your orders. I have been the one who has sent you behind the lines on these jolly little jaunts. Number 4 Commando is mine and I want it to be the best! Now that we are all together, no matter how briefly, I thought we should get to know one another. We won't always work together. That isn't the Commando way but you will find that I am not a staff officer who sits on his backside sending others to do his bidding." There was a ripple of laughter. "I am going to be with you on these raids. Not all of them," he smiled, "I don't want to hog all the glory but I will be there. And when we are not sneaking in and we are attacking like other soldiers then you will know where I am for you will hear the pipes of Billy Millins here. You won't need to look for me. You will hear me and I will be ahead of you. That is my way. You will follow the pipes. If you go forward when we go to battle then you can't go far wrong."

Despite the glares from Sergeant Major Dean everyone cheered.

Lord Lovat held up his hands for silence. "You have done some damn fine work up to now. The raid on those guns at Calais was particularly good. But I have to say that was just the start. We are going to raid and the raids will be bigger and more spectacular. We have shown Whitehall what we can do and they want more of it! Tomorrow a large number of you will be boarding a train and heading north with me. In fact, the majority of you will be doing so. The rest will have other important jobs to do so don't feel neglected," he paused, "and those jobs won't be in England. They will be where the Germans don't want us to be, in occupied Europe."

Again, we cheered.

He looked up at the circle and down at the stalls in the cinema where people had laughed at Will Hay and George Formby, "Some of us won't survive this war. We all know that and only a fool would think otherwise. You have proved you are no fools already. Those who fall know this; we shall never forget you and you will have died to keep this island, our home, free from the German jackboot. We are soldiers of the King and we will fight. Gentlemen, it is a privilege and an honour to be your commanding officer." He saluted and strode off. He went to applause such as might have greeted a movie star or a footballer scoring a winning goal at Wembley. We had a real leader!

Major Foster stood, "Sergeant Major Dean will read out a list of those troops which will need to pack for their journey north. As for the rest you need to stay where you are. You are the ones who will be remaining here in Weymouth. "He pointed to the circle, "When the others have left those who are in the circle come down to the stalls."

Reg Dean stood in the centre of the stage and bellowed for silence. It was instantaneous. He read out the names of the Commandos who would be leaving. It was a large number. "You will all draw cold weather gear from the Quarter Master. You will not need your digs for some months!" He actually smiled. It was both intriguing and enigmatic. Where were they going? "Good luck and off you go!"

There was a hubbub of noise as they departed. Some were leaving friends and there was a ripple of goodbyes. The rest of those who would be staying gradually filtered down from the circle and filled in the seats in the stalls. Soon we were ready to find out what we would be doing. Major Foster stood. He gestured to the side and a Major with the red collar of a staff officer came out from the wings. Sergeant Major Dean unfurled a large map of northern France which had red dots close to the coast and swastikas dotted all over.

Major Foster said, by way of introduction, "This is Major Howard and he will explain, in broad details, what we will be doing for the next few weeks."

I wondered if this staff officer would be the usual type, totally out of touch with ordinary soldiers. As soon as he spoke I knew he was not.

"The job you are going to do over the days to come will be both highly dangerous and difficult. I want none of you under any illusions about that. The battle over London and the airfields means that every aeroplane we possess has to be used for the defence of this island. We have not aircraft to spare to reconnoitre behind enemy lines. I daresay there will be French and Belgian resistance groups soon but the truth of the matter is that until we defeat the Luftwaffe and get intelligence from the ground it will be up to you to give us that information. You will become the new eyes and ears of the whole country. But it will be dangerous. If you are picked up behind enemy lines the odds are that at best you will be a prisoner of war and at worst, shot!"

He turned and took a pointer before going to the map. I liked his honesty. "We know that there are German troops in all of these places marked with a swastika. The trouble is we don't know if they are an army, a corps, or a regiment. They are the soldiers who will invade England should the RAF fail. The red dots mark the places you will be landed. We need you to find out as much information as you can. And I mean any information. Position of camps, names of regiments, airfields, petrol dumps, anti-aircraft guns; everything! If you can get a prisoner then so much the better but you will be behind enemy lines for at least twenty-four hours. Jerry has had months to begin making defences. We know what was there we now need to know what is there. The Navy will drop you off and pick you up."

There was a hum around the cinema as that information was taken in. "Quiet!" Once again, the stentorian tones of the Sergeant Major affected silence.

"And it is for that reason that you will be landed in ten-man sections." He walked to the front of the stage. "Lord Lovat just told you that many of you will not survive this war. I am here to tell you that I do not expect all of you to return. If half of you make it back then I will regard that as a success. It is cold and it is hard but it is also the truth. I wish it were otherwise but we need to face the facts here. Jerry has kicked our arse good and proper. We need to stop him from invading and then find a way of hitting back and finally, a way to retake France. It will be a long job. You are the boys who are up to it." He nodded as though he was punctuating his speech. "Now you gather every tiny piece of information you can: paths leading from beaches, woods, hedgerows, where there is water, villages, sign posts, everything. So long as one man from each group makes it back then we will have a better picture of what we face. That is the reason we chose the Commandos for this job. You can think and you have shown you can survive behind enemy lines." He pointed to Major Foster. "The Major here has your section assignments. Good luck and I hope to see you again."

As he strode off I heard Norm Ford grumble, "Cheerful bugger, isn't he?"

I hissed, "Shut it!"

Once we were given our maps and orders we dispersed to different parts of the cinema, the foyer, the circle, the concession stands, the manager's office so that we could discuss our mission. The redcaps still prevented anyone from entering.

Daddy read the orders. "Right lads its looks like we go in without an officer. I will take that as a compliment. It means they trust us. And I trust you to get it right." Everyone nodded and smiled. "We have got the area north of Boulogne and south of Dunkirk." He nodded to me, "Which is handy as Tom here knows the area. We will be dropped off after dark and picked up twenty-four hours later."

Bert said, "I would have thought they knew all there was about that place. For God's sake, last summer there were three hundred thousand lads on those beaches!"

Daddy filled his pipe. His wife was trying to get him off cigarettes. "You got me there, Bert. But if I heard the Major right then we don't know what Jerry has done since we were making sandcastles and waiting to be picked up off the beach."

While he tamped down his tobacco I said, "We know what it looked like. Jerry has had months now to make it his own. I can't imagine he would leave it the way it was. It is the closest part of Herr Adolph's empire to England. And besides it is the size of the army that might be coming over that's important. The Major was on the money; we need to know who is coming over."

With his pipe now drawing Daddy had had time to think, "The Corporal is right and any road up we have a job to do. There's blokes with more brass on their collars who decide these sorts of things. We just do our bit." He pointed with his pipe at me, "And another thing while I remember Tom and me have decided we all ought to speak a bit of Frog and Kraut. It might come in handy. Every spare minute Professor Harsker will run a language class."

Surprisingly enough they all seemed keen.

Lieutenant Reed came by, "Everything tickety boo, Sergeant Grant?"

"Yes sir, we have our objectives. The lads know what we are to do. Sorry you won't be with us this time."

He nodded his agreement. "They are short of French speakers and they have put me with another section this trip. Harsker here is as good as any. I won't lie. I wish I was coming with you boys but next time eh? You need to go to the Quartermaster and draw your rations and ammunition. We are to board the MLs as soon as it is dark. We sail overnight and we will wait off the south coast of Kent tomorrow. The intention is hide up in the river close to Rye and set off again after dark. German reconnaissance aeroplanes have been flying over our bases. You will all be issued with camouflage nets."

Polly said, "Two days on an ML sir? That seems a long time. They are only little boats."

"I am afraid so Poulson. With so many German aeroplanes flying overhead we don't want Fritz to know there are almost twenty launches waiting to pop over. At least we only have one night in the Channel. Anyway, chaps, if you are all done you had best pop over to the QM."

We had been on raids enough times to know what was useful to take and what was not. You could never have enough ammunition and Mills bombs. You could forage for food and find water. You could improvise shelter but you couldn't conjure up ammo. We made the men pack their Bergens in front of us. There was no rush. We were the first ones at the stores. Daddy and I went around and added extra ammo and grenades in the Bergens which had less in them. When we left, hefting the camouflage nets, all of us had full packs. We headed for the harbour. There was an empty building we were using to assemble while we waited for dark.

"Tom, you are a good scrounger, take Gordy and see if you can rustle up some grub eh? We'll get some from the Navy but..."

I dropped my Bergen and weapons, "Righto Sarge. Come on Gordy. Grab a bag eh?" As we left I said, "We'll just go and give the MLs the once over. It is always good to know where they are."

We headed down to the harbour. There was a substantial wall which made it a calm anchorage. I saw the MLs, MTBs, and MGBs moored in neat lines. The MLs looked naked compared with the other two types of vessels which bristled with weaponry. All of them were protected by barrage balloons and I saw anti-aircraft guns ringing the harbour. We walked down the harbour wall until we came to a fishing boat which had just tied up.

"Here is a likely candidate. We'll just hang around."

"They'll not give us fish, Corp. They'll wanna sell it."

"You never know." We lounged against the wall and watched. They were sorting the fish out into those they would sell and those they would throw back. When one of them picked up the box with small fish ready to throw them back I said, "Instead of throwing them out could we have them?"

"There's bugger all on them laddie."

"Aye I know but..."

He shook his head and gave me the box. "You lads must be bloody hungry if you'll eat a bit of skin and bone."

"You'd be surprised."

I watched as he took the heads off the large fish. This time I didn't say anything. "I am guessing you want these too?"

"Got it in one." He added them to our box. I gave him a quick salute, "Thank you kindly captain!"

The crew laughed. Gordy said, "I agree with him. This won't feed the lads."

"Oh, ye of little faith. Back to that green grocer we saw." When we reached the green grocer, I managed to cadge the outer leaves from some cauliflowers, a few potatoes which were starting to shoot, and some old onions, also growing old and furry. The greatest treasure I found was a bulb of garlic. For some reason, the British had never cottoned on to that member of the allium family. I got it for nothing. I pointed to his shelf. There was a rusting tin of tomatoes. "How much for the tomatoes?"

"Tuppence."

I handed over the money and we took it back to the empty building. There had been a kitchen and there was a large pot. I set to work. Everyone gathered around and wrinkled their noses. "I'm not eating that Corp!"

"Listen Bert when I have finished you will be asking for more."

I chopped the onion and the garlic. We had no oil and so I used a little water to cook and soften them. Finally, I added the chopped cauliflower leaves and potatoes and the tomatoes. "Gordy see if you can find another pan and something to strain the water."

By now everyone was so interested that Gordy had company for his hunt. When he returned I chopped up all the small fish and fish heads and cooked them in the water. He had found an old colander, which was perfect. After twenty minutes, I strained the fish through the colander and then used my hand to press the bits through as well. It got rid of any bones. The fish soup could have done with herbs and a little bread but it would have to do.

"Right lads, grub up. Fish stew."

Bert sniffed, "Smells better than it did when you started."

Sergeant Grant shook his head, "Just get it down your gob. Tom's given us all a good lesson in how to forage. Well done Corporal." They all ate heartily and that pleased me. "Where did you learn to cook like this?"

"We had a cottage in France and mum watched the locals make this. I used to help her make it." I pointed a spoon at Bert. "If we are in France and Belgium they have different food. You can't be squeamish. You eat what is available." I grinned, "Wait till you try snails in garlic."

Even Daddy was shocked, "You are joking!"

Shaking my head, I said, "No. They are delicious."

The food filled a hole and, I think, taught a lesson. We couldn't expect to eat and live the same way as we had done at home. We then spent an hour learning foreign words until it was time to board the ML.

The building was bursting at the seams when we left. We were assigned to ML 22. I recognised one of the sailors. We had sailed with him before. "Afternoon Reg."

"You are Bill's mate, aren't you? Already for the Skylark?"

The Lieutenant said, "Get a move on lads. Stow your gear below decks."

We stowed the camouflage net and our Bergens in the cabin and then went back on deck. The Lieutenant said, "All ready, Sergeant?"

"Yes sir."

"Then we'll push off. Hold on chaps!"

When the launch was clear of the jetty he gunned the motors and the launch leapt like a greyhound towards the narrow entrance. The sailor I recognised, Reg, said, "He's a mad bugger this one. Thinks he is driving a bloody racing car!"

I laughed, "How is Bill Leslie these days? I haven't seen him in a while."

"Oh, he's the Killick now on an MGB. They are giving us cover tomorrow night."

"Able Seaman Thompson, when you have quite finished lollygagging go and make a dixie of cocoa eh?"

"Righto Lieutenant Williams."

It was a choppy night and we bounced over the waves. It was not a pleasant voyage and I was glad when the young lieutenant slowed the launch down as we reached the river where we would lay up for the day.

"Right lads, get the netting rigged." We took out the nets and began to cover the deck. It would disguise our profile. We could still see through it. Dad had told me that he had taken part in its trials. From the air, it made it almost impossible to see what it hid.

Lieutenant Williams yawned, "Sergeant, have your chaps keep watch. Two men and a four-hour shift should do it."

"Right sir." He turned to me. "Organise that, Tom."

I knew from Dad that the worst watches were the ones in the middle no matter what time of day you were doing it. I gave them to myself and to Daddy. It was only right. It also meant that only six of us would actually need to watch and the rest would get more sleep.

I had been in the army long enough to be able to fall asleep anywhere and anytime. The fact that we slept under camouflage netting helped. It made the deck of the boat darker. I woke equally quickly when my shoulder was shaken and joined Gordy on the river bank. It was a pleasant enough day. Then we heard the drone of engines and saw the German bombers heading back east. They had finished their bombing raid on the south east and were going home. One or two were smoking and the formation looked irregular.

"I wonder if London copped it again."

"I reckon, Gordy, that the RAF will be happy if they do leave the fields alone and concentrate on London. I know that our people are suffering but if the air force can't fly from our airfields then we are done for. The Spitfires and Hurricanes are all that will stop the Germans. The Navy wouldn't be able to stop them if they ruled the air. They not only have bombers they have paratroopers. If they could drop a few hundred paratroopers they could control the ports and their barges sail in without losing a man."

He nodded as he took that in. "How come you didn't become a pilot like your dad, Corp?"

"I am not really certain but I am glad I chose the Commandos. I like the life."

"But you could have been up there; one of the Brylcreem Boys. Every girl would have been after you then." Gordy was obsessed with attracting women.

I laughed, "I don't think so." I stretched, "Come on I'll teach you a few more words while we watch." It was easy to keep watch while Gordy learned a little more French. I knew, from my own experience, that it was listening to French and becoming accustomed to the sound which helped you to speak it. Gordy was getting better. He was a quick learner.

We woke Daddy after our four hour stint. I was not sleepy and so I stripped my Thompson and my Colt and cleaned them. I took every bullet from the magazines and replaced them. It took time but I knew I wouldn't get a jam. I had nothing better to do. Then I went over the maps again. It looked likely that we would be exploring the land around the River Aa and Gravelines. Daddy had been wrong. I didn't know this area. It was further south that I knew better.

Lieutenant Williams began to prepare for sea as dusk fell. We had discovered that although each launch would make its own way across there would be four Motor Gun Boats ready to intercept any E-Boats which intervened. We would be sailing in a narrow corridor which the MGBs could protect. We might not see the other launches but they would be close to us.

Daddy yawned, "Right, Tom. Have the lads check their weapons. When we have to move there won't be a lot of time."

"Will do Sarge. You heard the Sergeant; the last thing you want over there is a jammed gun." I made sure that I oversaw the men. A second pair of eyes could often spot something.

It would take a couple of hours to make the crossing, perhaps more if the weather was against us. Every Commando had his Bergen and his gun ready to hand. The journey across might be more dangerous than the actual landing. We just didn't know. This time we were going into the unknown. Before we crossed the Channel, we blacked up our faces and hands. We had to be invisible when we landed.

The young lieutenant sent the launch speeding across the waves. I saw the leading seaman, Reg Thompson, shake his head. A few knots less would not hurt our time and the noise of the engines was louder at high speed. The Lieutenant seemed oblivious to danger. If we had had an officer I am certain he would have advised a slower speed. However, he had to take no such advice from a lowly Sergeant and Corporal. I expected the sound of German cannon fire at any moment. The engines sounded so loud that the Germans would have had to be deaf not to hear them. Amazingly we made it to the French coast without attracting undue attention. With his engine barely idling we edged in towards the beach. I could see the white of the river surf as we closed with the shore. My time studying the maps had not been wasted. I now knew exactly where we were.

We slipped silently into the sea holding our guns and our Bergens above our heads. We waded ashore. We had no need for words. The ML would return at the same time the next night. By the time we were on the sand we heard the powerful engines disappearing into the distance. Inwardly I cursed. The lieutenant might have brought us in silently but his roaring engine would wake any sentries.

My fears were realised when a powerful searchlight illuminated the beach to our right and began to move along the sand. Daddy and I waved our men forward and we ran as fast as we could for the sand dunes where, I hoped, we could find shelter. I reached them first and I turned and saw the beam of light reaching for us like a finger. As the rest of the section hurtled beyond me I saw, to my horror, the light stop at the footprints in the sand. They would send men to investigate and they would know that someone had landed. We had only just reached France and already we were in more danger than we needed to be. The Lieutenant might have doomed the mission before it had even started.

Chapter 2

I tapped Daddy on the shoulder and pointed to the top of the dunes. He nodded. We were Commandos and we didn't cry over spilled milk. The mission might be jeopardised already but we would still try to complete it. He led the section off and I knelt and brushed the sand where we had hidden as smooth as I could. The prints we would make from now on would not last long for they were in dunes. We had to delay the pursuit until we could hide. The dunes soon gave way to a low turf ridge which was covered with sand. As we reached the top I saw, to our right, the German anti-aircraft position and the searchlight. Already the Germans were summoning men to search the beach. Making a mental note of the emplacement I pushed Norm Ford in the back to hurry him up. The Germans were looking down at the beach and we had moved so quickly and quietly that we were beyond them.

Half a mile later we found the road and halted. Sergeant Grant waved me forward and I sprinted into the middle of the road and looked up and down. The road led to Gravelines. I saw nothing coming and, with my gun cocked, I waved the section across the road. It was not before time for I heard the sound of an engine and saw two tiny spots of light coming from the south. I dived into the ditch with the rest of the section. The Kübelwagen chugged along the road. I heard it stop and risked a glance. It was about four hundred yards south of us. Two Germans got out and scanned the land and the dunes to the west. After a short inspection, they returned to their vehicle and moved towards us. I ducked down again.

To my dismay it stopped next to us. They got out again but thankfully must have looked to the west again. They spoke. Their accents and the Kübelwagen's engine made their words hard to hear clearly. I did hear the words '*English*' and '*landing*'. They had found our foot prints on the beach. Those, allied to the sound of the engines would mean only one thing, us! Then they mounted up and drove down the road. They stopped every four hundred yards or so. I guessed they were using binoculars and the light mounted on the Kübelwagen to search for these English raiders who had landed on their beach. We were lucky that the one place they did not shine their light was at the side of the road.

Sergeant Grant tapped us on the shoulder and led us inland. When daylight came they would be able to examine, more closely, our prints in the sand, unless the tide had destroyed them and they would have an idea of numbers. Their cursory inspection would have shown them a landing had taken place. I had a feeling that we would have an interesting journey back to the beach and the pickup. The Germans would be waiting this time and we had no way of warning the crew of the ML that they were heading into danger.

We headed north paralleling the road. It was a risk but we had to reconnoitre Gravelines whilst it was dark. During the day, we would search the land to the south. There were houses and farms dotted along the road and we had to give them a wide berth. Farm dogs were always noisy. The Kübelwagen headed back along the road just when we were within sight of the outskirts of Gravelines. We ducked again and then breathed a sigh of relief as it returned to the emplacement.

We found a small copse close to what looked like a derelict farm. We knew which pair we would be working in and had been briefed on what to look for. They were Commandos and could operate without orders. "Right lads, you have an hour to recce the town. Take no chances. We meet back here."

I tapped Gordy and he followed me. We had divided the search area up before we had left England. I had the job of looking at the old fort defences at the mouth of the River Aa. The riskiest part was crossing the road. It was after midnight and there should not have been too many people about but any that were out were likely to be German. I smelled smoke as we approached the walls of the old town and we both dived to the ground. To our left, on the opposite side from the old town, two German sentries were having a cigarette just ten feet from where we were hiding. They had been obscured by a low wall. I heard them talking and knew from their words that they were looking out to sea. They were speaking of the invasion of England and one was saying how much he was looking forward to paying back the British for his crippled father who had been hurt in the Great War. The other was not certain that they would invade. Annoyingly they spoke for some minutes and enjoyed their illicit cigarettes before continuing their patrol.

When their voices receded, I risked rising. We hurried to the low wall and peered over. I hoped my blacked-out face would make us hard to see. I saw that they had many gun emplacements inside the old defences. They had sandbagged the 88s which could either fire in the air or, equally dangerously, be depressed to fire at Motor Launches! I could see helmets and knew that each gun was crewed even at this time of night. The machine guns which interspersed them were not. That intrigued me. Were they expecting a raid by the RAF? I was aware of the passage of time and I was about to leave when I saw a sign which sent chills up my spine. The land before the gun emplacements had been mined. I saw the skull and crossbones. I would have to note its position when we returned to the others.

I expected to be the last pair back but I was not. Smith and Griffiths were late. I looked at my watch. They had just five minutes to make it. There was a sudden noise from the town and what sounded like an alarm. Sergeant Grant looked at me and shook his head, "Looks like they've been caught. Tom, you have an eye for this sort of thing. Find us a way out of here!" Even as we went I heard firing and recognised the distinctive bark of a Colt. It confirmed my fears; Smith and Griffiths had been found!

I began running towards the far corner of the field. It was south west of us. North was Gravelines and trouble and the west was the coast where we had already woken them up. I prayed there was a gate or a gap in the hedge there. I ran hard. I knew that the rest of the men were all fit enough to keep up. There was a gap and we burst through. The next field was even larger. I kept to the same course. I did not glance around. The Sergeant would be at the back to chivvy up those who were slow. My job was to pull them along as quickly as I could.

This field had a gate and there was tarmac ahead. I held my hand up and peered down the road. There was no sign of anyone and I crossed it. I waved the rest across and waited while they all did so. We listened for any sounds of pursuit. There were noises to the north but they appeared to be some way away. Then I smelled fuel. It was aeroplane fuel. I saw, briefly, the shadow of a windsock. There was an airfield somewhere close by. I vaguely remembered from the map I had studied that there was a village nearby called Oye-Plage. It must have been there.

Norm said, "That was a bit of a cock up Sarge."

Daddy shook his head, "It is a lesson. Any of us can get caught."

Gordy asked, "You reckon they will spill the beans?"

Norm was one of Bert's mates, "Never!"

I caught Daddy's eye. We both knew that it was likely that they would say something which might put the Germans on to us. Daddy said, "We just keep on and do our job. We have the rest of the day and early morning to find out as much as we can. Then we make our way back to the coast."

Johnny Connor said, "In daylight? This place will be crawling with Germans."

"Then we have to hide."

It was too dark to read a map. I pointed south west. "As far as I can remember there is a main road over yonder. If we find a good place to hide we can watch the road. That will give us an idea of who is in the area." Pointing the other way, I said, "I reckon there is an airfield up there."

"Do you think we will be able to recce it?"

I shook my head, "We would be heading towards anybody searching for us. I am ninety percent certain there is a field there and we can mark it on the map. If the others hadn't been caught then we would be able to have a good look. Let's not push our luck eh Sarge? Let's just get away from here eh, Sarge?"

"That is as good a plan as any. Gordy, you take the rear, Tom lead on."

We crossed another field. I was glad that the weather had been fine of late. A muddy field would have left tracks for the Germans to find. I heard the sound of an approaching vehicle and I sprinted to the low hedge which ran along the side of the field. I waved my arm for the others to drop. Bill Becket landed next to me. He was one of the fittest men in the section. I put my finger to my lips.

As the vehicle was coming from the direction of Gravelines and might be looking for us I cocked my Thompson. It was a slow vehicle. I was desperate to sneak a view but that might have ended in disaster. As it passed us I began to slowly rise. I watched as it trundled down the road. I risked a peek over the top. It was a German truck. I glimpsed soldiers in the back and I ducked quickly back down. I waved the others forward and, as they did so, I began to work out what the truck meant. Had they been looking for us they would have had a Kübelwagen with them. The lorry was transporting Germans from Gravelines. Were they heading for Calais? It was only a few miles down the road. It was just possible that they were sending reinforcements to the invasion camps.

"Sarge, I reckon we go down this road a ways. I think we can risk the road and make better time. We will hear them and the lights on their lorries are dimmed."

I saw him chewing his lip. "Well you have been behind enemy lines more than I have." He turned to the others, "If you hear anything then throw yourselves in the ditch and stay there!" They nodded, "And another thing, we double time!"

With rubber soled shoes we made no sound at all as we ran down the road. It was easier than running across a field as we did not have to keep looking down. Miraculously we did not see anyone for an hour and made good time. I was at the front and I smelled the fires. There was something ahead. I held up my hand to stop the others. I looked for an entrance into the field on our right. I saw one just forty yards ahead. Relieved that I had found a way off the road I took the section into it. I waved the men into the field and when Daddy arrived I spoke in a whisper. "There is something on the other side of the road, Sarge. It could be just a patrol but it might be something else. I smelled smoke."

"Right then. We move down the edge of this field and find somewhere to lie up." Turning to the others, he said, "Keep in a crouched position. I want no one above the level of the hedgerow. Follow the Corporal."

It was agony to run like that but we had no option. I spied, set back from the road about sixty yards ahead, a bombed-out building. I made for it and the others followed. It had been a house or a small farm. That must have been before the war. Now it looked like it had been damaged for some time. It was certainly empty. Two roosting pigeons fluttered noisily off as I went in. I cursed my lack of caution. If there was a sharp eyed German sentry close by then he would have heard the disturbance. I held my breath as I waited for a challenge. There was none.

It did not take long to establish that it was empty and that it would be a good place to rest. I went to what had been the back door and scouted around. There was an untidy mixture of wrecked buildings, broken machinery, and bushes to the west. We had a way out if we needed it. As I waved the others in I saw that dawn was about to break. We had barely reached our sanctuary in time.

Sergeant Grant nodded his thanks to me. "Becket, you and Connor take first stag." He pointed to a half-wrecked staircase. It led to the partly demolished first floor." Get upstairs. The rest of you get some grub and then some sleep."

I shrugged off my Bergen and took out my canteen. I needed water. I was dehydrated. Food could wait. Sergeant Grant took out his pipe. I shook my head, "If there are Krauts nearby Sarge they will smell English baccy for sure."

He nodded, "You are right. Ford was right too. This is a bit of a cock up."

"I wouldn't say that. We have established where the German gun positions are."

Just then we heard the rumble of approaching German aero engines. We went to the back of the house and saw the shapes of bombers above us. They were returning from a raid on England. I realised that they were very low. "They are landing Sarge. There is an airfield nearby." I worked out that we had passed one, to the north, during the night. This was a second. Sure enough even as we watched they lowered their landing gear. They flew over us in the direction of Lille. We did not see them land but I knew that the bombers' field could only be four or five miles to the east of us. "That is useful intelligence Sarge. We can report two airfields. There was one at Oye-Plage and the other must be yonder, towards Lille. Less of a cock up now, eh Sarge?"

"Aye. We had better get our maps updated and then let the other lads copy them. Bearing in mind what happened to Smith and Griffith, we need to prepare for the worst." It did not take us long but, even so, dawn had fully broken by then and it was daylight. "Sarge?"

"Yes Becket?"

"I reckon you ought to come and see this."

I followed Daddy and we carefully climbed the half-wrecked staircase.

"Bugger me!"

I looked over his shoulder. Across the road were lines of tents and the smoking chimneys of mobile field kitchens. It was a German camp. It was just four hundred yards from where we were. During the night, we had passed within shouting distance. We had found one of the Corps or Armies which were going to invade England.

"Well Sergeant, it looks like we have some valuable information after all." I had brought my map with me. "That is Marck to the west of us and I saw a sign before we turned off for Offerkerque. That puts the camp here." I drew a cross on the map. "Now all we need is to identify how many are in there."

Daddy nodded, "You two, count the tents and see if you can work out how many men are in each one."

"How do we do that, Sarge?"

"Use your brains! Find a tent and count the men who come out. Do it a couple of times and you will get an average. Then count how many tents there are. You just need a rough figure. See if you can identify what units they are too."

Becket grumbled, "I was always hopeless at sums."

"Well now is your chance to get better at it eh? Come on Tom. We'll get the others to copy your map."

It was while they were copying that my nose caught the smell of aeroplane fuel drifting from the opposite side from the camp. I had grown up on airfields and I knew the smell. It appeared to be coming from the west. "Sarge I am just going to have a shufti out of the back. I will stay hidden but there's something I want to look at."

"Aye all right but be careful. Give me your map. One of these copies has to get back to England or those two poor lads are in the bag for nothing."

I slipped out of the back and moved to the edge of the bushes and buildings. In the distance, I could see wire. To my left was a hedge and the end of the land which must have belonged to the farm at one time. I kept low and ran towards it. I felt exposed but there was no vantage point from which I could be spied. I moved down the hedge line as quickly as I could. The smell from the aeroplane fuel became even stronger as I headed towards the fence. I knew what I would find but I had to confirm it. When I heard the Daimler-Benz engine fire up I knew what I would see. I crawled the last ten yards and peered through the fence at the German fighter airfield. They were Messerschmitt 109s and it looked like the squadron was about to take off. This was another airfield but at least we knew what type of aeroplanes used this one. The 109 was not a night fighter and did not accompany bombers on their night raids but they would during the day. There they would try to match the Spitfire.

I counted the aircraft and then made my way back to the others. Daddy looked at me curiously when I entered. "Well?"

"There is another German airfield at the back of us. It is filled with German fighters."

He nodded, "And this is a German Corps in front of us. We have the numbers now. The question is what to do. I don't think we could get much more information. Not without a prisoner."

I looked at my watch, "It is nine o'clock now, Sarge. The ML will be back at midnight. I think it will take us eight hours to get back there. That means if we do want a prisoner we will have to get one now and then take him back with us." I saw Daddy's face. "I think that is a tall order, Sarge, but that is just my opinion."

"I agree with you. I also think we will be lucky to get back without trouble. Smith and Griffiths might have told Jerry about the rendezvous."

Norm had been listening and he said, "He wouldn't! I know Bert!"

I shook my head, "And I have seen the SS at close hand. Believe me they are hard men."

"Are you saying we shouldn't go back to the beach?"

"No, Sarge. We have to. It isn't fair on the ML crew if we don't. They would be waiting for us. And besides we have no other way out have we? We have to go back but I think we should leave here earlier and get to the beach so that we can check that it is safe."

"That means moving in daylight."

"I think we have to do that in any case. It is light until about eight or nine at night. We can't get there in three or four hours."

"You have thought this through, eh Corporal?"

I nodded. "The proximity of the airfield and the camp means that there will be Germans all over these roads. We will have to use fields and natural cover. That is why I said eight hours. If there were no Germans we could be there in two hours no problem."

I saw him weighing it all up and then looking at the faces of the others. "You are right. The rest of you get some shut eye. Tom and I will watch." We went to the first floor. "We need to talk. No matter what Ford says the Germans will know about the beach. They would be fools not to put the tracks on the beach and two captured Commandos together. I know Smith and Griffiths are good lads but it wouldn't take much to get information from them. The Germans are clever. What did you mean about getting there early and checking if it is safe?"

"I don't think they will open fire on ML without us being on the beach. If we get there and there are no extra patrols then the Germans know nothing about the landing beach. If there are then we need to take the offensive and hit them first. We know where the Kübelwagen came from. That is what we need to hit. The last thing they will expect will be us attacking them. They will think we are hiding. If we knock that post out we have a chance."

"That is very risky with only eight of us."

"Eight ordinary squaddies might have a problem, Sarge, but we are trained for this. We go in and use our knives. They will think they are safe on the landward side and we will have the element of surprise. We approach the post from the west. They will be looking east and north."

"You have a lot of faith in these lads."

"We trained them. We have to believe in them. What's the alternative? Give ourselves up? If we don't go to the beach, that is our only option."

He nodded, "You are right." He swept an arm around us. We were hidden from view. "This is a bit safer here. We have been lucky. I'll risk a pipe while we watch. Helps me think." We kept watch in silence. I was thinking through all the problems we might encounter and how we would deal with them.

I woke the others at three. Daddy had smoked a pipe and was a little more optimistic about our chances. "Right lads, we are heading back. Tom will lead. I will be tail end Charlie. We keep ten yards between every man. That way if Tom gets hit we can all escape."

They all looked at me. I shrugged and grinned, "I have no intention of getting shot but this way we will be harder to see. We use whatever cover is out there."

Daddy and I had eaten and drunk some water. We had refilled our canteens from the old pump in the kitchen which, miraculously, had survived. I stepped out of the back. We had heard the fighters returning not long before we woke the others and we knew that we would not be spotted from the air. That had been my worry. We had had plenty of time to study the map. By heading north east we would be travelling across fields. The only danger was from the road which ran along the coast. If Germans looked south they might see us.

I ran from the building and used it as cover from the German camp. I kept looking and listening towards the road which ran obliquely away to the north and east. Consequently, each time I heard a vehicle I waved my arm and dropped to the ground. The others did as I did. We appeared to be hidden by the sides of the hedges and walls but we had to drop every time we heard a vehicle. It was slow going. We also skirted any farms or houses. Although I was fairly confident that we would be given assistance I did not want to risk the locals incurring the wrath of the Germans. We took detours whenever we came close to a building. We reached the coast road at seven in the evening. Despite the vehicles we had made better time than I had anticipated.

A road joined the coast road. It came from Offerkerque. Although a small road it complicated matters. There was a wood on the far side. It was not a huge one but it would hide us while we worked out our next movement. I checked the small road and then ran across. We all made it.

Daddy took out his dagger and used it as a pointer. "The Germans have a post here. They were the ones who sent the Kübelwagen after us. It is a mile and a half away. If we can we eliminate the Germans there we can then wait for the ML. It will be here in just over four hours. We will need to do a recce to see how many men there are."

"Suppose there are too many of them?"

"Then Norm, old son, we are up shit creek without a paddle and no mistake." Daddy was not sugaring this particular pill. The men had to know how serious the situation was.

I went to the edge of the wood and, lying down, peered up and down the road. It appeared to be clear of traffic. Perhaps they were all eating; it was a meal time. I waved the men across one by one and we ran into the fields on the opposite side of the road. There was a farmhouse to our right. We could not risk speaking with them and we went, instead, towards the dunes and scrubby trees. It took half an hour of stopping and starting as we heard voices and saw movement. I was glad that the sun was slowly setting behind us. When we reached the dunes, our lives became a little easier. We were able to use the dips and hollows to disguise our progress.

I held up my hand when I heard the German voices in the dark. We had found the post. I slithered out of my Bergen and left my Tommy gun with Daddy. I took my dagger and bellied along the sand. I slowly raised my blackened face and, peering over the sand, I saw that there was a machine gun before me in a sandbagged emplacement. There were two Germans manning it. There were four tents further along and then another machine gun. The second was unmanned. The Kübelwagen was parked near a small track.

I turned my head to the right and saw that there were eight Germans in all. The light from their oil lamp helped me to see them clearly. They were under an awning and eating. They were quite raucous. We had at least ten men to eliminate silently. I saw a tent some way off by itself and there was a light within it. Perhaps that was an officer's tent. How many officers were there? It would be an almost impossible task for just eight of us to do. I checked my watch. It would be completely dark in an hour. The ML would be here in three. Doubts assailed me. Would these Germans have a relief? Were there others not here? The tents looked to be six or eight men tents. That suggested twenty-four men. Then I thought again. The officer had his own tent as would the NCOs. Twenty men seemed a better number but it was still too many.

I made my way back to the others and then led them down to the edge of the beach. This was one was mined; I had seen the signs when I had gone to reconnoitre, and I felt safe waiting there. No one could flank us. I whispered to Daddy what I had seen. "That is not good, Tom." He looked out to sea. I think he was visualising Lieutenant Williams sailing towards us. "I think we wait until eleven. We can take out the machine gunners from behind with knives. By that time the others should be asleep anyway."

"Unless they know we are coming."

"Cheerful bugger, aren't you? Well I can't think of anything else. We try this and maybe go out in a blaze of glory." We made our way back up the dunes to wait. Our plan to escape secretly and silently would not happen. I know that I should have felt pleased that we had not just walked back to the beach to await the ML. That would have guaranteed we were either killed or captured but this hopeless situation did not sit well with me.

The Kübelwagen's engine started at ten forty-five. Daddy and I peered over the dune. The officer and three men got in the vehicle and drove off. I saw that the other machine gun was now manned. Eight of the soldiers were preparing to leave with their guns slung over their shoulders. We watched four of them make their way down the dunes towards the beach. The other four headed along the road. Presumably there was another path down to the beach there. It was a trap. They were expecting the ML. The numbers ahead of us were, however now halved. If there were twenty odd men in the camp then half had just left.

He looked at me and pointed to the two German machine gunners who were in the far emplacement. He made the sign to kill them. I nodded and, after sliding down the bank tapped Gordy on the shoulder. I took out my dagger and pointed to him. He nodded. I headed below the line of the dunes. Gordy and I would have to avoid being seen by the nearer of the machine guns. I hoped that their attention would be on the beach below. If there had been just one emplacement then we might have risked using our toggle rope or just choking them to subdue them. We could not risk noise for it might endanger the ML crew. I did not think for one moment that we would be able to kill these guards and still make the ML. What we should have done then was head away from this ambush and try to work out another way home but we were Commandos. We would dare. I was aware of the passage of time. Daddy and the others would be overcoming the other machine gun but we had to get rid of ours and then get to the beach before the launch returned to pick us up. If we were silent then we might succeed. The eight men who had gone down to the beach would have to be killed with guns and we would have to hope that there were no others waiting to catch the ML. It would be tight.

I heard the Germans above us. They were talking of the ambush. It became clear that they knew the Navy were coming back but they did not know exactly when. I heard them talk of troops from Gravelines. Even if we disposed of these then it would still be unlikely that we could escape on the launch. I forced myself to think of the job in hand not the problems ahead of us. I tapped Gordy and signalled for him to go to the left and take that German. He nodded and I moved to my right.

Both Germans were wearing helmets and that would help us. I rose like a wraith behind my German as Gordy did behind his. I reached over and pulled back hard on the front of the German helmet. The strap bit into his neck and stopped him shouting. His hands came up to stop the choking and I pulled the razor-sharp knife across his throat. Hot blood spilled on my hands and he shuddered before dying. I saw that Gordy had succeeded too. I dragged the body from the pit and rolled it down the dune. It tumbled and fell silently to the beach below. Gordy copied me.

I was just about to sneak back to Daddy when I heard the roar of an engine. It was the ML and he was coming in hot. In the distance, I could hear the sound of German E-Boats. To my horror a flare flew into the sky illuminating the beach. The ML was a hundred yards from the beach. The whole of the beach opened up with machine gun fire which ripped into the wooden launch. I watched as the two gunners on the Motor Launch were scythed in two by machine gun fire. The young Lieutenant tried to turn the stricken launch. From the sea came the sound of a German cannon and the launch exploded in a fireball. Mercifully any left aboard would have known nothing.

Just then the Germans, who had been in their tents, emerged. The flare illuminated Gordy and me. I drew my Colt but before I could fire, the rest of the section ripped into them with Tommy guns. All was silent but as the flare began to die I saw the Germans on the beach pointing up. They had seen us. We were trapped in France and they knew where we were.

Chapter 3

I ran to Sergeant Grant who was at the far side of the German encampment, "The boat has been destroyed. There is no way home there and the Krauts are coming."

Daddy was a calm man, "We have two choices: surrender or get the hell out of here." He pointed at the dead Germans. "I don't think they will take too kindly to what we have done here so let's go."

Bill Becket said, "Where to? There are Germans everywhere!"

Bill was right. We were surrounded. Then I thought of the only safe place we had found. "Back to the wrecked house."

"Are you sure, Tom?"

"It is so close to the German camp that it is the last place they will think to look." I gestured to the Channel with my machine gun. "They will expect us to go towards the sea. They might think we have a back up ship to pick us up."

"Lead on!"

We had no reason to hide. We had to get inland before the Kübelwagen and the other Germans returned from the beach ambush and we ran as hard as only Commandos can do. We hurtled across the road and dived through the gaps in the hedges. I wanted to get to the safety of the woods as soon as possible. The Germans would go to the machine gun emplacements first and if we could make the woods in which we had sheltered we would be hidden from the road and we could crawl across the fields. Now that it was dark we might escape observation. It would be slow but the undulations in the fields would hide us. So long as it was dark we had a chance. We had to be back in the wrecked house before dawn or we would be either killed or captured.

In the distance, I could hear the whine of the engine of the Kübelwagen as it screamed up the twisting trail from the beach. I also heard the deeper noise of a truck engine. It moved towards us and then receded into the distance. We reached the woods and I waited until Daddy joined us. He nodded. There was no sound of an engine closing with us and I decided to run while we had the chance. The Germans would be searching the tops of the cliffs. We ran across the fields. We managed to cross three fields before I heard the engines. It was a vehicle and it was closing with us. I dived to the ground and the others followed suit. I led us at the crawl until we reached the hedgerow which marked the next field.

I risked standing and peering through the thin branches. I saw the lights of vehicles on the road and the shadows of Germans. They were searching the crossroads close to the wood. As I had only seen them in the light of the vehicles I thought we might be able to run a little more. The searchers would be blinded by the lights they were using and we would be hard to see and impossible to hear. "Sarge, if we run at the crouch I reckon we can make the farmhouse in under a couple of hours. Better than crawling and risking them catching sight of us."

He nodded, "Right lads, we run at the crouch. I know it hurts but a bullet hurts worse."

He was right. With the Bergens on our backs and our Thompsons in our hands it was agony. But we kept on running and all those five mile runs in full kit paid off. We were rewarded, after an hour and forty-five minutes with the smell of the German cooking fires and the faint aroma of aircraft fuel. We were close to our hidey hole. As soon as we saw the wrecked back door we threw ourselves in. Daddy pointed to Bill Becket and Ken Curtis and then upstairs. They nodded and disappeared up the damaged stairs to keep watch.

He spoke so quietly that we had to lean in to hear him. "The rest of you check your food and water. We may be here for some time." We took off our Bergens and he led me to the back of the building. Here we could talk a little easier. "This is a right pickle. You have done this before. Any chance of us stealing a boat like you did and sailing home?"

I shook my head, "If they are going to invade then every port will have more guards than fleas on a dog. We would stand no chance not to mention the fact that they now have more guns along the coast. And there are too many of us. We would need a big boat."

"What then?"

I could see that he was worried. This was way beyond anything he had experienced before. "Dad was in a position like this. And I was when I was stranded here before. The worst thing we can do is panic. So long as we have food and water we can survive. We have shelter and we are hidden. When daylight comes we will have a better idea of our position. If we can survive for a couple of days until the hue and cry has gone down then we might be able to come up with something better. We just have to keep our eyes, ears, and minds open. While we are alive we have a chance."

"So, your plan is to sit on our arses and do nowt?"

I grinned, "There is no real alternative is there, Sarge?"

"I suppose not."

Because we had not eaten all day we still had rations. The water supply still worked. Daddy worked out that by eking out our supplies we could last three more days. That, of course, all depended upon the Germans. If they searched every building close to the beach then we were in trouble. We took a two-hour watch each. When Gordy and I were on duty I heard the sound of aeroplane engines and went out of the back to look towards the airfield. The fighters were taking off. I looked at my watch. It was eight o'clock. That information might prove useful.

At the end of our duty we were relieved by Poulson and Connor. "Just going for a leak."

I headed out of the back and went towards the airfield. It was a risk but the fighters had taken off. The mechanics would be having their breakfast and the guards would have their attention on the roads. I was a little bolder than the last time and I crawled to the wire fence. The fence was not of German manufacture. In places, it was rusted and I deduced it was the original one. The barbed wire at the top was broken in places. I crawled along and found a section which was overgrown with wild blackberries, nettles, and grasses. There was a drainage ditch which ran alongside and it too was overgrown. Animals, probably rabbits and rats, had burrowed beneath the fence. I took out my home-made wire cutters and, by feel alone, I cut some of the fence above the hole. I did not think it would be seen. They would have to clear the vegetation first. I took a deep breath and then wriggled down under the fence. A couple of wires caught on my neck and I realised I had not cut enough of the wire. However, I was able to look through to the airfield. There appeared to be no guard post at this end of the field although I could see, in the distance, patrolling sentries. If I could make the hole bigger then we could get into the airfield.

I crawled back and cut more of the wire. When it was done I raised my head to inspect the airfield. There were three fighters close by and they were covered by tarpaulins. They were obviously being repaired. I saw two, two seater trainers. If there were just two of us we could have stolen that and flown home. There were too many of us for that option. Then I saw a JU 52. It was just forty yards from the fence. This was a quiet corner of the field. The JU 52 was the German workhorse. It was used both as a bomber and as a transport. It had been the three-engine transport aeroplane which had dropped German paratroopers into the Netherlands. Two mechanics were working on the port engine. They were the only aeroplanes on the field. I slithered back down the hole and then crawled. I headed back to the farm.

When I entered Gordy, who was having a cigarette out of the back, said, "Your neck is bleeding Corp."

I put my hand up and it came away bloody. "Bugger! Have you a dressing?"

He stubbed his cigarette out, "Aye. Let's get it cleaned up. Can't have you injured. You and the Sarge have kept us alive up to now."

He began to wash the wound and then applied the gel we had been issued. It would prevent infections. When he had finished he tapped me on the back. "All done."

"Thanks, Gordy."

He packed the medical kit away. "You reckon we can get out of this situation?"

I think Gordy was looking for a miracle from me. "We have been trained so that we can get out of most situations which would seem impossible to other soldiers. That run from Oswestry to Poole showed that. The problem here is that we are in the dark about what is around us. I guess that is why they sent us in. They need to know what is here. The next set of blokes will find it easier because of the info we take back."

He laughed, "So you think we will get back."

Just then Polly whistled. Danger. We grabbed our guns and ran to the windows. A Kübelwagen had pulled up at the end of the track leading to the farm. If they came as far as the building and entered they would discover that it had been used. I went to Sergeant Grant and shook him awake. He did not need my finger on my lips to tell him there was danger. We could hear the German voices. As they approached I took out my knife. The gun would make too much noise. If they discovered us we would kill them silently and try to escape before the others in the vehicle realised they were dead. We had one chance in ten of doing so. I went behind the door. I heard them approach, their footsteps sounded on the gravel path. It was only when they tried the door and found it locked that I remembered that we had entered through the wrecked part at the back.

I heard the Germans talking, "I told you Hans, it is a shell. There are rats and mice only. No one is here"

"The Feldwebel said to check. We will go around the back."

I turned and made the signal to hide. It was one of the many things we were good at. We could hide in plain sight. I heard them as they moved around the back. Then the thought struck me. Gordy had discarded his cigarette. If they looked down and discovered that they would know that someone had been there recently.

I dared not risk looking but I could hear them as they stepped over the broken back wall. "There is no one here."

I heard a match strike and then smelled smoke as they lit cigarettes, "This would have been a nice farm before the war." They were taking the opportunity of a quiet smoke. Their laziness might yet save us.

"It could be again. When we have invaded Britain and conquered it, the war will be over. I could bring Freya here and farm. I like the sea and this land is easier to farm than in the Tyrol."

"You don't think the likes of us would get the chance of living here do you? You would have to be an officer."

Just then a voice barked out, "When you ladies have quite finished! What have you found?"

"Nothing Feldwebel."

"Then get back to the car. We have just heard that more of these Commandos were seen south of Calais. We will search there!"

I waited until the footsteps had receded before I risked lifting my head. The back was clear and I went up the stairs to join Poulson and Curtis. "They have gone Corp." Polly pointed to the truck and the Kübelwagen heading in the direction of Calais.

I went back down. "We are safe for a while Sarge. Some more of our lads have been spotted south of Calais."

"Well I am sorry for them but it has bought us some time."

I turned to Gordy, "You smokers will have to stop throwing away your cigarette ends. If they had seen your old butt, Gordy, they would have known someone was here."

"Sorry Corp."

It became clear, as the afternoon wore on, that we had escaped detection. We heard the fighters return and the airfield was filled with the noise of engines being repaired. Leaving Gordy on watch Sergeant Grant gathered us all together. "Right lads, I am open for suggestions as to how we get out of this fix."

Bill Becket nodded in my direction, "How about Tom's trick of stealing a boat."

"He has already told me that will be impossible now and I agree with him."

Ken nodded, "Then how about heading further north. Maybe they won't be as vigilant nearer to Denmark."

"Nice idea but that is a bit far. We have no maps and when we started to steal food they would soon find us. No, we have to get out from here and in the next two days."

When I had woken from my nap the bones of a plan had begun to come together. I had seen the aeroplanes but no clear idea of how to use them. Now I did. "I have an idea, Sarge. It is risky and it might not work so if you don't want to try it then say so."

He smiled, "It can't be any worse than mine. I was going to suggest walking to Switzerland or Spain. Go ahead."

"We break into the airfield and steal an aeroplane. We fly home."

They all looked at me as though I was mad. Sergeant Grant shook his head, "A grand idea… if one of us could fly!"

I nodded, "I can."

"What?"

"When my dad was a squadron leader he taught me to fly. I even sat next to him when he flew a twin engine Wellington. I can get us off the ground and, with any luck I can land it." I shrugged. "At the very least I might be able to get us down in the sea closer to England." I saw the doubt on their faces and I stood, "But you are right it …"

Daddy laughed, "No, Tom, I am well happy about that. It is just that I am surprised. I don't know about you lot but at least we have a chance this way."

"Before you get excited we have to get into the field. I have already found a way. There is a wire fence and I have cut a hole in it but we will need to make it bigger. Then we have the problem of starting the aeroplane."

"You have found an aeroplane?"

"They have a JU 52. They were fixing one of the engines. It still has two so even if they don't repair it then we can still take off."

Bill said, "What about the fighters? Won't they shoot us down?"

"Definitely so we have to steal the bus during daylight when the fighters have taken off and left for England. The field is quiet once they leave. That is our best chance."

Daddy looked around, "Right we will do it. After dark, we all go with Tom and find the way in. What do we need?"

"Wire cutters."

As the afternoon wore on we rested and made sure we had enough wire cutters between us. Most had homemade ones like mine. They were light and serviceable. We left Ken Curtis to watch the farm while I led the others to the fence. It seemed further in the dark but I knew that was my imagination. I had told them what we needed to do and Poulson and Barker went down under the fence to enlarge the hole. The rest kept watch. If their cutters broke we had spares. We took the opportunity to familiarise ourselves with the ground. The two came back and nodded to us. I led them back along the ditch to the farm.

Once back in the farm, Daddy and I decided when we would make the attempt. "We have to be at the hole before dawn. We have to get in within minutes of the fighters taking off. The field will be busy as a beehive before they take off and some eagle-eyed mechanic might just spot us. Everything will need to be done really quickly. We have to use surprise."

"Right. We will get some shut eye now. We leave at three."

I managed an hour or so at best. I was too nervous. It was some time since I had flown. Dad had told me it was like riding a bike. Once you had done it you never forgot. I hoped that he was right. Of course, with a large aeroplane I would need someone to help me operate the levers. I decided I would choose whoever the first one in the aeroplane was when we succeeded in gaining entry.

There was a chill in the air as we left our wrecked farm. The clear skies and cool air suggested a fine day ahead. That was good. It had been some time since I had flown and flying an unknown German aeroplane now seemed a more daunting prospect. I wanted an empty sky when I took off and no tricky side wind. As we moved down the field I took heart from the fact that my dad had done the same thing. There was always hope. We reached the fence and took off our Bergens. We would not get under with them on our back. The waiting was the hardest part. We had to be as still as possible. However, the skill of comrades was shown when birds above us happily whistled their dawn chorus. We had become part of the land. No eagle-eyed sentry would wonder why the birds were not singing.

The field came to light as mechanics noisily began work. I heard lorries as the fuel bowsers came to fill up the fighters. The smell drifted across to us. It was maddening not to be able to look at what was going on but we did not want to be seen. I, alone of the section, knew what was going on. For them it would be even worse. We had to lie in the ditch and beneath the bush and wait. It was while we were waiting that I thought of the camouflage netting we had had on the ML.

Something like that would have hidden us well. It would be something else to carry but it would be worth it.

At last I heard the fighters' engines started and knew that they were going to take off soon. I wriggled, as slowly as possible, towards the hole we had made in the fence. I gently lifted the cut section and bent it up so that I could get my head underneath. My face was still blackened and I just peered through the long grass on the other side. I saw the fighters taxiing. The mechanics were standing around and watching. It was the same on a British field. Aeroplanes had been known to develop a fault while preparing to take off. The mechanics would only go for their breakfast when the aircraft were all in the air.

I glanced to the right and saw the mechanics still working on the JU 52. One was leaning out of the cockpit. I saw him shout something and they tried to fire the port engine. He shook his head when it did not.

There was a sudden increase in engine noises and a wave of heat as the squadron all took off. It took a few minutes and then the noise receded as they headed west. I waited until the mechanics began to meander towards the mess tent. As I turned to tell the others it was time I heard a bang and then the splutter of an engine trying to fire.

"Up now!"

I forced myself under the fence and pulled my Bergen and gun behind me. As the others followed I stared at the JU 52. The port engine fired. I saw the mechanic in the cockpit bang the side with glee. The rest of the section rolled from under the fence. We were still hidden by the undergrowth but the minute we stood we would be seen. I pointed to the aeroplane. It was just fifty yards from us. Then the other two engines were started and I saw the four mechanics patting each other on the back. This was too good a chance to miss. I stood and, holding my machine gun and Bergen in my left hand drew my Colt. The others followed me as I ran towards the aeroplane. It was the fifth mechanic, the one in the cockpit, who spotted us. He pointed and shouted something. By then I was twenty yards from them. I pointed my Colt at them and shouted, in German, "Down on the ground or we will shoot you!"

They were unarmed and when our machine guns were levelled at them they obeyed. I pointed the gun to the mechanic in the cockpit.

"You stay there!" Without turning I shouted, "Gordy, cover the one in the cockpit. If he moves his head then kill him!"

So far our little vignette was being played out just for us. I knew that eventually someone in the tower would spot our uniforms. We had to move and quickly. I kicked one of the chocks away from the port wheel. "Bill, get rid of the other chock."

Daddy shouted, "Ken keep them covered and the rest of you get on board."

I jumped into the hatch and dropped my bag and machine gun. I went to the cockpit. I said, to the mechanic. "Sit there and put your hands behind your head!" I pointed to the well of the cargo bay.

"You will not get away with this."

I smiled, "Then you will die with us, Fritz! Now move!" He did as I said. I went to the window as Polly jammed his machine gun next to the mechanic's head. "Gordy, get on board." Just then a klaxon sounded. We had been spotted.

Daddy shouted, "Right lads on board."

"Norm, get up here and sit next to me! I'll need your help to fly." He sat down and looked in terror at the gauges and levers. I smiled and pointed to the levers next to his right hand. "All you need to do is to push them forward at the same time as me." He nodded and put his hands on them.

I saw, a Kübelwagen racing down the airfield. "Sarge they are coming for us. Better start making a noise. Here we go!"

Dad had always said that flying was like riding a bike or driving a car; you never forgot. I hoped he was right. This one had more controls than the ones I had learned in but essentially, they were the same. My German came in handy. I read the German instruction and I pushed the levers forward. We began to move down the bumpy grass. I heard the sound of German machine guns and then the chatter of Tommy guns. I ignored that.

"Norm put your hands on that stick in front of you. When I give the word pull back gently on it."

"You sure Corp?"

"You are doing fine." I prayed I would have the right revs when it came time to lift the nose or this could be a very short and explosive flight.

Suddenly the mechanic behind me made a lurch towards me. I half turned as he leapt towards me. His fist caught the side of my head. I elbowed him and then Polly smashed the stock of his machine gun into the side of his head. "Sorry Corp!"

I felt the blood dripping from my nose. "Not to worry. Hang on lads!" We were bouncing down the runway and it felt like I was clinging on to a runaway horse. "Ready Norm?"

"I suppose so."

I saw that the revs were getting almost into the red zone. "Now!" We both pulled back on the yoke. The nose didn't seem to move at first. The engines were all screaming and the whole aeroplane was shaking. The other wire fence was a hundred yards away. I was not certain that we would clear it. I saw that I still had more power available and I pushed the levers forward. The nose began to rise and we stopped bumping. We were airborne. I felt something bang into the fuselage. We had been hit by bullets. "Okay Norm, you can let go now." As we cleared the fence I began to bank to the right. I decided not to risk lifting the undercarriage I might not be able to get it down again. I brought down the power. One of the engines had been recently repaired. It would not do to risk damaging it. Behind us I heard the pop of anti-aircraft fire. I put the nose down. We would fly as low over the sea as we could. If we were attacked then I would put her down; the sea was safer than crashing into the cliffs or being shot down.

Daddy came behind me and slapped me on the back as the section all cheered. "Well done, Tom!"

"We aren't safe yet. We are flying a German aeroplane. Our own lads will try to shoot us down."

"What's your plan?"

"The nearest field, as far as I can remember, is Eastchurch in Kent. We should reach it in fifteen minutes but I would use the side windows to watch for German fighters. They may not take kindly to us stealing one of their aeroplanes."

"Right." He turned, "Right lads get to the side windows with your machine guns and keep a sharp eye out for Jerries."

I focussed on the distant coastline. "Norm, find the maps. Find Eastchurch. Use Calais and Marck as our starting point. I have been flying north west; three hundred and five degrees."

Although our maps were of France they also had part of the Kent coast. "Got it." He peered forward. "You need to go left a bit!"

I laughed, "I think you will find that they say port. How many degrees?"

"Just five degrees and you should be able to see it."

"Keep your eyes open for the field. There will be buildings and a windsock."

"Righto."

I saw the coast drawing nearer and nearer. I estimated that we were but ten minutes from Blighty when Ken shouted, "German fighters, three of them!"

Sergeant Grant said, "Give them short bursts. Let's discourage them."

"I can see the field, Corp. It is to port."

I saw it too and I dipped the nose. I heard bullets strike the fuselage and heard a shout as someone was hit. I could do nothing about it. I began to reduce speed and corrected my approach. The field was intended for Spitfires and not a bus as big as a JU 52. More bullets struck us but I could hear the Thompsons chattering in reply. The small aeroplane I had learned in and flown was much closer to the ground than this lumbering beast. I had to work out how high above the ground we were. I reduced speed even more. I was acutely aware that if we stalled then we might flip and kill us all. It seemed hard to control and I was fearful of over-correcting.

The men on the ground began to fire; thankfully it was not at us but the pursuing fighters. The JU 52 hit the ground and bumped back up in the air. Dad would have tutted at that point. I put the nose down again as I reduced the airspeed even more. We hit the ground hard but stayed on the ground. We were travelling too quickly and I reduced the engines as far as I could. I saw some tents looming up and I kicked hard on the rudder. I had not needed to do much when I had landed the single engine trainer. This JU 52 was an altogether different animal. We spun around and I worried that we might catch the ground as I felt a wheel lift and the starboard wing lurch towards the ground. Then the wheel bit and we stopped. I turned off the engines and sat. Behind me I heard cheers. Then I heard a voice from outside, "Alright Fritz! Your war is over." I glanced out of the window and saw ten guns pointing at the hatch. I began to laugh.

Chapter 4

Our injury was Bill Becket who was hit by pieces of metal from the corrugated fuselage of the German aeroplane. He was lucky it had been a direct hit from the bullets. The fragments of metal were bad enough. He would live. When the Royal Air Force police realised we were British then we were lauded as heroes. The adjutant of 266 Squadron could not believe that a Commando knew how to fly. When he discovered my name he laughed, "I knew your father. I served with him in Russia just after the Great War. Now it makes sense! Well done. You are a credit to your old man. We have rung intelligence and they are sending someone down for your prisoner. You chaps can use the Sergeants' Mess until your transport arrives."

Daddy said, "They know then?"

"One of the MPs saw your shoulder flash. Someone called Major Foster said he would come personally!"

Even though we were safe in England we were still Commandos. Daddy made sure that Bill was being looked after in the sick bay and we all kept our equipment with us. The Sergeants' Mess was filled with a barrage of questions. We, of course, had to be discreet with our answers. All that they got out of us was that we had been in France and stolen the aeroplane in order to return to England. That proved enough to satisfy them. What fascinated them more than anything was the range of weapons we carried. The Thompson machine gun and the Colt were the only such weapons they had seen.

We were rescued from further interrogation by a lorry driven by Sergeant Major Dean and with Major Foster in tow. The Intelligence Officer from London also arrived and we were taken to the pilot's briefing room so that Captain James from Intelligence and Major Foster could both debrief us at the same time.

The information we had about the camp was particularly important and the captain was disappointed we had not identified the Corps. Major Foster became both protective and annoyed, "Good God man! How in the hell would they manage that? They did damn well to stay behind enemy lines for almost three days. The fact that they know it is a Corps and not an army is important, right?"

The Captain was young and, I suspect, had not seen active service, "Quite right Major. Damned fine show chaps."

"I think, sir, that if you question the mechanic he might well know the identity of the Corps. The camp and the airfield were only a couple of miles apart."

The Captain nodded gratefully. Major Foster sniffed. "And that, Captain, is how a Commando thinks! He uses his head."

Captain James said, "And dashed important too that you identified the two fields. I dare say we might send over bombers to raid them."

"Sir," I ventured, "They are both very close to both Calais and Gravelines. There were plenty of civilians and buildings close by."

"Good point Corporal." He turned to Major Foster, "You are right. Your chaps are thinkers. Well done. That's all from me but if I have any more questions I'll give you a bell eh Major?"

Major Foster nodded, "Right chaps. Let's get you back to base. Everyone there thought we had lost you." He glanced at the Captain, "That is all isn't it Captain?"

"Oh yes, Major. And we have an aeroplane as well as a prisoner!"

Just then we heard the sound of the returning Spitfires. Major Foster laughed, "I wonder what they make of Jerry on their field eh?"

"Sir, can we go and see if Beckett is fit to travel?" Daddy would not want to leave one of our own behind."

The doctor had finished with Becket and was dealing with the German who had received a blow on the head from Poulson. "Sir, is Private Becket ready to travel back to the base?"

The doctor looked up and shook his head, "I would prefer to keep him under observation for a day or so Sergeant."

I saw Bill's face, "It's alright sir. I feel fit as a fiddle. You have done a good job here." He began to get off the bed. "Besides you will need these beds for your lads eh sir?"

I picked up his Bergen and Daddy his Thompson. The doctor shook his head, "It is right what they say, you Commandos are as mad as a pocket full of frogs! Be off with you." He wagged a finger at Daddy, "You make sure your doctor gets these notes." He handed him a manila envelope.

"Yes, sir. We will."

"Bye Fritz."

The German scowled. I said, in German, "You will get better attention here than we would if the SS had captured us. Think on that my friend." He looked up with an angry scowl upon his face. They had a different philosophy than we did.

Once in the back of the lorry and trundling down the road the lads began singing. They were just music hall songs but the fact that we had survived when we had expected to die was the difference. They were just pleased to be alive. Less than a few hours ago we had all faced death and, against the odds, we had survived. When we stopped at a checkpoint Major Foster clambered in the back with us.

"If you chaps have got the songs out of your system I will have a little chat with you. I didn't want to wash our dirty linen in front of that staff officer. What happened to Smith and Griffiths?" He held up his hands, "I think you did a first-rate job and there should be medals for this but we need to know what went wrong and then we can learn lessons."

Daddy lit his pipe. I smiled. That was his thinking time. "We reached Gravelines and we split up to recce the town's defences. It was our orders, sir."

"I know Grant. Carry on."

"We gave each pair an hour. After fifty minutes, they weren't back and we heard the alarm go off. There was the sound of firing. We scarpered. They didn't show."

Major Foster nodded. "Textbook stuff, Grant. Now the Navy is not happy because it lost an ML and crew." Daddy looked at me. "Come on lads. Out with it."

I spoke, "It's just that it doesn't do to speak ill of the dead sir and Lieutenant Williams, well sir, he was reckless. His crew told us he always went too fast. We were watching from the cliff and we heard him before we saw him. He came screaming in; he gave the engines full revs and we all know that you go in as quietly as you can. When the flare went off he had no chance."

"They were waiting then?"

Daddy nodded, "Oh they knew we were going to be there but they didn't know the time."

"So, our lads talked?"

I shook my head, "Sir, we left prints in the sand. The Germans heard the boat when we landed and came to investigate. Even if they hadn't captured our lads they would have known something was up."

He smiled, "I think I can see it now. How could we have done it differently then?"

"We need the tide times. It is better to go in when the tide is about to turn. It covers up our prints and we need a backup plan to get out. I was lucky to find that JU 52 and to fly it out It is hard to see how we could have got out otherwise."

Major Foster nodded, "We lost two sections on the raid and another ML. They might have been like you but had no means of getting out. Anyway, the position of the airfield and the camp is like gold dust. I dare say it will be bombed now."

"When I was flying out sir I saw the cliffs close to Calais were covered in 88s."

Norm nodded, "Aye sir and that camp was ringed with them too. I saw that from the co-pilot's seat."

"Nevertheless, the RAF will want to have a go at them." We must have all looked deflated. I know that I my euphoria had deflated hearing that there were almost thirty men who had been lost on this mission. It was a waste. "Come on chaps, cheer up. You look like you had a disaster when you have had a great success. We will have a couple of weeks of training and then see what our lords and masters want of us eh?"

Daddy nodded, "You are right sir. We must be tired. We haven't had much sleep in the last three days."

"Of course! I am an idiot. You can all have the day off tomorrow to recover."

"Thank you, sir!"

The chorus was drowned out by Sergeant Major Dean's voice from the front seat, "But the day after you report at six a.m. in full kit for a five-mile run and I still have the first time you set. You have to beat it!"

I smiled at Daddy, Reg Dean never compromised. If you were a Commando there were certain standards and he would make sure that everyone kept to them.

After we had dumped our bags we managed a quick swill in the sink. Hot water was a luxury and there was a rota for the bath. We would have to wait for the immersion to heat our share. We did, however, manage to put on clean clothes. That made a difference. Daddy and I headed down to the Red Lion for a pint. We had an unwritten agreement about which pubs we would use. The NCOs used the Red Lion, the Privates the Black Swan or as it was known, The Mucky Duck and the officers used The Hope and Anchor. It made discipline easier and the brewery was the same for all of the pubs.

Our late arrival and our ablutions meant that we were the last two to make the pub. Sergeant Major Dean was there, having beaten us by minutes. He had two pints on the bar when we arrived. "Here y'are lads. I reckon you deserve this."

We took the pints and raised them in a toast. "To the lads who didn't make it back!"

Everyone raised their glass at Daddy's toast and we drank in silence. The silence was broken by Wally White. "So Biggles, you can fly an aeroplane. You kept that quiet!"

There was some laughter at the reference to the boys' fictional flying hero, Biggles. Daddy said, "I for one am bloody glad he can fly. We would have been in the bag otherwise, or dead."

There were nods all around. Wally asked, "What about the two lads?"

Reg Dean tapped his glass on the bar, "White! Not in public eh?"

"Sorry Sarn't Major, I forgot." There was a rule that we didn't talk about missions where civilians could hear.

Finishing the beer Sergeant Major Dean said, "Not too many eh lads? We have a run first thing." He actually smiled at Daddy and me, "I have given these two the day off!"

After he had gone Jack Johnson said, "Bloody Hell, you must have impressed him. We didn't get a day off when we got back."

Sergeant Peter Wilson said, "Well none of us had three days in France, did we?"

I was always uncomfortable when the attention was on our section and so I changed the subject, "Have we replacements yet for the lads who were lost?"

Jack shook his head, "A new batch is due in next week." He grinned at Daddy, "That means you will have to train up two new lads."

Daddy shrugged, "We have a good section. They will help. Did you know Bill Becket caught a packet but wouldn't stay in the RAF Sick Bay? We have sound chaps."

"Aye y'have." Wally pointed to the bar with his glass, "Fancy another pint you lads?"

"We'll get these. My dad always told me to stand my own corner. It is our round. What are you on?"

The second pint went down as well as the first. The warm smoky atmosphere and the beer soon had my eyes drooping. Wally said, quietly to me, "Seriously Tom, how the hell did you manage to fly a bloody big German aeroplane and why aren't you in the air force?"

"Flying isn't that hard. Remember my dad taught me almost before I could drive. And as for the size and the type; an aeroplane is the same no matter what the size. I am just glad that we were lucky enough to get one. I didn't fancy spending the war behind bars."

"I heard a rumour that the Germans are shooting Commandos."

"That wouldn't surprise me. I met the Waffen SS and they were more than happy to shoot ordinary soldiers. I think if they could get their hands on one of us they wouldn't think twice about it."

"You reckon your lads caught a packet then?"

"The soldiers we saw in Gravelines weren't SS. On the other hand, we did hear shooting." I shrugged, "I like to think they made it and are safe. They were good lads."

"Amen to that."

The next morning, we took back the Mills bombs we had not used. I asked the Quarter Master's sergeant, Fred Jones, "Have you any gash camouflage netting?"

"Might have. What for?"

Daddy said, "We had to spend a few hours in a ditch with Jerry twenty yards away. Netting would have helped."

"I'll go and have a butchers out the back for you."

He came back ten minutes later with a roll of it. "We have this. Any good to you?"

"Perfect." Daddy reached over for it.

Fred put one hand on it and held open the other, "Fair exchange and all that lads."

Daddy looked at me and I reached into my battledress pocket and pulled out a pack of cigarettes. Fred held up two fingers and I took out a second packet. Fred quickly pocketed the packs and released the netting. As Daddy took it he mumbled, "Robbing bastard!"

Fred just grinned, "You have to look out for number one in this war, mate."

When we were outside I said, "Why are you worrying Sarge? I don't smoke. I just keep the rations for the lads."

"I know but," He turned and looked back at the hut. "He sits on his arse over here and never risks anything. Poor Bert and Ian are now in the bag or dead. It isn't fair. He is like one of those Black-Market spivs. He'll end this war a rich man."

"You know what they say about fair and the army. Don't let it get to you. Dad said that worrying about dead mates was a luxury you couldn't afford in war. Just remember them when it is all over he said."

"Then he is a better man than me. I can't get them out of my head."

"You've lost mates before though."

"Aye but then I wasn't in charge," he tapped his stripes, "these weigh a lot more when they are on your own arm."

"I know. Come on let's get some scissors and see how many bits we can get out of this."

We unrolled the netting and worked out how many pieces we would be able to get out of it. There was no point in making it too small and if it was too large then it would add weight to our Bergens. We managed to make six good sized cloaks from it. When we rolled them up we found they were quite light. We had four spares to give to the lads but we would wait a while before we distributed them.

After a bath, we both washed the uniforms we had worn in France. A Commando received more pay. We could have paid someone to do it but we both liked looking after our own equipment. Then we stripped and cleaned our guns. I sharpened my dagger on my whetstone. The blood of the dead German was still there until I cleaned it off. It was a reminder of what we did.

We were up bright and early the next day for the new routine of a five-mile run in full kit before breakfast and then a day of learning new skills and honing old ones. The new intake arrived at the start of October. To us they looked young but we realised that they weren't. Many were the same age as us and had transferred in from other units. It was just our faces showed the war we fought. None of these had seen action yet.

The two replacements were Harry Gowland and George Lowe. Harry was a northern lad from Sunderland and George came from near Carlisle. These were young and had volunteered as territorials. They were keen to learn and that always helped. After a week, we realised that they weren't as fit as we were and we used Ken and Gordy to keep an eye on them and act as a sort of big brother to them both. It paid off and by the second week they were no longer falling behind on the five mile runs.

Many lads thought they were fit until they came to the Commandos. We knew the value of the five mile runs. If we had not been as fit as we were then the Germans would have captured us already.

With the replacements, the two troops under Major Foster were back up to full strength. The rest of the Brigade was still in Scotland and we wondered what our function would be. When we debated the future most of us were agreed that we preferred working in smaller groups. The idea of going ashore in hundreds rather than tens did not appeal to us. It was, perhaps, because we had been one of the first troops to start raiding and that had been, perforce, in small numbers. Many of those with Lord Lovat had never fired a weapon in anger yet. There was a rumour that Lord Lovat was going to invade Norway with the rest of our Commando. I didn't believe that but it provided much discussion. What were the others training for?

Towards the end of October Major Foster sent for the NCOs from two sections. One was ours and one was Jack Johnson's. We met in the Troop office. Sergeant Major Dean and Lieutenant Reed were both there. "Right chaps." He nodded to Daddy and me. "Thanks to you two we sent bombers over to attack the airfields you identified and the army camp. You were right Corporal Harsker. It was heavily defended by guns and by fighters. The Wellingtons took heavy losses. It seems the only way to attack them safely with bombers is at night but the accuracy isn't very good at night and with Calais and Gravelines close by the brass don't want too many civilian casualties." He paused and I knew what was coming. "We have to go back in."

Daddy could not contain himself. "But sir, with just two sections we wouldn't stand a chance of destroying the airfield!"

Sergeant Major Dean snapped, "Grant!"

"That is all right Sergeant Major, the sergeant is quite right. No Grant, the two squads will go and illuminate the fields for the bombers."

Jack asked, "Illuminate sir?"

"Yes, send off a Very Light when you hear the bombers. It will show them where the field is."

I remembered the flare at our beach. It had only shone for a few minutes. I knew how long it would take the bombers to pass. "Sir, that won't work."

I received a glare from Sergeant Major Dean but Major Foster just smiled, "Go on, Harsker. Your contributions are always worth hearing."

"Well sir, even allowing for wind drift and the like the flare will only burn for a couple of minutes. You have just as much chance of missing the target as hitting it. It seems a risky mission with little chance of success."

The Major looked disappointed, "You are saying it can't be done because if you do then I have to tell you that you are wrong. This has come from Commando Headquarters."

"But not Bomber Command eh sir? If we fire the flares when we hear the bombers then by the time they get over the target the flare might not even be visible. No sir, I am saying we need to start a fire. That way it will burn long enough for the bombers to target the field. A fire will be visible for miles."

Jack said, "How would you start a fire?"

I smiled, "Aeroplanes use petrol and the hangars are made of wood. I reckon we could rig something up to burn."

The Major was intrigued and he leaned forward, "Go on, how would you get inside the field?"

"I am not sure about the one at Oye-Plage but the one at Marck just had a wire fence and we got in that way before."

"Wasn't it mined, Harsker?"

"No, Lieutenant Reed."

I saw the two officers exchanging looks, "That might work. It is no more risky than sending a flare up."

Sergeant Major Dean said, "Less risky sir. A flare doesn't give the lads much time to escape. They could use a timer for the fire."

"You would need to have more than one fire. There would always be a chance that just one timer might not work."

"You are right, Lieutenant Reed." The Major looked at Daddy and me; I suspect because we had had eyes on the field. "Could you do more than one fire?"

I had seen Daddy thinking during this conversation and he nodded. "They looked to have the fighters dispersed, sir. Three fires near three aeroplanes should be possible. One man to each aeroplane and the rest keeping watch. The thing is sir we would have to know when the bombers were coming; I mean to within ten minutes. We would need to get away fairly sharpish."

"We can do that."

I coughed, "And, sir, how do we get off."

"I know Harsker, you had problems the last time. We have had a word with Navy and there will be a backup pick up point too."

"We can't use the same beaches we used last time, sir. They will have them guarded tighter than a Waaf's knickers."

Major Foster laughed, "Very colourful Sergeant. We are working on that. The Navy has been over to recce suitable sites." We all nodded, "Any further questions?" We shook our heads, "The mission is scheduled for the thirtieth. You may need to do a cliff assault. We have Lulworth Cove close by. You had better use that to practise. Lieutenant Reed will command."

We gathered the two sections and drew ropes from the QM stores. As we headed for the cliffs around Lulworth Daddy said, "We have all done the basic climbing course, sir but cliffs..."

"Don't worry Sergeant, I did a fair bit of rock climbing before the war. Besides I have had a look at the maps and the cliffs are not as intimidating as those around Dover. There are more beaches than cliffs where we are going."

Jack asked, "And which field will we be doing sir?"

"I will be with you at Oye-Plage. Grant and the others are familiar with Marck." He looked at Daddy, "You have a way in I take it?"

"Unless they have bolted that stable door then yes sir, but if not then we can always make another. I am guessing that we get landed one night; hide during the day and then escape the second night?"

"That is about it."

"Then we should have enough time to recce the fence the first night." He grinned at Jack, "Unless they have demolished it we have a nice little hidey hole for the day."

Jack sniffed, "You know you have more luck than is good for you."

"What explosives will we be taking sir?"

"T.N.T. again, White. Clock timers." Wally groaned. "I know they are heavy but they work."

"There is a backup we could use sir."

"And what is that Corporal Harsker?"

"The aeroplanes will have fuel in them. If we open the drain then we could use that to set them on fire."

Daddy shook his head, "That would be no good. We would have to be close enough to light the fuel."

"Both airfields are close to roads; we could shift down them quicker than across country. We could wait until the timers set off the charge and then run. It would only need two to wait behind as insurance. If the timers didn't work they could resort to lighting the petrol." I shrugged, "Besides spilling the petrol would guarantee a good fire."

"If we knew where the drain was."

"We ask the RAF. They will know."

Lieutenant Reed nodded. It was good working with Jack Johnson's section. Daddy and I had been in that section until our promotion. My closest friend had been Sean and he hoped to be a corporal like me. He was the senior Commando in the section after Jack and Wally. Our close links made the training easier somehow. We needed all of our camaraderie and shared experiences to get us through the cliff climbing.

By the time we had finished on the cliffs our hands were red raw and bleeding. We had had all taken a tumble, Lieutenant Reed apart. But we all felt more confident. We finished up learning how to abseil down the cliffs. That was frightening for you had to step out over nothing. Lieutenant Reed said, "That won't be a problem lads."

"Why not sir?"

"Because Barker, we will be doing it at night. It will be pitch black and you will see bugger all!"

If he thought to cheer us up then he failed. However, we all became quite adept and the Lieutenant even showed us how to do it quickly by bouncing down. "It is risky at night as you might not be able to see what is at the bottom but it is the quickest way down and that might be important. You will all have your own rope. We might need to look at what we are packing in the Bergens. The ropes will be vital." John Connor was given the extra weight of the Aldis signalling lamp. If we ran in to trouble we could send signals to the Navy who would stand off the pickup beaches.

On the way back I ran through this risky plan in my mind. It seemed to me that there were more opportunities for things to go wrong than to go right. We had to find a beach which was not patrolled. We had to revisit somewhere we had already raided. We had to use timers and we had to escape by a different route from the one we took to get in. Added to that was the fact that we had to time the raid to coincide with a bombing run. We would need all of Daddy's famous luck and then some.

Chapter 5

With just two MLs we were able to load and set sail in daylight. Daylight was something of an exaggeration. It was a murky grey day with drizzle. It was a long voyage and we would not be lying up in Kent. An MGB accompanied us and I was delighted to see Bill Leslie. He was still alive. We had little time to talk but I told him of the disaster on our last voyage. "It wouldn't be down to your lads, Tom. That Williams was a mad bugger. He seemed to treat the war as a game."

"You sailed with him?"

He shook his head, "He was in the flotilla for a while and I got to see him in action." He pointed to our officer. "Lieutenant Jarvis is sound. He might look like he hasn't started to shave but he is a good sailor."

As we bounced across the Channel I mentally ran through all that I would need to do. We were landing at Sangatte just south of Calais. The meteorological boys had worked out the tides and we would be able to leave from the same beach at Sangatte. It meant that the other section and Lieutenant Reed would have a longer journey but that could not be helped. The backup plan was for us to be picked up from the cliffs at Gris Nez. I, for one, was hoping that we would get off from Sangatte. It was close to where Louis Bleriot had flown across the Channel for the first time. A beach departure was preferable to a cliff climb. The thought of descending a cliff at night to catch a launch was a frightening prospect.

Our packs were heavier than ever. Despite our best efforts we had had to bring more than ever before. The ropes, the TNT, and the clocks were all invaluable. We would just have to tough it out. Bill had been right. Our Captain knew his business. His leading hand came to us and said, "Just half an hour to go lads. Get ready."

This was our second such landing and we knew what to expect. The tide was on the turn and the young lieutenant was able to run us in a little closer so that we barely got wet. The water came to just above my knees. I was the first ashore and I ran up the beach and then crouched with cocked gun. I scanned the shoreline but saw nothing untoward. More importantly I heard nothing either. It was a narrow beach and the road, according to the maps, was just fifty yards from the beach. Connor ran up to me and tapped me on the shoulder. I ran the fifty yards to the road and threw myself to the ground. There were a couple of houses but neither was closer than a hundred yards from our position. The Navy had done their job well. They had landed us at an isolated section of occupied France.

I half stood and, without turning, waved the others forward. We would travel together as far as Marck and the others would then make their own way to Oye-Plage. It was only three miles from our target and would just take them an hour longer. I would be the scout for this raid. My knowledge of French and the fact that I had scouted before made me the obvious choice. We had studied the old road maps from before the war and we had decided to risk using the D 247. I took it as a mark of the Lieutenant's confidence in me that he thought I would be able to spot danger before it struck us.

I led us towards Coquelles, a tiny hamlet. The late hour and the curfew ensured that no locals were out and about. There might be German sentries and patrols but I hoped that I would see and hear them. We were wearing our rubber soled shoes and we were silent as we almost crept along the tarmac. Each time we neared a house or a building I slowed down. Our equipment was so well designed that it did not make a noise but I was taking no chances. I had a great responsibility upon my shoulders.

We reached the outskirts of Calais. I smelled tobacco and wood smoke. I waved the others to get into a ditch. I crawled snake like, towards the road junction. There was a sentry box and a brazier. It was a check point. I turned and waved Gordy forward. I pointed ahead and made the sign that we had to disable the guards. If we killed them then that might cause a bigger hue and cry. Dead men would enrage their comrades. This was not a good start to our raid but there was no point in making it into a disaster.

We moved together and separated close to the sentry box. I heard them speaking. I calculated that my target was just to the right of the box and was poking the fire. I ran up to him and, wrapping my left arm tightly around his neck with my forearm on his Adam's apple I put my right arm behind his neck and pulled hard. The move was called the Japanese strangle. I had not yet used it in action. I knew that too much pressure would kill the guard and not enough would enable him to shout. I needed to make him lose consciousness.

When I felt him go limp I released him and lowered him to the ground. I took his belt and fastened his hands together. I used my knife to cut two long pieces of leather from his equipment and tied his feet together and then his hands to his feet. Finally, I ripped his shirt in two and gagged him. Polly had joined me and we dragged the unconscious sentry into the ditch where we hid him with his greatcoat. Norm and Gordy brought the other. The Lieutenant nodded his approval and waved me forward again.

We managed to make another two miles before I saw in the distance the dim lights of a vehicle and heard the sound of a Kübelwagen. I waved us all into the ditch. I hoped they were heading for Calais. If they went to the crossroads they would find the unconscious sentries and would then search for us. After it had passed I rose and I began to run. It was time for double time. To my left I could see the airfield in the distance. We were close to our target. I expected more signs of German security nearer to the field and, sure enough, I heard dogs barking in the distance. I left the road and led the two sections across the field to the distant road, the D 940. I doubted that the Germans would be patrolling the fields but the road was a different matter. As we crossed the field I was aware that it was trodden down and, even in the dark, I could see the patches where tents had stood. We were crossing what had been the camp we had seen. As we approached the road I gave the signal to halt and then made my way to the hedge which ran along the road. I peered over it. I could see, less than six hundred yards away, the airfield. I looked to the right and saw the dark shape which I now knew to be the wrecked farm.

The road was empty and no one was coming and so I clambered over the hedge and then waved the others forward. I watched in the road as they crossed before me and disappeared into the field on the other side. Gordy led them to the wrecked farm. He took them around the outside to the back door where we all gathered our wits.

Sergeant Grant said, "Right, sir. You keep on this road for three miles and you should find the other airfield. There is a hedge and a ditch if you need to hide."

"Understood Sergeant. Good luck lads and see you on the beach."

As my old friend, Sean Higgins, passed I clasped his hand, "Good luck Sean."

He grinned, "Don't forget Tom I have Irish blood in me! We were born lucky."

They slipped out of the back and disappeared. We took off our Bergens. My shoulders ached. I pitied the other section. They had three more miles of travelling with their heavy Bergens.

"Curtis, you stay here with Gowland and Lowe. The rest of you bring your pistols and wire cutters."

We left out of the back and made our way to the airfield perimeter. The first thing I noticed was the barbed wire on the top of the fence. They had also cleared the undergrowth from the bottom. That was a problem. As I had feared they had replaced the damaged section. However, what they had not done was stop the animals from burrowing their way in. The ground at the bottom was soft and easy to shift. We did not cut out a whole section of wire. The wire was hexagonal and we cut through three of the strands in each section. A cursory glance would make a sentry think that the wire was whole but when we came to break in, half of our work would be done. We cut a section which was six feet long and two feet high. It took time but we would be able to get inside quickly the next night.

We wearily made our way back to the farmhouse and I saw the first hint of dawn in the eastern sky. I was not certain that the other section would have achieved what we had done in the time available. We had had the advantage of knowing where we had to go and what we had to do. The Lieutenant and the other section would have to discover this for themselves. We had set up the sleeping rota before we left England and I crashed out almost immediately.

Daddy woke me with some tepid tea. We had brought a flask with us. It was a luxury but, at that moment, it was worth it. "Everything all right, Sarge?"

He frowned, "I am not sure. There was a great deal of activity on the road just after dawn. Lorry loads of troops heading towards Gravelines. I am guessing that they found those sentries."

"Sorry about that. If we had killed them they might have thought it was the resistance."

"That would have made it worse for the French. No, you did the right thing. It was just unfortunate."

"Have the fighters taken off yet?"

"Nah, it's pissing down, like it was yesterday. It looks like they are grounded."

"That's good then."

"Why?"

"They are more likely to have full tanks."

"That makes sense."

We had been shown by an RAF mechanic where the drain tap on the tanks were. We were lucky; we knew the type of aircraft we would have to deal with. The other section had more variables. If they had not flown then they would still be ready to fly with ammunition and petrol loaded.

"The problem is this rain, Sarge. If we open the tanks too early it will mix with the water and might not burn."

He shrugged, "We will have to wait and see."

We spent a tense day worrying if the Germans would come down the track and find us. They didn't.

As soon as it was dark we left the derelict farm and made our way to the fence. It was still raining; it was a fine rain. It was the kind my grandmother had said, 'soaked you'. For us it helped. Any guards on the field would not wish to venture far from shelter. And visibility would be down to a few yards. We were less than a hundred yards from the place we would enter when I heard the dogs. They had three German Shepherds, Alsatians. I was glad that it was wet. The rain would have washed away any trace of smell we might have left when we had cut the fence. After they had gone we hurried to the fence. The trouble was that they would return and that could cause a problem. We did not have the luxury now of setting our bombs, opening the tanks and then most of the section leaving. We would all have to wait longer and that increased the danger.

It took forty minutes to finish cutting through the wire so that we could slip through. I went with Ken and Bill to set the charges in the aeroplanes. I had told them how to open the cockpit. As I was placing mine in the cockpit of the 109 furthest from the fence I saw that Ken could not open his. I signalled for him to put it next to the wheel. We had been told that the bombers would be over at midnight. It was now almost eleven. I set the timer for eleven fifty-five. When I heard the reassuring tick tock of the clock I climbed out, shut the Perspex and went to the drain hole. The rain was even lighter now but I waited. I saw the other two watching me. It was my responsibility. I watched the fingers of my watch edge around. I knew that the bombers could come a little early or a little late. It would depend upon the wind and the air.

At eleven thirty I could wait no longer. I signalled to the other two and unscrewed the drain cap. The petrol flooded out. The tank was, indeed, full. We each had an old pan we had taken from the farmhouse and I now filled it with the fuel. Although there was a slight slope I needed to make a petrol fuse to the aeroplane. When I saw the shimmering river of fuel I made my way to Bill's aeroplane. The fuel from my 109 had flowed towards his. We hurried to Ken. Bill poured some of his fuel so that there was a line of petrol from my aeroplane to Ken's. We used almost the last of the petrol to lay a trail to the fence. I kept a little in mine to make sure the fire started.

Daddy waved half of the men to form a semi-circle some thirty yards from us. Our escape route would take us back to the road and was the reverse of the route we had taken coming. I had tried to dissuade Daddy telling him that our attack on the sentries would have alerted the Germans but as the alternative was going through Calais, he was adamant we would risk our original plan.

At eleven forty-five I happened to look at my watch. I thought I heard the faint hum of engines to the west but then I convinced myself I was imagining it. Suddenly, to the north, in the direction of Oye-Plage I heard the sound of small arms fire and then the crack and bang of grenades. I turned to look and saw a sheet of flame leap into the air. There were more explosions and I saw something large explode.

"That's done it! Right Tom, set off the petrol!"

"Hang on Sarge. We still have a little time. I can't hear the bombers yet."

I saw him chew his lip. A klaxon sounded inside the field at the same time as the air raid siren went off.

"Well it's too late now to worry. Do it!"

The sirens told me that the bombers were on their way. I took out the matches and lit one. I threw it on to the petrol. The water had thinned it out, as I had feared. I threw another two matches and then the half pan of undiluted fuel. It caught. As the flames danced towards the first 109 I saw German lorries leaving the airfield. They were going to the aid of Oye-Plage.

"Sarge, we can't go the way we came, the Germans are on the road. We will have to go towards Calais, through the town!"

Just then the flames struck the first 109 and engulfed it in flames. "Follow me. To the west!" Daddy led the way. I took out a Mills bomb and put it in my pocket. I cocked my Thompson. I had gone no further than a few feet when Bill's bomb went off. He must have set the timer too short. The first 109 went up and the explosion knocked me from my feet. That probably saved my life for when Ken's aeroplane went up the wall of flame washed right over my head. Finally, my 109 went up and I heard the bombers overhead.

I struggled to my feet, my ears ringing and ran after the rest of the section. The German dog handlers had raced out when they heard the explosions. I saw the three dogs leaping towards my men as the Germans unslung their guns. I dropped to my knee and fired four short bursts. Two dogs went down and two of the handlers. The third turned to fire at me and I emptied the rest of the magazine into him. I quickly changed magazines and caught up with the others just as Gordy shot the last dog.

Then the bombs fell. The section hit the ground. "No lads! On your feet! This is our best chance to get through Calais while the air raid is on."

Daddy nodded, "The Corporal is right keep running!"

It made all of our training runs seem easy by comparison. Our fires meant that the bombers could see the field clearly. They had come in lower than I had expected. The German searchlights danced around in the sky looking for them but the gunners had less success than in daylight. The sudden attack had caught them unawares. Even though the bomb run was accurate the shock waves of the explosions were close enough to knock us from our feet a couple of times. As we approached the road which ran between the field and the coast I saw a German machine gun post less than a hundred yards away. They saw us and traversed the gun. God smiled on us that day. The last bomb in a stick scored a direct hit on the emplacement and killed all within.

Daddy ran directly down the road towards Calais. We knew that the town was in no danger but the locals did not and those who had been on the street were desperately taking shelter. Any Germans were running to the airfield to fight the fires. There were so many fires now, as ammunition and fuel caught fire, that it was almost like day. As we ran through the French town I almost smiled. No one was looking at the road. Their attention was either on the skies or on their own safety. The odd person we saw did not even seem to see us.

I heard the bombers receding. Daddy halted us close to the harbour. It was partly to regroup but mainly to get our bearings. The port was a complicated place. We had to get across the port, the ancillary buildings, the suburbs, and then drop down to the beach. That would enable us to run along the shoreline to Sangatte where, hopefully, our MLs would be waiting. He took out the map and pointed to the far side of the harbour. I nodded and we set off once more.

Here there were more Germans. The port was closely monitored. Fortunately, most of the guards were inside the port complex and their eyes were on the sky. In the distance, we could hear the sudden crackle of gun fire as ammunition went off at the field. However, I also heard the bark of small arms fire too. Was it our mates having to fight their way out?

I don't know if it was his old wound or carelessness but Bill Becket suddenly tripped in front of me. I had to hurdle him to avoid falling. I stopped and helped him to his feet. "Are you hurt?" He shook his head. "Then let's go we are losing the others."

The short delay meant that the others were almost eighty yards ahead. I saw Daddy's arm as he waved it to the right. We were heading for the beach. I knew, from the mental map I carried in my head, that we had just three hundred yards to go before we reached the relative safety of the sand. As the rest of the section began to cross the bridge over the small canal which ran into the dock four Germans emerged from a guard hut. There was a crack of rifle fire and I saw someone go down. Bill and I kept running, firing short bursts as we ran. Two dived back into the hut and two fell. I drew my Mills bomb and pulled the pin. Without breaking stride, we passed the guard hut at full speed and the two dead Germans. I rolled the grenade into the building. Ken and Polly had picked up Connor who had been hit. As we reached the other side of the bridge there was a crack and an explosion behind me as the hut was blown up. We were showered by falling wood.

We had no time to tend to Connor. Bill and I turned to look back. There appeared to be no pursuit. Daddy took the section ahead and we followed. When I felt sand beneath my feet I felt a little happier. Fifty yards down the beach we stopped and Daddy looked at Connor's shoulder. It was a mess.

"Gowland, Lowe, watch the road. Ken, get the Aldis lamp from Connor's Bergen. You are signaller now."

"Right Corp."

I changed magazines and fitted a full one. I had one full one left and a half used one. If we had the chance I would reload my magazines from the spare ammunition in my Bergen but I hoped that I would not need it. I looked at my watch. It was two o'clock. The MLs were due between two thirty and three. Their orders were to stand off until we signalled and then close with us.

I heard Daddy's voice, "That is all I can do. Poulson, you carry his Bergen." He threw the Tommy gun to Gordy. "Here you can be Two Gun Tex!"

"Right Sarge."

"Corporal, you and Becket are tail end Charlie!"

"Righto!"

"Right lads, down the beach and let's find these boats!"

As I looked north and east I saw the glow from the burning airfield. I saw flames shoot up and then die back. We had achieved our objective but I couldn't help thinking about the lieutenant and the other section. The early attack was ominous. It suggested that something had gone wrong.

We moved backwards down the beach until I heard Daddy say, "Mines! The beach is mined! Head to the road and be sharpish!"

When we reached the road Norm said, "I can see a light flashing. It must be the launch."

"Curtis, signal them and tell them the beach is mined. Tell them we will go to the backup point at Gris Nez. We'll be there in an hour!"

As the Aldis began to chatter I said, "We have a wounded man."

"I know and dawn will break in two or three hours. We have to do it in an hour."

"It is almost six miles and we have to do a descent down a cliff too!"

"We are Commandos, Tom, and we don't give in."

I nodded, "Then take them down the road. I will catch up with you."

As we had approached the beach I had spied a clutch of buildings just off the main road. It looked to be a garage of sorts. I ran back to it. Approaching it cautiously I slung my Tommy gun and drew my Colt. I moved towards the building cautiously. I spied a car but it was too small to carry all of us. I went around the back to see what else was there. Suddenly there was a light from behind me and I turned to look down the barrel of a shotgun. It was the garage owner.

I did not have time for any kind of deception. "I am a British Commando. We have a wounded man and I need a vehicle to get away from here."

The barrel of the gun was dropped and a grin appeared. He nodded to the north, "Your work?" I nodded, "Well done. Follow me." We went out of the back and there was an old beat up Citroen tow truck. I looked at him, doubt written all over my face, he shrugged, "She goes."

I threw my Bergen and Tommy gun in the back. "Thank you. I hope you won't get in trouble for this."

He laughed, "What can I do if the gangsters from England steal my truck?" He shook my hand, "They have my land but I can still fight. Good luck my friend."

I got behind the wheel. It was not the smoothest gearbox in the world and had no power but it went. I headed along the road. I did not use lights but I had the window down and said, every hundred yards, "It's me lads!"

Half a mile down the road the section rose like ghosts from the ditch. "Lift anyone?"

Daddy grinned, "A bloody miracle worker is what you are old son. Put Connor in the cab with Tom; the rest in the back."

We were close to Wissant when I heard a crack from the beach at Sangatte. I wondered if a German had followed us and triggered one of his own mines. I hoped so. When we reached Tardinghen I turned off the main road and drove gingerly along the smaller, spiralling road. It twisted and turned until it passed through the tiny hamlet of Framezelle and then we were at the cliff top. The rather dubious brakes barely stopped me. We emptied the truck and then, with Daddy guiding me I backed it up close to the cliff edge. Reverse gear was hard to find! The tow truck's hook would be used to secure the rope. It meant we could abseil down with a securely fastened rope.

"Corporal, you take charge here. Curtis, you and the lamp will be the second down after me. Poulson and Barker, rig something up so that we can lower Connor down the cliff."

"I'm fine, Sarge. I can make it on my own."

"You are fine when a doc in England says you are. Until then you are an invalid."

"Sarge I can hear the ML engines." Becket pointed out to sea.

"Right Curtis, let's go. Harsker, you take charge here."

Daddy slipped over the cliff closely followed by Curtis. Poulson and Barker had made a sling for Connor. "I feel like a bloody mummy in this!

"Good that means you can't move. Polly and Gordy, you abseil down next to him. Gowland and Lowe you lower him gently." I watched as the injured man disappeared over the top.

There was just Norm and I left to watch. Suddenly Ford said, "Corp I can hear something coming along the road. It sounds like a motor bike."

I turned, "As soon as Connor is down you pair follow and tell the Sarge we have company. We will follow when we can."

"Right Corp!"

I joined Ford at the top of the road. I could see three pairs of headlights, dim though they were, and there was a motorbike and sidecar, without lights well ahead of two other vehicles. One appeared to be another motor bike while the second looked to be a German vehicle of some description. I took out a grenade and laid it on the ground before me and then cocked my Thompson. "Wait for the order eh Norm?"

"Right Corp."

I lined up my gun so that I could spray the bike and side car. I was just about to shout, "*Fire!*" When I heard Sean's voice shout, "Commando Higgins inbound!"

I took the situation in a flash. The motorbike had the remnants of our friends. "Norm, it is a friendly but the ones behind aren't!"

Sean and his motorbike spun around behind us as the first Germans appeared. We fired our guns in short bursts. Norm hit the rider with his first volley. We had to dive out of the way as the bike kept going with a dead rider. The gunner tried to jump out but his webbing got in the way. It plunged over the cliff.

The Kübelwagen behind had a machine gun. They made the mistake of firing too soon before the barrel could depress enough to hit us. We both fired and then, as my gun clicked empty I reached down and pulled the pin on the grenade. The Kübelwagen did not follow the motorcycle and the driver spun it round, barely avoiding the tow truck. The grenade landed in the vehicle and we threw ourselves to the ground. The concussion from the explosion made my head ring and the debris flew the air. I stood and drew my Colt. There was no one else following.

"Keep watch, Norm!"

I turned and ran to the motorcycle and side car. Sean and Jack Johnson were leaning over Lieutenant Reed in the sidecar. Jack shook his head, "He's dead."

Sean said, "Poor bugger. He was hit and it saved Wally's life then Wally went to the beach to signal the launches and stood on a mine! A bloody waste."

Norm ran up. "Corp, more Krauts coming. I can hear their engines. It is a lorry this time."

"Right let's get down the ropes."

Jack said, "We take the Lieutenant with us!"

Norm looked at me as though he was going to object, "Right. We leave no one behind. Here take my rope and lower him with this one."

"What about you Corp?"

I will go down with the others on this last one. Go on Ford, you get down and tell the Sergeant what happened."

We tied the rope under the Lieutenant's armpits. The blood had congealed on his back and was sticky. We began to lower him. I heard the engines of the German vehicles. "I'll go and delay them."

I ran to the Kübelwagen. Two of the Germans had been thrown clear. I found three of their potato masher grenades. I broke the porcelain tops and attached the toggle to the next grenade so that there was a line of them I placed them at the top of the path so that when the Germans ran to the cliff edge they would set them off. I saw that Sean and Jack had already descended. I was the last one on the cliff top. Taking out my last two Mills bombs I went to the edge of the road. The Germans were some fifty yards down the slope and struggling to get up in their truck. As the vehicle moved towards me I took out the pins and lobbed them one by one high in the air. Then I ran for the rope; I pulled it and it was free. The other two had reached the bottom. There were two explosions in quick succession as the grenades went off. I had no idea if I had caused damage. I just wanted to slow them up.

I had no time for a steady descent and, after wrapping it around my back I stepped over. I flexed my knees and then sprang back and allowed the rope to run through my hands. I had not had time to don gloves and I knew that I would burn my hands when I slowed down. Burned hands were something I could live with. The cliff came up and I flexed my knees and kicked again. I heard a series of explosions from the top of the cliff. They had found my booby traps. I glanced down and saw the ground less than thirty feet away. I gripped the rope and, ignoring the pain, pulled it across my chest. I stopped instantly. I slowly lowered myself the last ten feet or so.

As I dropped, bullets sprayed from above. I turned and saw the others making their way to the two MLs. I aimed my gun at the top of the cliff and emptied the magazine. It worked for all the heads ducked back. As I waded through the surf I saw the wrecked remains of the German motorcycle and sidecar. The spread-eagled Germans told their own story. After hurling myself into the water I clambered on the ML. I heard bullets hit the water and the MLs' gunners fired their machine guns. They hauled me aboard; the Lieutenant spun the wheel and we surged away from the coast of France. We had escaped. The fact that only two of the other section had survived was a disaster but we were heading home. We had survived and that was important.

Chapter 6

The rating rolled me over. "Well jumped Corporal, you were cutting it fine."

"Thank the Lord we are safe now."

He shook his head, "Don't tempt fate, Corporal. There are a couple of E-boats out to sea. We have been ducking and diving to avoid them all night." He jerked his thumb back at the coast. I daresay Fritz will have told his mates where we are. They will be after a nice juicy target like a Motor Launch filled with Commandos."

I slithered down to where the others were waiting. There was just Sean, Jack, and Norm Ford on this launch. The rest were aboard the other ML. "What happened, Sarge?"

"We were unlucky. We had cut the wire and had just set the charges when the dogs found us. We used the Tommy guns and grenades to escape. The grenades set fire to the bombers and then we ran. Jerry was all over us and we had a running fight. We headed towards the road. We lost Jenkins and Dixon there. The Lieutenant wanted to head for the beach. He thought we had a better chance that way."

Sean shook his head and took up the story, "Aye and we might have made it if it wasn't for the troops coming down the road. There were two motor cycle combinations, a Kübelwagen, and a lorry. They opened up. We killed the crew of the first motor bike. There was a fire fight. Jerry dived out of his vehicles to try to surround us. There were just the four of us left by then. Lieutenant Reed told us to get aboard the motorcycle. He and Wally threw four grenades. They dived in the sidecar and we headed for the rendezvous. We were overcrowded but we escaped."

"I reckon you were lucky. You could be in the bag by now. I know you lost some lads but you did bloody well to escape."

Jack nodded, "So we thought. There was confusion in Calais and we breezed through. I couldn't believe it. No one was looking at us. I reckon they heard the bike and thought we were Germans. Then we came to a bridge over a canal and there were krauts there looking at some dead sentries. As we passed them we were fired at and that was when the Lieutenant was hit."

I had a sickening feeling in my stomach. That had been my decision. "That was my fault. I killed the sentries."

"It wasn't your fault. You were trying to escape. It was just bad luck. When we reached the beach at Sangatte, Wally was so keen to send the signal that he didn't see the sign for the minefield. He knew nowt about it. He just went up. Then the others caught up with us and, well, you know the rest."

"We were luckier than you then. We heard the explosions and we escaped after the bombers came over. If you hadn't stopped Jerry he would have caught up with us. We ran through Calais and it was only when we reached the canal we hit trouble. We told the MLs that the beach was mined. I borrowed the tow truck and we made it to the rendezvous."

Jack looked at the body of the Lieutenant. It had been covered by a blanket, "Do you reckon it was worth it? We left a lot of good lads behind."

"It is a trade-off really. What were they on your field, bombers?" They both nodded. "And we had fighters. That is two squadrons of aeroplanes that won't bomb London or shoot down our Spitfires and Hurricanes any time soon. There are fighter pilots who will have a better chance of survival."

"But they'll replace the aeroplanes soon enough."

"Not as soon as you might think, Sean and they will have to repair the airfields. Goodness only knows how many personnel they will have lost. We might have lost a couple of bombers although I didn't see any but if they had gone over in daylight then more than half wouldn't have returned." I pointed to Lieutenant Reed, "You know that he would say it was worth the sacrifice if he was here."

"You are right but it is such a waste."

"And you are thinking about Wally too."

"Aye you are right. We had been together since we joined up. When he had his wound, I thought that was it. He would go through the rest of the war and survive."

I lay back on the pitching deck of the launch. "Don't make plans. Don't think about tomorrow. Just survive."

I noticed, behind us, that the sky was lightening. We would soon be home. I had just closed my eyes when I heard, "E-Boats!" I had tangled with these powerful beasts before. They were faster, bigger and better armed than anything we had. "Hang on!" The young lieutenant threw the boat hard over.

The launch heeled to port to take us away from the E-boats which were coming from the north east. I put my half full magazine into my Tommy gun. It would only be useful if they closed with us but it was reassuring having a weapon in my hand; no matter how inadequate. I looked astern and saw the huge boats closing with us. The ML was fast but the E-Boats could catch them.

The Vickers gunners were already in position. The Hotchkiss six pounder would be no use as it was forward of the bridge. The two E-boats were travelling almost twenty miles an hour faster than us and catching up rapidly. They had twenty-millimetre cannons and they would tear through the wooden hull of our launch. Our young Lieutenant was doing his best. We were swinging from side to side to avoid giving the enemy a target but they were gaining so rapidly that it would soon not make any difference how much we swung our stern. I felt helpless. There was nothing that I could do.

When the leading boat opened fire, I saw the tracer as it arced towards us. The skill of our Lieutenant was shown when the shells struck the space we had just occupied. Lieutenant Jarvis in the ML ahead was also weaving his way home. The others had a better chance of survival as they were ahead of us but as I could not even see the English coastline it was likely that we would both end up in a watery grave.

I noticed that the leading E-Boat was not catching us as quickly and I began to hope that, perhaps, it had suffered some mechanical failure. When I saw the second one draw abeam of the other I knew that I was wrong. The Germans wanted to end this quickly and for that they wanted two ships to fire at us. The converging fire of six cannons tore through the starboard Vickers gun and the two crew were cut in half.

I jumped up to the gun. "Norm, you load and I'll fire!"

I was not going to sit idly by. If I was going to die I would, at least, die fighting. I reached the Vickers gun. The dead rating had not even had the chance to fire it. Dad had told me how reliable the Vickers was and that it had a long range. I would find out for myself now. "You feed the ammo, Norm."

"Right Corp!"

I tapped the side of the barrel to align it with the port E-Boat. I hoped they had tracer rounds. I squeezed the triggers gently and saw the rounds arc towards the German. They had tracer and I saw where they hit. I had the range. The gunner on the port side opened fire too. I adjusted my aim. I was firing too high. I gave a longer burst. Unlike my dad in the Great War I could reload. He had had to conserve his ammunition. We had belts of the stuff. My aim was better and I struck his bow. The other gunner joined in and we were able to fire at the cupola with the cannon in. We must have upset his aim for the shells stopped striking our launch. As we hit a wave my next burst hit the bridge. It was pure luck but I guess I hit someone for the E-Boat veered a little to port.

Every gun on the two German boats was now directed at Norm and me. We had no cover. I felt the rounds as they thudded into the hull. Suddenly smoke began to drift from the rear. I shouted, "You have smoke, sir!"

As the two E-Boats closed in for the kill I heard the double crack of two three pounders. The water spouts told their own story. Sean shouted, "It is a couple of MGBs! Well done Navy!"

We redoubled our efforts as the two MGBs poured their shells and machine gun bullets into the E-Boat I had already hit. It began to smoke and turned to port. We raked the side with the Vickers and I saw German sailors fall into the sea as we cut them down. The second E-Boat was now outnumbered and it, too, turned and headed home. The MGBs leapt after them. They would soon have to give up the chase for the E-boats were much faster but they would enjoy the brief reversal of fortunes.

The engine room rating came up, "Sir, the engine has been damaged. We'll need a tow."

"Thank you, Anderson." He picked up his megaphone; Lieutenant Jarvis had turned around to see what the damage was. "I'm afraid we need a tow old boy."

"Happy to oblige!"

As the sky lightened we chugged our way home. The two MGBS raced on either side of us and took station to escort us back home. They circled us like sheepdogs. I saw Bill and waved. There was something reassuring about seeing the same faces each time we sailed. We were like a large extended family.

It took us until almost dark to reach Weymouth. We could have put in at any number of ports but I think everyone wanted to take Lieutenant Reed home. Lieutenant Jarvis radioed ahead. Although we had seen to Private Connor's wounds all of us wanted him looked at by a doctor. There would be one waiting. I knew, even before we reached Weymouth, that Major Foster would be there. He and Lieutenant Reed had been friends. Lieutenant Reed had been immensely popular with everyone and would be sadly missed.

As we passed the outer harbour Jack said, "You did well Higgins. I am going to recommend that you be made up to Corporal."

He did not look thrilled at the prospect. "They'll all be new lads, Sarge. It won't be the same."

I pointed to Norm, who was sound asleep. "All these lads were new to Daddy and me. They are a good bunch and I wouldn't swap any of them. The two new lads who replaced Smith and Griffiths are good blokes too. I don't reckon we will get through this war with the same men we have now. If you wanted that you should have joined the Catering Corps."

Sean laughed, "You are joking! No, you are both right. Perhaps Major Foster won't want me as a Corporal."

Jack laughed, "I think you'll find that he will!"

There was a sombre mood as we took off the dead body. I looked at Lieutenant Jarvis. He had lost two men and had no bodies to return; they lay in the Channel. In the heat of the battle he had not noticed their deaths but I had seen the change on the voyage back. He was realising that they were gone. We stepped ashore and followed the stretcher bearers carrying Lieutenant Reed and Private Connor. Major Foster came over to Jack, Daddy and me.

"The RAF said that the bombing raid was a success. Both fields were destroyed. You can be proud of what you achieved."

Jack nodded and spoke for the three of us, "We are sir but we left a lot of good lads back there so don't expect us to be happy about it."

"I'm not and I, for one, will raise a glass tonight to Lieutenant Reed." He held up a manila envelope. "He was just promoted to Captain. I knew before you left but kept it as a surprise. Perhaps I shouldn't have."

It was strange to think of officers like Major Foster having regrets. He always seemed so confident.

That night, in the pub, it was a quiet atmosphere. The last time we had been there Wally had been with us and now he was gone. No one spoke about the death or about Wally. We didn't do that. Nor did we banter, as we usually did. There was some desultory talk about football but as there would be none for the duration that petered out. A couple of the younger corporals tried to talk about films but the exploits of John Wayne in 'Stagecoach' and Errol Flynn in 'They died with their boots on' were seen as unrealistic and that conversation died out too.

The Quarter Master asked, "Did you lads use those bits of camouflage netting?"

"We didn't need it but it will come in handy."

Surprisingly that made everyone take notice and we were grilled about how we would use it. We were on safer ground when discussing professional matters. When we left the air of depression had been replaced by optimism. That was the kind of warriors we were. None of us dwelled too long on the past. It was the future which counted.

We had little ordinance to return but I pointed out to Daddy that we needed more ammo. "I was out on the way back. We need another two magazines each."

"Extra weight."

"I'd rather carry extra weight than be dead weight."

Once again, we had a day off and once again we used it for laundry. We were busy washing when Sean breezed in. "Right Tom, you and me are going on a bender! I made Corporal!"

"Give me a hand with the washing and you are on!"

When we took the washing back to my room we passed the room which would be Sean's new digs; it was Wally's old room. He would have a constant reminder of the man he was replacing.

When we resumed our training and the daily five mile run it became more relevant than ever before. If we had not been so fit then we would not have escaped the airfield. We began to finish first each day and the other sergeants asked Daddy how he managed to get so much out of the section. Even though he was the most recently promoted sergeant events had conspired to make him one of the most experienced. He had tapped out his pipe and said, "There is no substitute for being over there. We can tell them until we are blue in the face that they need to do what we say but until they are under fire, and not on a range, then they will never understand."

The replacements for Jack and Sean's section arrived at the end of the first week of November. It was cold it was dark and it was wet. I had always found November a depressing month. We also heard that troops were being sent to Greece to help them fight the Italians. It was not enough that we were fighting the Germans alone, now we were fighting Italians as well. It seemed Britain and the Commonwealth were taking on the world.

Major Foster tried to find inventive ways of enlivening the training but it was hard work. The new Lieutenant, Marsden, arrived with them. He was young and he was keen.

With Lord Lovat and the majority of the battalion in Scotland we were a very small troop. We became even smaller when, towards the end of November, the other sections were sent to the area to the east of Boulogne to do as we had done and raid the airfields. The three days they were gone showed us what it must have been like for them when they had waited for our return. Major Foster accompanied them and we were left under the close scrutiny of Sergeant Major Dean. When we discussed the raids in the pub, being vague about the details, Jack Johnson couldn't understand why the RAF didn't bomb them in daylight.

As usual when we discussed the RAF all eyes turned to me. Because of my dad I was considered the expert on such matters. "It's dead simple really. We have not got enough aeroplanes yet to risk losing them on daylight raids. You saw the number of batteries they have around the Pas de Calais. The bombers we have wouldn't stand a chance and you can't risk civilian casualties. Having us as human beacons is the most effective way of bombing accurately. It works, Jack."

Sean stubbed out his cigarette, "I am just surprised they haven't sent some of us to North Africa to fight the Eyeties. We could do some real harm out there."

Reg Dean gave a thin smile, "How do you know there aren't Commandos there?"

"Well we would have heard."

He shook his head and, lowering his voice added, "You haven't read about your raids over there have you?"

"Well no but…"

"The public know about us but there is no point in banging on about what we do is there? The whole point about Commandos is that they work in secret, in the dark. There won't be much glory, Corporal Higgins, if that is what you are hoping."

It was food for thought. Before the Major and the rest of the troop returned Sergeant Major Dean summoned Jack and Daddy to his office. When they returned they had orders. "Right lads we have a little trip up north. We are going to RAF Ringway near Manchester."

Sean looked confused, "RAF Ringway, Sarge? What the hell for?"

"We are joining some of Number Two Commando to be trained how to use parachutes. They are going to throw us out of aeroplanes!"

Chapter 7

The two sections headed north towards the place I had enlisted. It felt strange. Once again I was interrogated by the others for it was an RAF base and I was the font of all aeronautical knowledge. "Why the hell do we have to jump out of planes? I thought we landed by boat."

"Well, Norm, the trouble is that some places are too far to reach by boat. Norway, for example. If we went there we would be at sea for days. The only way would be if the whole battalion went over on those LCAs. The problem is they would need ships to escort them and I reckon they are being used to protect convoys." I smiled, "Anyway this time when you are in the air you will have a proper pilot and not me!"

Gordy said, "You did all right, Corp. You saved our arse anyway."

I wondered, as we headed up through the Midlands, if I would get the chance to see Aunty Sarah. It was some time since I had been at Burscough. The thought that we might get Christmas leave also flickered across my mind. I knew that Mum and Mary would be missing Dad and worrying about me too. If I could get off for a couple of days it might reassure them. Poor Mum had had to endure this during the Great War too.

This time we would not be getting our own digs. For the three weeks we were to be there we would be in the barracks at the base. This was a brand-new airfield and Dad had never been stationed here. I felt relieved when no one recognised my name. I preferred the anonymity of Corporal Harsker, Commando. There were more than just Commandos here too. There were Poles and Norwegians although they were kept away from us. There was also, at Bowden, a small group of trainees who, it was rumoured, included women. We never saw them but, sometimes, when we went training we caught the faint whiff of their perfume. They had been there before us. As the training progressed we sometimes saw other aeroplanes and parachutes. They were smaller in number. Gossip was rife about their identity!

We were not at the Tatton Park establishment. That was reserved for the foreign trainees and the mysterious women. We were with Number Two Commando at the main base. When the other

Commandos discovered that we had been on a number of raids in France our standing went up. They had only recently been formed and had spent all of their time training. When we were not learning about parachutes they were asking us about the weapons we used and how we had managed to survive behind enemy lines.

The first day we were shown how to fall. It was an extension of the unarmed combat training and we found it easy. When we progressed to the small tower it became slightly harder although our rock climbing and abseil experience stood us in good stead. They taught us things which, in hindsight, were quite obvious, like bending the knees, keeping arms in tight and so on. At the time, it was all new. By the end of the first week we had progressed to the huge tower where we could experience a fall from a great height. When we were shown how to pack our parachutes I heard grumbles from some of the other Commandos.

"Won't someone do this for us?"

The senior instructor, a small man with the thinnest moustache I had ever seen, said, "Sonny I don't know about you but I, personally, would rather pack my own parachute. That way I know it will open although in your case I am not so sure!" Sergeant Major Taylor rarely shouted but he was well respected and his advice heeded. We each packed our parachutes carefully.

Then one day we went to a new tower. This one was a fuselage from a bomber. It was inside a hangar and there were mats on the floor.

"Right my lovely lads, we are going to simulate leaving the aircraft using a static line." He was standing at the top of the tower and addressing us all. In his hand, he held a rope attached to a metal clip. He held it up. "First you clip it onto this cable. Then you check that the man in front of you has his line secured to his parachute. The man behind will do yours. You step up to the door." He moved forward. "And then, when ordered, you will jump." He jumped. The fall was only a few feet and he rolled to the ground and stood upright. "Now the difference will be that when you do this tomorrow a parachute will billow beautifully above your head. Otherwise there is nothing different to what you have been training to do for the last few weeks."

A Commando raised his hand, "Sergeant Major what do we do if it doesn't open?"

"Good question laddie!"

There was a silence. The Commando asked, "No, seriously Sarn't Major, what happens?"

"You will reach the ground a lot quicker." He smiled, "Don't worry; it will open and if it is any consolation there are some boffins working on a spare parachute which can be opened manually."

The next day we were taken up in a balloon. A winch attached it to the ground and it rose slowly once we were all inside. Four of us were seated around an opening with a Corporal Instructor. We were winched up to a thousand feet. The Corporal grinned at me, "I am guessing, Corporal, that you will lead from the front and take this leap of faith."

I nodded. I said nothing for I was nervous. The instructor clipped my hook on to a cable running around the balloon. "Ready when you are."

"What do I do?"

"Just stand up and jump through the whole. The parachute will do the rest. Remember your training and when you near the ground relax and bend your knees. You'll be fine."

I stood and, folding my arms across my chest stepped out. I fell like a stone. I was going to die and I could nothing about it. Just when I thought that the parachute had failed to deploy it was though a giant hand had scooped me up. I looked above my head and saw the huge mushroom of the parachute above me. Just in time I glanced down and saw the ground approaching. I bent my knees as ordered but it still jolted my body as I hit the ground. The Sergeant Major said, "Now pick up your parachute and get out of the way Corporal so your lads can follow you!" I did as I was told and as I passed him he murmured, "Well done, son."

I had done my first jump. The rest all managed it. In the afternoon, we did our second jump from the balloon. This time I actually enjoyed it because I knew that the parachute would open!

That evening Major Foster and Lieutenant Marsden joined us. "How is it going chaps?" We were all full of enthusiasm for we had all successfully had two jumps. "We will be playing catch up. I daresay we will have a successful jump such as you have had."

Sean said, "It's a piece of cake sir. Nowt to it!"

Jack said, "You were a bit green before the first jump Higgins."

"It was something I ate. I didn't throw up, did I?"

Daddy asked, "How did it go sir? You know…" It did not do, even on an RAF base, to talk of missions in detail. Daddy wanted to know if the others had taken casualties when raiding the airfields.

The Major frowned, "Not a great success but we got back, at least most of us did."

That was all he would say. We later discovered that five more Commandos had either been killed or captured and only one of the squadrons had successfully bombed the airfield. With winter upon us such raids would be put on hold.

That evening we were assembled in a hangar. "Well, my lads, you all did well today. Tomorrow we go up for the first of your jumps from a real aeroplane. You will each complete seven and then you will be given your wings which mean you are a paratrooper. Get a good night's sleep and just do what you did today and everything will be fine."

There were six Whitley bombers waiting for us the next day. They had been modified to take men. There was a hole where the bomb doors had been. Our two sections were amongst the first to be loaded. I was happy to see the Sergeant Major was aboard our Whitley. He leaned against the bulkhead as the pilots went through their pre-flight checks. He waved a hand at us. "You are now a stick. It is what we called the lads who jump." He tapped the cable to which we would attach our hooks. "You hook up here. I will check that you are secure. The man behind will check that you are secure. We look after each other. I know that you Commandos live by that creed. That is good for it works here too. You exit through this bloody big hole in the floor. It is a tight fit. We had two Poles last week who broke their noses; it was not pretty. I will tap you on the shoulder and tell you when you have to jump. If you hesitate then I will push you. If our taxi drivers get it right and the wind isn't blowing too hard then you should land back at the airfield. Even if you don't the procedure is the same. Gather your parachute and fold it up. Bring it back here. It is a valuable item! Women can't wear silk stockings just so that you can have a safe landing!"

The co-pilot shouted, "All ready, Sarn't."

"Right, hold on to something. This can be a bit bumpy and noisy."

He was not joking. The JU52 had been silent by comparison. The pilots were building up the revs and the whole aeroplane shook and rattled so that I was convinced it would fall apart. Then we began to bounce down the runway. I am certain that Daddy was saying something to me for his mouth was moving but I heard nothing. When the wheels finally left the ground, the noise diminished somewhat although the smell of fuel almost made me vomit. The 'Flying Coffins' as they were known had notoriously leaky fuel systems. It was no wonder they were being phased out.

The Whitley spiralled up to the height we needed for a safe parachute jump. The co-pilot said, "Almost there Sarn't Major. Get them ready."

"On your feet, my lucky lads." He nodded to me. "You're first. Hook up."

I clipped my static line on to the cable. He tapped me on my shoulder. Then I felt Daddy as he tapped me too. I was ready. We almost had no time to think. When the Sergeant Major had been down the stick to check the cables and the parachutes he returned to me. The co-pilot gave us the thumbs up and I heard the shout, "Go! Go! Go!" A hand propelled me forward and I barely had enough time to tuck my head in and prevent my nose from striking the aeroplane. And then I was falling. There was a slight jerk and then, suddenly, I slowed. I looked up and saw the creamy canopy covering the sky. My chute had opened. I held on to the lines holding it and I found that, if I pulled on one side and not the other, then it changed my direction. My canopy obscured the others but I could feel the wind shifting me. There was a wood to the right of the field and I pulled on the chute until I had managed, more by good luck than anything, to correct my descent. The ground was coming up rapidly and I prepared to do the forward roll when my bent knees hit the ground. I hit heavier than I had intended. I quickly scrambled to my feet and began to gather in the silk. I had done my first jump! It was exhilarating.

I looked up and saw the others drifting towards the trees. Only Norm actually landed in them. I heard his curses on the wind. The instructors on the ground watched as we folded and repacked our chutes. They would be done properly by the Waafs who would do the job far better than we would. Gordy said, "I thought we had to pack our own?"

"That was just the Sergeant Major's way of making sure that you knew how to do it. If you want to pack your own then go ahead but, trust me, the women are the best packers there are."

As if to prove the point the third Whitley which appeared in the skies above us disgorged its stick and we knew straightaway that something was up. Two of Number Two Commando had parachutes which didn't open. They just spun around without billowing open. The instructor next to me said, "Shit! Roman Candles! Poor buggers."

There was nothing anyone could do and they struck the ground with a sickening splat. Mercifully they must have died instantly. When the Sergeant Major came over, after his Whitley had landed, I could see that he was shaken. His Corporal said, "It isn't your fault Sarn't Major. They mustn't have packed them right."

He stiffened, "Don't make excuses for me, Corporal. I am the man in charge and I will carry the can for this."

We had a two-day hiatus while there was an inquiry into the fatal accidents but the Sergeant Major was cleared and we resumed our training. I for one was nervous on my next jump until the silk opened and I landed safely. My second landing was better than my first. By the time I came to the last of my seven landings I even managed to land on my feet. I could jump.

The Major and the Lieutenant had used the two days of the enquiry to catch up with us and they did their last jump just a day after us. We were all paraded on the airfield and presented with our paratrooper's wings. For some of Number Two Commando it was a change in direction. They would become Airborne soldiers rather than Commandos. For our sections, it was just a new skill. We were packing our gear into our bags when Major Foster came in. "Well chaps, I have some good news. You have all been granted leave until New Year's Eve. You report back to Weymouth on New Year's Day."

That pleased everyone. It had been some time since we had had a leave.

"However, you should then prepare yourselves for some intensive training. We may have a mission and it will come as no surprise to tell you that it will be behind enemy lines." He was being enigmatic but we knew he could not tell us anything more.

I didn't bother to telephone Mum. Manchester was on the mainline and I wanted to get the first train home that I could. Christmas at home was a luxury and I would not squander the opportunity. I wanted some quality time with my family. I was lucky enough to catch a fast train and make a good connection. It was worth it just to see the look of surprise, joy, and tears on my mum's face when she opened the door. She burst into tears and hugged me so hard that I felt I could hardly breathe. She pulled back and held my shoulders in her hands. "You should have telephoned! I could have aired your bed and got extra food in!"

I shook my head, "These days I can sleep on a clothes line, and I have brought my ration book home. We will go shopping tomorrow eh? I am just glad to be home." She nodded. "Where's Mary?"

"She volunteered for the Women's Land Army. She will be back at five."

"Good for Mary!"

"She can't wait until she can join the ATA."

"ATA?"

"The women who deliver fighters to the squadrons. She thinks it is the only way she will be able to fly,"

I dropped my bag at the foot of the stairs. "What does dad think of that?"

She looked worried as she grabbed my hand and said, "I don't know, Tom! We haven't heard from him for six months."

That wasn't like dad but I smiled, "You know Dad. He probably has a bunch of letters already written but he hasn't got round to posting them. He is worse than me."

She shook her head, "We have friends at the Air Ministry. Group Captain Marshall was evasive when I rang him. Randolph is never evasive. Your dad has gone and volunteered again in the Middle East and now the Italians have invaded Greece as well as Africa!"

I could hear the panic in her voice, "Mum, calm down. You don't know anything yet." I took a deep breath. "Look I have been up to stuff and I haven't told you about it. Dad is like me he doesn't want to worry you but," I put my arm around her shoulder, "I am like him. I am a survivor and dad is too. He has a sixth sense." I laughed, "If you listen to Uncle Ted and Uncle Gordy he has a sixth, seventh and eighth sense."

When she smiled I felt a sense of relief. I hated the thought of mum worrying about anyone. I could see that she had aged in the last year. I had worried that it had been my fault. Now I discovered that dad was just as much of a worry as I was.

"How long have you got at home?"

"I am here until New Year's Eve."

The look of joy on her face made her look ten years younger, "Oh that is wonderful; Christmas together!"

I changed out of my uniform. It felt strange not to be in khaki! Mum pottered away in the kitchen. I knew she would be fretting about the food she would be offering. I poured myself a whisky. I felt I had earned one.

When Mary breezed in, shouting cheerily, "I'm home mum!" I said nothing. She came into the lounge and when she saw me she squealed. "Tommy! How fantastic!"

"Look at you! A Land Army girl. Give me a twirl!" She was wearing the uniform which I had seen all over the country. Women and girls were doing the jobs which men had done. The men were at war and the women took up the challenge.

She obliged me with a spin, "How long are you home, Tommy?"

"Almost a fortnight!"

"Splendid! That will be fun."

Mum's voice came from the kitchen, "Mary, can you give me a hand?"

"Will do! I brought home some potatoes and carrots. They are going off a bit but they will fill a hole."

This was England in nineteen forty. We made do and we got by. It was the way we were and no one would complain. That was not our way. That was why we would win this war. Churchill embodied the spirit of the people and we reflected his tenacious spirit. I felt quite hopeful.

When they put the dishes on the table mum was quite apologetic. "I only managed to get four ounces of beef but the butcher let me have two calves' feet. Sorry."

I rubbed my hands. "What are you talking about? I love this! It is one of my favourites!"

"I know but that was before the war when I would have used two pounds of beef."

"It will still taste the same!"

And I was not lying. I loved it. I cleaned the plate and the dish with bread. I knew I had pleased mum. She liked clean plates. She and Mary took the dishes out. As she left the dining room she said, "You can smoke if you like. Your dad does."

I shook my head, "I don't. I never started and you know what they say. What you never have you never miss."

Mum brought in a pot of tea after the dishes were done. "Sorry there is no coffee. You can't get it and tea is on the ration too."

"Well use my rations while I am here. I insist."

We spent a delightful evening; the two of them filled me in with the mundane and the dull; the life in the village and in the extended family. "Aunt Alice is coming for Christmas. She will be thrilled to see you. I bet she doesn't even recognise you. I know I can see a change."

"I can't believe how young I looked." I pointed to the photograph they had had taken before I went away to University.

"Now I will do your washing tomorrow. Do you have any sewing? Socks, that sort of thing?"

I reached into my pocket. "You could sew this on my battledress if you like."

I handed her my paratrooper wings. Mary took it. "What's this? Are you a pilot now, like dad?"

"No. I have just finished a paratrooper course. I am now qualified to jump out of aeroplanes!"

Mary looked envious; mum looked sad, "You are your father's son."

I thoroughly enjoyed my leave. When Aunty Alice arrived then it became almost perfect. It was only dad's mysterious absence which spoiled things. Aunty Alice was everything a boy could want in an aunt. She was vivacious and she was fun. She liked fast cars and knew film stars. For the four days she stayed with us I forgot all about the war. I went with her to the station to see her off. She kissed me on the cheek. "You are a handsome young man, Tom. Dashing! You remind me of Charlie. I like to think that if we had had children then our son might have grown up to be like you. You will take care, won't you? Don't be a risk taker like your dad."

"I promise."

She took out her handkerchief and wiped the lipstick from my cheek, "Liar!" I laughed. "Then just take care. Your mum worries about you."

"I know."

"All aboard!"

The Guard's whistle made her slam the door. "And write to me!"

"I will… when I get the chance!"

She laughed as the train chugged down the platform, "Men!"

Chapter 8

When I reached Weymouth, I discovered I was one of the first of our section to return. It was New Years' Day and most of the country had been celebrating. New Year was dad's favourite celebration and with him absent we had had a quiet night and I had got the earliest train south I could. War had made many changes in our country. One was that people celebrated even harder. The last year had been a disaster. Our little island was alone save for the Commonwealth soldiers who were gradually joining us from their distant homes. Since the fall of France, the U-Boat menace was growing. The Germans now had access to the Atlantic coast of France and U-Boats no longer had to run the gauntlet of the North Sea. Our convoys were suffering more and the materials and soldiers who travelled from Canada, South Africa, and Australia were suffering. The train had been full of doom and gloom about the shortages. My happiness gradually evaporated as I headed back to Weymouth.

As we chugged south I saw the effects of the German bombing raids. The Blitz in London was devastating but nowhere was immune. The factories in the Midlands were a tempting target for bombers. Smoke still billowed from the latest raids as we passed through Birmingham and the Black Country.

Reg Dean was in the office when I reported. He noticed the wings on my battledress and frowned, "Does the Major know about those, Corporal?"

"Yes, Sergeant Major. He has some too."

He sniffed, "I don't know what is wrong with boats."

"Have the replacements arrived yet, Sarn't?" Although we did not need any in our section there were gaps in the others.

"No, they will be here by the end of the week." He opened a drawer and took out a sheet of paper. "Here is this week's training schedule. Give it to Sergeant Grant when you see him. You might as well give it the once over."

I looked down the list and it looked much like the kind of training before we had gone to Ringway. "Major Foster said we had a mission when we got back."

For the first time since I had known him Sergeant Major Dean looked surprised, "He didn't tell me."

I shrugged, "It was something he said when he and Lieutenant Marsden joined us."

He relaxed a little, "Aye well they did go up to London before they joined you." He tapped the sheet of paper. "Until you hear otherwise those are the standing orders, right?"

"Right, Sarn't!"

I had dropped my bag off at my digs and I went to the armoury to pick up my weapons. They had been stored under lock and key but I needed to clean them. If we did have a mission coming up then I wanted to be prepared. I stripped them both down before giving them a thorough clean. I reassembled them and then took every bullet out of my magazine before cleaning and reloading them. It took time but I had little better to do and I had yet to have a gun jam on me. Uncle Lumpy had impressed that upon me. What he didn't know about weapons was not worth knowing.

Gradually the base filled up as men returned. All had dropped their kit off and, like me, came to get their weapons. When Daddy arrived, I handed him the sheet of paper. He gave it a cursory glance and pocketed it. "Good leave, Daddy?"

Daddy had a family and his grin spoke volumes. "It would have been perfect but for the bombing, oh aye, and the shortages. We are luckier than the civilians you know Tom. At least we have rations. They have to queue for everything."

"I know." Changing the subject, I went on, "Reg Dean knew nothing about this mission the Major mentioned."

"Might be secret then. There must be tons of stuff going on that we know nowt about."

I thought about my dad. From what mum had said he was doing something which was secret. That was the only reason she could not find out more information but what was it? He was no longer a front-line pilot. He was a Group Captain. They sat behind desks.

When the rest of the section arrived, Daddy told them of our orders for the following week. "But for today, I reckon we might be a bit rusty with our weapons. We will go to the firing range."

The real reason we went was to get the smell of cordite in our noses once more. There were many soldiers in England who had not fired a gun in anger since Dunkirk. We were the fighting edge in England. There were soldiers fighting in Africa and Greece, according to the newspapers Italians were being captured not in their hundreds but their thousands. That did not help the mood in England. Once again, especially in Greece, we were helping our neighbours. Others were standing idly by and watching. They would wait to see if Little England could survive. It was ever thus.

To make the training interesting Daddy and I promised a shilling each to whoever was the best shot that day. It was little enough but it would buy a couple of pints. It was more the victory that the men would want. Gordy won. He normally did. I had discussed with Daddy the possibility of getting him a Lee Enfield Rifle No.3 (T). That was a sniper's rifle with a three times magnification telescope. Daddy maintained that we wouldn't need it. He preferred the firepower of the machine gun. It was one of the areas of disagreement. The machine gun had the problem of range. The Lee Enfield was more accurate at longer ranges.

After our five-mile run the next morning we saw the effects of too much drink over Christmas. Even I felt a little out of condition and I had barely drunk. Daddy shook his head, "This won't do lads! The WVS could run further than we could. Instead of the range this afternoon we will have a ten-mile run in full kit."

Lieutenant Marsden joined us for the unarmed combat training. Having used it effectively we were even more enthusiastic about the training. When Daddy put the young Lieutenant on his back for the third time Lieutenant Marsden rose, laughing. "With all due respect Sergeant, how can someone who is ten years older than me manage to put me down three times!"

Daddy smiled, "Put it down to experience sir. We have been doing this a wee bit longer than you."

"Yes, I heard from the Major about the prowess of your section. You have quite a reputation."

"Yes, sir. These are good lads."

We were heading back to the armoury when we saw Major Foster return and he had a Royal Navy Commander with him. They had an official car too. Although the others did not pay much attention to it I knew, from my father, that such things were important.

The last event on Reg Dean's list was a talk about map reading. It was a skill which not all of our men possessed. I had always found it easy. I even had an expensive Silva compass. Dad had bought it for me when he attended a conference in Sweden in the nineteen thirties.

Half way through the lecture Major Foster came in. Behind him came a Captain of Commandos. He stood at the front, "First of all, Happy New Year."

We all chorused the response.

"Secondly, well done to those, who, like me, achieved their wings. Many more of you will be undergoing the training. Thirdly our replacements will be arriving this week." He gestured with his arm, "This is Captain Willoughby. He is Lieutenant Reed's replacement." The Captain stepped forward and nodded. He was older than Lieutenant Reed had been. It was hard to read a man from his appearance alone. We would see how he fared on a run in full kit before we judged him. "Thirdly I shall be away for a while and so Captain Willoughby will command. Finally, Number three section, would you come with me please."

We all stood and every eye was on us. As I edged down the row Sean said, "Good luck Tom." He knew what that meant. We were going on a mission.

When we reached the Troop Office Sergeant Major Dean and the Lieutenant Commander were there waiting. When the door closed Major Foster turned and said, "No point beating about the bus chaps. We have a mission in France and it is a tad dangerous. I need four volunteers."

Before our hands could join those of the rest of the section Sergeant Major Dean said, "Sergeant Grant and Corporal Harsker you volunteered already!" he smiled at the frowning Major Foster, "Thought that would save time, sir!"

"Thank you Sarn't Major. So, I need another two."

There was a cough, "Sir, if you don't mind I would suggest, Privates Curtis and Barker."

Giving the NCO a wry smile Major Foster said, "And why are they the best choice, Sergeant Major Dean?"

"Barker is the best shot, by a long way sir, and Curtis is almost as good with explosives as the Corporal." The Major nodded. "Right the rest of you, back to the lecture and you join Sergeant Johnson's section for a while."

I saw the disappointment on their faces. It was a measure of the men that they had all volunteered. "This is Lieutenant Commander Collins of the Royal Navy. He will give you the background to our mission."

The Lieutenant Commander gave the major a look which suggested the background was unnecessary but he nodded and carried on. "As you know the Navy sank a pocket battleship, the *'Graf Spee'*, in the early years of the war. Although we sank her quickly her raids showed that the Germans could tie up great numbers of our vessels and do a great deal of damage to our commerce with such attacks. Now we have learned that the Germans are building two ships which are bigger and better armed than anything we possess. They are called the Bismarck class. One of them finished its trials in December but, thanks to the Kiel Canal being damaged, it has not been able to leave. We believe it is due to leave soon. In fact, that is the reason the Major here was on standby in case it did leave its harbour. When it does it will be able to raid at will. Now the only place such a ship can repair is at the Normandie dry dock in northern France at a place called St. Nazaire. We have heard that the ship has finished its sea trials and is preparing to leave."

Daddy shook his head, "You want us to blow it up?"

Major Foster said, "Just wait, Grant, until the Lieutenant Commander has finished will you."

"When we found out that this beast had been launched we sent bombers over to bomb the dry dock. Less than half returned. We have yet to find out what damage has been caused to the dry dock. Every aeroplane we have sent to photograph has either had to turn back because of low cloud or has been shot down. We asked the French Resistance to have a look and they were all captured." He nodded towards the Major. "Some of your chaps even tried to get in by sea and all of them were either killed or captured. We are blind."

The Major nodded, "Number One Commando."

"Things are desperate. If we send more bombers in then they will suffer just as the first raid did."

He looked at the Major who continued, "That is the main reason you were sent on the Paratrooper course. Lieutenant Marsden and Sergeant Johnson's squads are the backup in case we fail. We are going to parachute behind enemy lines. Then we will get into St. Nazaire and see what damage has been done. We are there to observe and report back. We come out by sea. The Navy will pick us up. There is small bay some twenty miles from St. Nazaire. A submarine will surface there for three consecutive nights. We just parachute in, have a quick shufti and then nip over to the coast."

Even Sergeant Major Dean shook his head at the Major's words. He made it sound like a walk in the park when, in fact, it was anything but.

"Questions?"

Daddy said, "And we are going in by air because?"

The Lieutenant Commander said, "Because the other Commandos were caught on the beaches. The Germans have them sewn tight shut."

Daddy shook his head, "Then how do we get off?"

The Major said, "You lads showed us that at Wissant. It is another reason why you were chosen. The Germans are stopping people landing; not stopping them leaving."

Raising my hand, I felt like a schoolboy again. "Sir."

"Yes Harsker?"

"Does it matter if the Germans know we have seen the dock?"

The Navy man shook his head and snapped irritably, "What difference does that make, Corporal?"

"Let him speak, Lieutenant Commander. In my experience Corporal Harsker normally has intelligent things to say. Go ahead, Tom."

"The odds are that we will be seen at some point. It has happened to us on every mission we have been on. I am guessing this will be the same. I am suggesting that we take timers and explosives. We make them think that we were trying to blow it up. We make the bombs look as though they are booby trapped. That will make them take longer to defuse them and they will spend time searching. I am just trying to buy us time to escape. Twenty miles is a long way in occupied France."

"Interesting. Well it wouldn't hurt to take explosives and timers. Anything else?"

Gordy put up his hand, "Sir, any chance of a sniper rifle? It might come in handy. We don't need firepower, do we? But we might need to keep someone at a distance."

Reg Dean nodded, "I'll get one."

"Anything else?" We shook our heads and the Major looked at Lieutenant Commander Collins.

"The only thing you need is the password for the submarine then. It will lie off the coast from midnight until four a.m. for three nights following your landing. The password you will send is 'Tiger' and the response will be 'Burning'. They will send a rubber dinghy for you." He looked at us all. "I cannot stress enough the importance of this mission. It is vital that one of you gets back. Thank you, gentlemen."

He left. We all looked at each other. The Major said, "Smoke if you like." He smiled, "Now you see why I asked for volunteers."

I was the only one who laughed. "I think we can pull it off, sir."

"Really? You surprise me. I thought it has more chance of failure than success."

"There are just five of us sir. That is an easier number to hide than a full section. Two of us speak French well and the others understand it. I speak German and... well... we are Commandos!"

The Major laughed, "Optimism. I love it. Let's get down to details. Sarn't Major how about a pot of tea?"

"Good idea sir." He stuck his head out of the door. "Jenkins, a pot of Sergeant Major tea and six mugs."

The Major unrolled a map. "This is from before the war and might not be accurate. It is, however, a starting point." He pointed to an empty area just north of the port. "This forest is a mile or so north of the river. We will land just south of it. I know it is risky. Private Ford had a collision with trees as I recall. However, we will be jumping out at a thousand feet. That is quite low and, so long as the winds aren't too strong we should land safely enough. We will be landing at ten o'clock at night which means that we should be able to get into St. Nazaire by midnight at the latest."

The tea arrived and there was a hiatus while it was poured. It was Sergeant Major tea. You could have stood a spoon up in it. I saw Major Foster wrinkle his nose but it was the way the lads liked it. They all used at least three spoonfuls of sugar!

"Sir, won't there be a curfew?"

"Yes Curtis, there will be. I am afraid we will have to use deadly force on any Germans we find. If we are caught we will be shot; be under no illusions. As with our raids around Calais we need as much information bringing back as we can. If the dock is not damaged then someone will have to think of another way to destroy them."

We spent the rest of the morning going over what we knew. When the Major and Sergeant Major Dean were certain that everything had been covered we were taken to collect our equipment. The clocks and TNT were waiting for us, as was the sniper rifle. Curtis had an Aldis lamp and we had rations for four days. My section still had their camouflage netting. It was small enough to hide in the bottom of our Bergens. As the weather was likely to be unpredictable we took oilskins which could be used as a temporary shelter. There was a lorry waiting to whisk us away. The other Commandos watched as we boarded. They waved. Sergeant Major Dean saluted us as we climbed in the back, "Good luck, sir. Do your best lads!"

The Major rode in the front with the driver. I turned to Daddy, "You could have refused you know. You are married. You have a family. Us three are single."

He shook his head, "I joined the Commandos. I don't hide behind our lass!" I nodded. He smiled, "Besides you reckon this is going to be easy."

"When did I say that?"

Ken Curtis laughed, "Back there! You made it sound like a stroll along Blackpool Promenade."

"Just trying to be positive. There's no point in thinking it can't be done."

"But it is going to be hard, Tom. I reckon they will have guards and sentries all over the dock."

I had had a good look at the map. "The Old Town is the place to go. If it is anything like the other old towns I have seen in France it will have lots of narrow twisting streets and narrow alleys. And it doesn't need all of us to go in. To be honest this job could be done by two just as easily as five." I shrugged, "All the jobs we have done have gone awry at some point and we have adapted our plans. That is what we will do here." I put my hands behind my head and leaned back. "I am going to catch forty winks. We will get no sleep tonight, will we?"

I must have dozed off but I woke when the lorry lurched to a halt. The Major appeared at the tailgate. "Right lads, this is our stop."

We were at an airfield somewhere but it could have been anywhere. The lorry was next to a Whitley just like the one we had trained in. It would be a noisy and uncomfortable ride. A Royal Air Force Warrant Officer in flying gear welcomed us and handed us our chutes. After we had thrown our Bergens on board and placed our guns at our feet we put them on. I hoped that they had been packed well. "If you could get a move on, sir. These are not the fastest aeroplanes in the world."

We picked up the cables and our guns and clambered into the aircraft. There was more room than in the one we had used at Ringway. There were just five of us. We sat on the benches at the side and jammed our Bergens underneath them. When the engines spluttered and then roared into life it became almost impossible to talk. I knew that once we were airborne it would be marginally easier. Ken went to put a cigarette in his mouth. The Warrant officer shook his head and mouthed, "Petrol!" He stuffed it back in his battle dress.

The hatch was closed and we braced ourselves for the take-off. This one was not as bad as the ones in training. I suspected it was because we had a lighter load and the runway was a little longer. When we reached our cruising altitude the pilot came into the cabin. "Right chaps, Warrant Officer Marshall here will tell you when to jump." He pointed to the floor. I could see that this one had two doors there. "We have no time to hang around. They have increased the flak here. We might be lucky and they might not send night fighters after us. I will try to drop you where I am supposed to but..."

Major Foster said, "Just do you best eh?"

"Will do."

The Warrant Officer went to the rear of the aeroplane and brought back a huge flask and five mugs. "Might as well have a cuppa eh?"

He poured us a cup each and then took two more for the pilots. When he came back he said, "We are over the sea now."

I had calculated that it would take at least two and possibly three hours to reach the target. All of our journey would be over the sea. The pilot would take us south and then turn to head directly east. It avoided enemy fighters and ships. I savoured my tea. It would be the last hot drink we had until we got back to Blighty. Once you were used to the engines it became possible to have a conversation. I could see that the Major was nervous for he kept checking his Colt. Daddy played with his pipe. Ken and Gordy argued football. The aeroplane made me think about my dad and I wondered just where he was. That distraction took my mind from my mission and when the pilot put his thumb up at us I was surprised. I had felt us descending but I thought we had further to go.

Warrant Officer Marshall said, "Right lads hook up."

This was not training. This wasn't a stooge around the quiet Cheshire countryside. This was the real thing. As if to emphasise that we heard the crack of flak and the Whitley bounced up and down in the turbulent air. The Major hooked up and Daddy checked that it was secure. It went down the line until it came to me. The Warrant Officer checked mine. Major Foster had wanted me last as he said I had the most skill with a chute. With my Thompson around my neck and my Bergen on my front I worried that something would snag on the way down. We had not jumped with equipment before.

The flak became worse and the Whitley swayed alarmingly. Suddenly there was a crack as something hit the aeroplane. The Warrant Officer tapped Major Foster on the shoulder. And then he was gone and I was moving forward. The others leapt out quickly. As I reached the hole in the floor and there was an almighty crash as a shell hit the wing. The aeroplane began to bank and the Warrant Officer pushed me out of the door. My head cracked off the hatch and I blacked out.

Chapter 9

The jolt as the chute jerked opened woke me up. I saw that the Whitley was on fire and descending rapidly. The sudden movement of the aeroplane just before I had jumped meant that the other four chutes were far to the south and west of me. I felt blood trickling down my face but I had no time to worry about that. I tried to remember what I had done in Manchester to correct the chute. I tugged on one side and was rewarded by a movement in the right direction. I realised that the aeroplane had been lower when I had jumped. I would land when they did; just not necessarily in the same place.

The Whitley was mortally stricken. The best that the pilot could hope for was to crash land. That hope was dashed when, as it descended, it was hit again. This time half of the port wing broke off and the aeroplane went into a steep dive. At least they would know little about it when they hit the ground. There was a huge explosion. I saw that it had hit close to the town. As I made another correction the thought flickered across my mind that, if it crashed close to the port then we would not be able to get near. That would be ironic.

The ground was racing up and I saw the trees to my left. I made another correction and then braced myself for a landing. This would not be a pretty one where I sprang to my feet. I had extra weight and I could not see the ground. I just knew that we were landing in a piece of open ground. I hit and rolled. The stock of my Thompson smacked me in the face. I would not be a pretty picture when I returned home! I stood as soon as I could and began gathering the chute. That was more important than anything. If the wind caught it I could be blown along the ground. Once it was gathered I folded it and then took off my Bergen, machine gun, and parachute pack. I jammed the chute back in the pack and put it on my back. It was hard but I managed, by loosening the straps, to put my Bergen on top. The chute might come in handy and it saved me having to bury it.

I then had time to look around. The others were shadows to the south of me. I picked up my Thompson and, cocking it, headed towards them. Just then I heard, from my left, the sound of a vehicle. I saw a stone wall and the glint of headlights. I ran away from my comrades towards the wall and lay flat against it. The others had also dropped to the ground. I wondered if they would be seen. I knew where they were and it was hard for me to identify them.

The vehicle stopped. I guessed it was some kind of German lorry. I heard a German voice order men from the inside. Their feet clattered on the road. They were just on the other side of the wall. I mentally cursed myself. My Mills bombs were in my Bergen; I could not get at them.

I heard a German say, "Sir, I cannot see anything. Perhaps the airmen landed further west."

"I saw them. Use the light."

"But sir, the blackout!"

"Do as I say, Sergeant!"

The light shone out across the field. I knew it would find them. As soon as the beam picked out their parachutes the officer shouted, in English, "Put your hands in the air. You are now our prisoners!"

I saw the four of them slowly rise. Would the Major and the others fight? I knew from their voices where the Germans were and, as I stood, I began to spray my bullets in the direction of their voices. The officer and the sergeant were just feet from me and I cut them in two. I gave another burst at the cab and then a final burst at the light and the man operating it. A bullet pinged off the wall in front of me and I turned and fired at the German who had appeared from the far side of the truck. I sprang over the wall and checked to see if he had been alone. He was.

The others ran up to me.

"Well done Harsker! You saved our bacon." The Major looked at the bodies. "You men throw the bodies in the field. I will search the officer." As we picked up the sergeant I pocketed his Luger and his ammunition. One never knew when it might come in handy. I jammed it in my battledress. It was a bloody task but by holding the head and the feet between us we were able to dispose of the bodies. "Now the officer."

Curtis and Barker threw him over. I picked up three or four stick grenades. They always came in handy.

"Harsker, get behind the wheel. Sergeant you and the others get in the back."

We were too well trained to question our officer but I wondered if he had lost his senses. I did as I was asked. The engine was still running. "Where to sir?"

"First take off your hat." He gave me a German field cap. "Put this on." I did so. "Now carry on along this road. At the end you will come to a village, Saint-Andre-des-Eaux. There you turn left. If we reach any roadblocks we will try to bluff it out. Say we have captured the spies."

"Sir, they think we are the crew of the Whitley."

"Even better. If our luck holds we will take the turn for Le Passouer. It is less than half a mile from the port and we should be able to dump the lorry. This will save us a couple of hours of walking."

As I put the truck into gear I couldn't help thinking that the Major took more risks than I did. The road was hard to see with dimmed headlights and I drove gingerly. It was still faster than running. I saw the small huddle of houses at the crossroads. I put the wheel over and we trundled along the main road in the village until it broadened out into the D 47. This road was easier for it was straight. I kept glancing nervously at the side of the road, looking for Germans. There were none.

"You are doing well, Tom. That was smart and quick thinking back there."

I had no idea how far we would have to drive down the road and when I saw more buildings ahead I began to worry. It was St. Nazaire. "There, Tom, the next right!"

It was a very small road. We passed a track leading to a farm and I began to slow. "Look sir, a track leading to that copse."

"Will this fit down there?"

I grinned in the dark, "I am not worried about damaging the paintwork sir, are you?"

"Go for it."

We did indeed barely fit. The hedges scratched along the side but we made it into the shelter of the trees. There was a clearing. It looked like charcoal burners used this space in the middle of the copse but it was empty. I turned off the lights and the engine as the Major climbed out and said, "Right lads, we are here. Everyone out."

Before I left, I booby trapped the door of the lorry with a German grenade. It would let us know when they found it. I put on my comforter and jammed the German cap in my battledress. Who knew when we might need it again?

We gathered in front of the truck. The Major pointed to the east. "Our target is a mile and half that way. Jerry thinks that we were the crew of the bomber. They will find the bodies of their men and the truck but by then, I hope we have managed to do the job and get out. Barker, you take point. Sergeant, bring up the rear."

We moved through the woods and emerged into a field. It was dark and we hurried across it and the next two fields. Then we saw houses. It looked like a village which had been swallowed up by the town. Gordy waited for us and the Major waved him forward. We moved silently, on rubber soled boots, through narrow streets. It was all quiet although, in the distance, I heard the sound of a truck as it headed north. The small suburban streets soon gave way to wider streets. We had been lucky up until that point. Gordy stopped at every intersection before waving us forward. It was a good job he did; at one intersection, he put his hand up and we stopped. Ahead of us was a wire fence with barbed wire around it. It looked like a compound of some description with huts inside it. We immediately headed to the left, away from the potential danger.

At one intersection, the Major went forward. Instead of going straight he took us up a road to the left. Gordy waited for us and joined the Sergeant at the rear. I looked to the right and saw, less than two hundred yards away, the entrance to the basin where the ships tied up. We had come too far south and the Major was taking us north. The Major gave the signal for danger and we all ducked into doorways. I had recently looked at my watch and seen that the time was two thirty. Any delay now would mean we would be stuck in the town for the day.

Two soldiers tramped their way down the centre of the road. One of them was smoking and cupping the cigarette in his hand so that its glow would not be seen. They were complaining, as all soldiers do, about their sergeant. I think they had done this patrol so often that they were in a routine. Our blackened faces helped and we were stationary in our doorways. I hoped that we would not be seen. Their boots receded in the distance. I glanced behind and saw Sergeant Grant wave us forward.

At the next intersection, we turned right and I felt the sea was closer; I could smell it. Here we began to see the damage caused by the bombers. There were two houses which had been demolished by the bombing. Others showed the effects of the attack from the air. We passed through a small square. I daresay that in the summer it would have been filled with old men playing petanque but at that moment it was filled with leafless trees and looked sad. After we crossed it we found ourselves in higher buildings. Major Foster suddenly stopped. He held his hand up for us to wait and then disappeared. I glanced around the street for danger. These were commercial buildings. The area felt empty and derelict and yet not all of the buildings had been damaged.

Major Foster reappeared and waved us forward. Ahead of us was a wall of wire and, down the road I could see a guardhouse of some description. He waved us into the doorway of a building to our left. Sergeant Grant stayed in the doorway as the Major led us up some partly damaged stairs. We went one at a time to avoid further damaging them.

He pointed to the stairs which led up to the next floor and tapped Ken on the back. The Major pointed to the back and tapped me on the shoulder. The building looked to have been offices for there were old filing cabinets lying at awkward angles in the first room. Some of the papers had caught fire and there was the sign of burning in the room. The second room looked to have been a kitchen and dining area. There was a large table and some broken chairs. I spied a sink and a stove. I went to the sink and turned the tap. A trickle of water came out. It still worked. The last room was a French toilet. I smiled. I was used to them but the lads would not think that a hole in the ground with two places for your feet constituted a toilet.

I returned to the Major and gave the sign for safe. He nodded and said quietly, "Go and fetch the Sergeant. Close the door. It was closed before I opened it."

I gingerly went down the stairs and tapped Daddy on the shoulder. I pointed up the stairs. Before I closed the door, I glanced down the street. This time I saw German soldiers at the guardhouse. They had their backs to me and I quickly closed the door. Surprisingly the door still worked although as I pushed it too I felt the blackened wood where there had been some burning. I returned to the others.

"We are going to have to spend the day here. They have the whole of the dock area protected. You can see that from the street. Harsker, what did you find?"

"A toilet, kitchen, and an office."

"Barker?"

"An office and storage rooms. There is another floor but it looks like an attic. You get there by going up a ladder."

The Major nodded, "The front part is fairly wrecked. There is a gaping hole in the front. We will go upstairs. We might get a better view and we can talk. We will have less chance of being overheard." He turned to me and asked, "Any water in the kitchen." I nodded. "Good then we can refill our canteens. Let's go."

The top floor had suffered the most damage. Part of the roof, at the back had been destroyed and there were more signs of burning. I began to work out that the bombers had not been carrying incendiary bombs. They had wanted destruction of stone. That explained why there was so little fire damage.

The Major pointed to the front window. The glass had gone and it was open to the elements. "We watch from here. One man on the window at all times and another watching the stairs. I will watch first with Curtis. The rest of you get your heads down. I will wake Daddy in an hour. He will replace me; then Tom an hour later. That way we should all get two hours sleep. Mark anything you see on your maps." We heard an explosion in the distance. "I think they found the lorry!"

While the others prepared for bed I went down to the toilet. I couldn't sleep with a full bladder. Once I was back with the others I laid my Thompson next to me and I was asleep as soon as my head touched my Bergen.

Ken's touch woke me instantly. "It looks like they are changing guards. See you in two hours."

I joined Daddy by the window. He nodded and pointed to the stairs. I went to sit at the top of them with my Colt. I checked my watch.

It would be an hour before I woke Gordy and it would be my turn to go to the window. Time passes slowly when you are in a black hole watching for a sudden flash of light. However, your ears become attuned to the sounds you normally miss. There was movement in the roof above me. I suspected rats. I could hear distant vehicles and, just occasionally a louder one which must have been driving down the street below. After almost fifty minutes I heard the sound of the town coming to life. I went back to Daddy who was yawning. He nodded and rose, somewhat stiffly.

I took his place and sat so that I could see out of the window without being seen. Gordy had had the most sleep. I pointed to the stairs and he went. I took out the map and my pencil. Looking down the street I saw that it was lighter below me. Then I heard the sound of feet marching along the road. I risked a look to the right and I saw a column of men being marched by German guards towards the guardhouse. As they passed me I saw British uniforms as well as French and what I took to be Polish uniforms amongst them. I watched them pass and then halt at the guardhouse. I now saw that there was a barrier and it was raised to allow them in.

I was the lucky one who saw dawn break. I was the one who saw that the basin below was undamaged. The lock gates at the end still functioned. I discovered that when a small flotilla of fishing boats returned from a night's work. When I lifted the Major's binoculars to examine the Normandie dock I saw that it too was totally undamaged. Either the bombers had failed or the damage was so superficial that it had been quickly repaired.

I put down the binoculars. I did not want to risk the flash of light from the lens. There was no damage to mark on the map but there were gun emplacements. I marked them all on the map. The railway line still functioned. That lay just inside the wire. As the light brightened I saw a lighthouse at the end of a mole close to the entrance of the basin. I saw another entrance to the basin and it was quite close to the entrance of the Normandie dock. Once I had marked all on the map I turned my attention to the soldiers I had seen entering. They were not there to repair the damage to either the dock or the basin. They were undamaged. What were they doing?

I heard the sounds of labour but I could not see anything. What were they doing? About five minutes before I was due to wake the Major

I saw concrete mixers arrive. They were building something in the basin. When I woke the Major, I told him what I had seen and I handed him my map. I found a corner and curled up in a little foetal ball. I was asleep instantly.

I felt a hand on my shoulder, it was Daddy and, as I looked at my watch I saw that I had slept for three hours. "The Major let you sleep a bit longer. He wants us all awake and ready to move as soon as it is dark."

"It is still light. Is there trouble?"

"Dunno but there has been a lot of German troop activity in the street below. I think he is just being cautious."

"Better to be cautious than dead."

Just then I heard the sound of German lorries. Ken shouted, "Ey up sir, looks like they are searching houses."

"Right lads get into the attic and make sure that there is nothing down here which shows we were here."

None of the lads had smoked and the only thing I could see was that the dust had been disturbed. I found a curtain which had fallen to the ground and I lifted it up and flapped it. The dust from it flew into the air and when it landed, it disguised, somewhat, where we had lain. I threw the curtain on to the area we had used for sleeping. "Hurry up Harsker!"

I clambered up the ladder into the attic. It was quite bright as half of the roof had been blown off. We scurried to the part with the roof and sheltered where we could. I lay down and listened. My German might come in handy. They did not enter our house immediately. They were being thorough Germans and working their way down the street. I had no doubt that this was as a result of the dead Germans and the lorry. I heard the front door being kicked open and then the sound of boots on wood as they entered. I held up my hand for silence. I was hardly breathing. The voices were muffled as they searched the ground floor. They became a little clearer as they ascended. I heard the sergeant telling them to look for signs of British airmen. He was particularly keen for them to find parachutes. That was interesting.

Then I heard one shout, "Sergeant, there is a ladder to the loft!"

I heard the sound of feet moving along the floorboards. "Right Hans you and Frederic check it out. Better go up one at a time. The ladder looks rickety!"

I slid my Colt out and signalled to the others that we were about to be discovered. Just then I heard the rattle of rifles firing and the sound of shouts and screams from the street.

A German voice shouted, "Quick outside!"

Boots thundered down the stairs and then there was silence. I held up my hand for silence and then slid over to the entrance. There was no one on the floor below. I turned and said quietly, "They were about to search the attic."

The Major said, "Let's go down. I don't want to be caught like rats in a trap up here."

I was the nearest one to the ladder and I clambered down. As soon as I reached the floor below I swung my Thompson around. I saw no one. The Germans had all gone. While the others were descending I went to the window we had used to observe the basin. I saw four bloodied bodies lying on the road. There were Waffen SS laughing and pointing to the dead bodies. One of them, a Feldwebel, pushed one body over with his foot and then placed his boot on the dead man's chest as though he was a big game hunter and the body was a trophy. Sickened, I was about to turn and join the others when I saw the uniform of the man who lay below the German boot. He wore the badge of the 1st Loyal Lancashire; he was one of my old comrades. His face had been obliterated by bullets but I could have fought alongside him in the rear guard. I so wanted to poke the machine gun from the window and shoot the whole arrogant bunch of them but I was a Commando. I went and joined the others.

"It looks like they shot four of the prisoners. I don't know if they were trying to escape or what but they looked to have been shot in the back whilst running away."

"Will they search here again?"

"I have no idea but they are SS. I would not even contemplate surrender. If they come back sir, we fight."

"Let's hope it doesn't come down to that. We have valuable information here. We have to get back. We owe it to the dead crew of that Whitley." We crouched at the top of the stairs, guns ready to slaughter any who came in. The front door was still open; we could see the light shining in but no-one returned. Daddy went to check the road after we heard a German truck. The bodies had been removed.

Half an hour after the shooting outside we heard the sound of shooting close to the Basin. What was going on? As the afternoon waned we began to hope that the Germans had forgotten about searching for us and that there was something happening on the other side of the wire.

At six we heard the sound of orders being shouted. They were indistinct but I thought I heard English as well as Polish. Ken was on duty at the window and he came through. "They are marching the poor sods off down the road. It looks like it is getting dark."

One advantage of the blackout and the time of year was that there was little light after six.

""Everybody down to the ground floor. When the street is clear I want Tom to nip out and reconnoitre the street. We might just make it to the rendezvous if we have a clear run."

The Major was even more optimistic than I had been. As soon as the street was silent I slipped out of the open door. I expected a shout in German or a shot, at the very least but all was silent. I pressed myself into the dark wall. I could just see the head of a German in the guardhouse but his back was to me. I slid along the wall to the intersection where we had first seen the basin. I put just one eye around the corner. There was a German armoured car there. That way was blocked. I saw that it was just an armoured car; there was no infantry and no road block. I saw a German face looking in my direction; it was the commander in the turret. I remained still. My blackened face hid me. When he turned I ran across the road.

If we could not go back that way we would have to find another route. The wire on my left showed me that they protected the basin and the dock for its entire length. As I moved towards the sea along the derelict and empty houses and businesses I began to despair. That despair sank to new depths when I saw the barrier and the guards at the end of the street. They had a machine gun. There were sandbags and I counted at least six of them. Behind them were a gate and a wire fence with barbed wire at the top. It was where they housed the prisoners we had seen. I realised that it was the same building we had seen the previous night. It was impossible to get out that way. There was no escape route left to us. We were trapped.

Chapter 10

I managed to get back to the house safely enough. The eager faces of my comrades soon turned sour as I told them my news.

"I am sorry sir, but whichever way we go there are Germans. There is wire to the front of us, a guardhouse to the left, an armoured car to the right and a prisoner of war camp ahead of us."

The previous optimism of Major Foster disappeared in a flash. No-one said a word. Daddy suddenly slapped his head, "The back! We can go out of the back!"

"Go and recce it, sergeant."

While he was away an idea began to grow in my mind. I remembered a teacher at school who had been talking about logic and engineering. It went along the lines of eliminating the absolute impossible and whatever was left, no matter how improbable was possible. It seemed to me that the only thing which we could move was the armoured car. There were machine guns at the guard house and at the prisoner of war camp. They would not move and they would cut us down. We had to draw the armoured car to us and then destroy it.

Daddy came back. He was shaking his head. "There is a three-storey building behind us and it looks like it is occupied with barbed wire along the adjoining wall. Even worse, it is flying a German flag."

"There must be something! Come on Tom! What can your fertile mind conjure up?"

"I have one idea but it is madness."

"Go on. Insanity might be the only solution to this dilemma."

"We blow up this building. It is half wrecked as it is. We use the charges and the timer. If we wait on the far side to the road beyond the armoured car it will come and investigate. Their attention will be on this building. It is not a tank, just an armoured car. We can use grenades to destroy or disable it. There looked to be nothing beyond it. If we can pass it then I believe we have a chance to disappear into the dark. I have some stick grenades here as well as the Mills bombs. When we destroy it, we leg it down the road."

"It means we will be pursued."

I said nothing for no one had come up with an alternative. Gordy said, "I could use the sniper rifle to hit the guards near to the prison camp. They will think they are being attacked from all directions."

Ken added, "Aye and if we give them a burst or two from the machine guns it will add to the illusion. They will never believe we are just five men. It will be like a conjuror, moving his hand one way to distract you then pulling the rabbit out of the hat! It's worth a try sir."

The Major shook his head, "As I can't think of a better solution we will go with this one."

I took out the TNT and the timer. At least it would make my Bergen much lighter. I placed the bag under the stairs. They were already weak and they were made of wood. The force of the explosion would bring down the front of the damaged building. Before I set the timer, I said, "You have better get a move on, sir. I am setting the charge for five minutes."

The Major nodded, "Good luck Tom. Right lads."

I was alone. I set the clock and then attached the wires. I slipped the Bergen on. I already had my grenades in my battledress and I picked up the two stick grenades from the floor and ran. There was no one outside the front door and I scurried along the wall of the half-destroyed buildings. I saw the others on the opposite side of the road crouched against the wall. I peered around the wall and saw that the driver and the commander were out of the armoured car, leaning against the side and enjoying a cigarette. I waited until they turned away. I was aware of the passage of time. When they turned to look the other way, I ran. One of them turned back. I don't know if he sensed my movement or heard me, but whatever the reason, the outcome was the same.

"Stop!"

I made the other side of the road and I armed the two grenades by smashing the porcelain tops. The two men leapt inside the vehicle. I grabbed the two cords as the German armoured car came towards us. The others cocked their weapons. Gordy and Ken were aiming their rifle and Tommy gun at the machine guns by the prison camp. The Major and Daddy had their Mills bombs ready. The two guardhouses came to life as they heard the sound of the armoured car's engine. I put my head around the corner and pulled the cords. I threw them both underhand at a spot ten feet in front of the armoured car and then ducked back behind the end of the wall which would shield me from the blast.

The armoured car's gun began to chatter. Gordy and Ken fired at the far guardhouse and the Major and Daddy hurled their grenades around the side of the house to our left. The TNT exploded and, at the same time, my grenades went off under the armoured car. The two explosions lifted it in the air and sent it down the street. It rolled towards us and missed Gordy by feet.

"Run!"

We ran down the road which the armoured car had previously occupied. We would be running the reverse of the route we had taken the night before. The difference was we were now being pursued. We ran as only Commandos can run- hard! Hesitation would have cost us dear. We knew that attention would be on the armoured car and the demolished building. The smoke from the demolition and the armoured car drifted down the street making the visibility almost nil. It was, effectively, the fog of war. We had minutes to disappear. The suburb we had first passed seemed the best place in which to disappear. It was a warren of tiny streets and blind alleys.

As we passed what we now knew was the prisoner of war camp we heard shouts and the sound of gunfire. They must have been firing into the smoke trying to hit us. We did not mind. It would add to the confusion. Even though my chest was hurting I kept running. We heard sirens and the noise of vehicles behind us. When we reached occupied houses the odd Frenchman poked his head out and then ducked back just as quickly. Suddenly I saw a café ahead. When we had passed through the night before, it had been closed up. Now there were four old men sharing a bottle of wine. A waiter or perhaps the owner stood nearby. As we passed them the four of them raised a glass and toasted us. It was one of the more bizarre and surreal moments.

As soon as we passed the outskirts of the town we headed for the wood. I guess the Major, who was leading, hoped that, having removed the vehicle; it would be safe for us. I prayed that it would too. We crashed through the trees and found the blackened and burned clearing. The truck had, indeed, been taken away. The Major stopped and held up his hand. We all halted and began to suck in air. It was tempting to drink from our canteens but that would have been a mistake; we had run too hard.

Behind us we heard, in the distance, the sound of vehicles and gun shots. I wondered who they were shooting at. The Major got his breath back. "So far so good." He took out his map. "Curtis, keep watch while we check the map."

He jabbed a finger at a point on the map. "Guérande is about six or seven miles up the road. There are salt marshes to the south of the town and I think we could lose any pursuit there. It is then another eight or so miles to the pick-up point."

Daddy said, "Sir, it is gone seven. The submarine will only be there until three. That gives us eight hours to cover fifteen miles."

"We have done more than that in training."

"I know sir but that wasn't in the dark and we weren't being chased by Waffen SS."

"We will try, Sergeant. If we miss this one we lie up during the day and wait for the next pick-up."

Suddenly Ken ran up, "Sir, there are men heading in this direction."

"Germans?"

"Not certain. There are Germans but I think they are chasing someone."

"Spread out in a defensive semi-circle. Don't fire until I give the order."

I could hear them approach as I crouched with my Thompson aimed at waist height. There were German shouts coming towards us. They were telling someone to stop or they would shoot. I heard a crackle of rifles, a scream, and a shout. It was in English. I did not need to say anything. The others would have heard it too. There were Englishmen being pursued by Germans. Four men in English battle dress burst into the clearing. The Major shouted, "Get down!"

They were well trained men and they dropped to the ground. The Germans must not have heard the command or thought it was the men they were chasing who had shouted for they kept on running. As soon as they entered the clearing we opened fire. Five Thompsons can do a great deal of damage. Trees and leaves were shredded as the bullets tore into the German troops. We heard the wounded moaning.

"Cease fire! Harsker, check the Germans. Make sure we have them all!"

I dropped my empty Thompson and took out my Colt. I ran towards the dead and dying Germans. They were SS. I saw a German trying to hold in his guts. I gave him a merciful death. There were two Germans who were wounded in the legs. They were trying to drag themselves away from the scene. I remembered the Waffen SS with his boot on the body of the dead prisoner. I shot them both in the back of the head; it was a quick death for they were bleeding to death.

I ran back towards the edge of the wood but there were no more troops there. I heard firing to the west and the east. The prisoners must have used our attack to make a break out. I picked up another couple of stick grenades from the dead Germans as I returned to the others. The remainder of the grenades I rigged underneath the bodies of the dead Germans as booby traps. It would not hurt the dead soldiers and it would delay the pursuit. By the time I reached the rest of the section there were three English soldiers being given water. The fourth lay dead with a line of bullets in his back. Three dead Germans lay close by. They had been the first to die in the ambush.

I knew that this complicated matters. We would be slowed down by these prisoners of war but we could not leave them there. As I approached the Major asked, "Are we clear, Corporal Harsker?"

Even as I was saying, "Yes sir," the sergeant turned around.

"Tom?"

It was Sergeant Greely. It was my old sergeant from the 1st Loyal Lancashire. "Yes, it is Sergeant Greely, what happened?"

The Major snapped, "We will have time for stories later on. Tom, you and Barker watch the rear." He pointed to the three men we had saved, "You three grab a weapon from the Germans. We have a long way to go." They grabbed weapons from the dead and followed the Major as he led the section north.

I had no time to talk to Sergeant Greely even though a thousand questions raced around in my head. Gordy and I turned to face any threat from the south. We waited fifteen minutes and there was no pursuit; at least not in our vicinity. "Right, Gordy, let's go."

As we ran he asked, "Did you know the Sergeant?"

"He helped me to join up and I served with him in Belgium. I thought he was either dead or in the bag."

"They will slow us up."

"I know but do you want to leave them?"

"Of course not, Corporal. I am just saying!"

"Besides the sub will be there tomorrow night." I knew that I was clutching at straws; the odds were that they would slow us up too much and they were ordinary soldiers. They were not Commandos who were used to running for hour upon hour and disappearing in plain view.

It took us half an hour but we caught up with Curtis who was the new Tail End Charlie. "How they doing, Ken?"

"Your old sergeant is keeping them going but the other two lads are struggling."

"I suppose if we had been prisoners since May and suffered at the hands of the SS then we might be a bit out of condition. Don't worry. There is no pursuit yet."

We kept going for another hour and then we stopped. The Major waved me forward. "Have you still got your Silva compass Harsker?"

"Yes sir."

He took out his map. "Then you get to lead us through these salt marshes. I reckon it will be slow but they won't be able to follow us. This is the course we need to take." He pointed out the route on the map.

"You can rely on me." I turned to him and said, quietly, "It's Sergeant Greely, sir. What are the odds?"

The Major nodded, "I know, small world eh? Don't worry Tom, we won't leave an old comrade behind. If we do then we might as well give up because we will have lost the war. That is what makes us different from them."

The next hour was a nightmare. We kept twisting and turning on the dry parts of ground and I had to keep us heading the right direction. But for the compass I think we might have perished but it kept us on course and when we found dry land and the D 452 I knew that we had a chance. We stopped so that the three escapees could have some water and some of our rations. They needed it more than we did. They looked emaciated. I checked my watch. We had three hours to cover seven miles. If we did not have the three men with us then it would have been easy. With them it would be harder.

Sergeant Greely came over to me, "Corporal eh?" I nodded. "Commandos?"

"Yes Sarge, a new unit. We operate behind the enemy lines. Do you remember Major Foster, he was a Captain in Belgium?"

"Aye I thought I recognised him."

"How come you chose tonight to break out?"

The Major's voice was almost in my ear, "Right Harsker, you can catch up later on. Take the point. We will risk the road and try to make good time. You are our eyes and ears at the front. Sergeant Grant, take the rear with Barker. You three will have to try to keep up. There is a submarine waiting for us so if you can keep going it will be worth it."

"Don't worry about us sir. We won't hold you up." Sergeant Greely sounded determined. He was more like his old self.

"Good man. Harsker, a good pace if you please."

I was acutely aware that I had three weakened men behind me and I tried to keep a steady pace. I also had to keep peering and listening ahead. The three men had boots on and I could hear them thudding on the road behind me. We were silent. I stopped every half hour. Each time I did both the Major and Sergeant Greely waved me forward. I kept looking at my watch. We were tantalisingly close to the pickup point. It would be awful to miss the rendezvous by minutes.

We had been lucky hitherto and our luck had to run out. Just a mile from the beach and, with forty-five left before the submarine left, I spotted a road block and checkpoint. They had a motorcycle blocking the road between a derelict, bombed out house and a low wall. If we went around it then we would miss our submarine. I put my hand up and scurried back.

"Sir, there is a road block."

"How many men?"

Just two. They have a motorcycle."

Sergeant, go with the Corporal and Barker get rid of them. I am not going to miss the submarine just because two men stand in our way."

As we hurried up the road Gordy said, "I am not going to bring this rifle all the way here and not use it properly. If you two go left and right I can take out one of them with my rifle."

Daddy shook his head, "No, Barker. We do it silently. We use knives. You cover us."

He reluctantly nodded. When we were a hundred yards from them he dropped to a prone position and I disappeared up the right. I realised that the motorcycle might be a Godsend. We could reach the beach quicker. The rubber soled shoes gave good purchase on the slippery soil through which we moved and yet they were silent. I could hear the Germans and smell their tobacco smoke even though I could not see them. I moved towards their voices. With Gordy as backup I did not need to wait until Daddy was in position. I moved quickly behind the house to approach them from the coast side.

When I emerged around the corner of the bombed out building I was less than three yards from them and they had their backs to me. I laid my gun on the ground, drew my dagger, and then ran towards them. The shoes were silent and I pulled back the helmet of the man on the left to drag him towards me. I was aware that Daddy was not in position. I had to focus on my target. He put his hands up to help himself balance and to try to grab me. I plunged the knife into the side of his neck. There was a sudden crack as the Lee Enfield fired and the second German fell dead. I dragged the body of my dead German and pushed it into the derelict building. Daddy emerged from behind the wall and shook his head, "Sorry, Tom."

"Don't worry about it. Get this body out of sight."

The others raced up. "That's torn it." The Major turned to look back down the road. "That will have every Kraut for miles here in minutes. Curtis, take the bike and get to the beach. One of you get on the back. Signal the submarine. We will follow. Come on, we double time from here on. Corporal you and Barker watch the rear."

There were more houses ahead. I knew that the gunshot would have alerted any of the inhabitants. I prayed that they were French and would stay within doors. I could smell the sea and the road was descending slightly towards it. Then I heard in the distance the unmistakeable whine of a truck as it climbed a gradient. It would be Germans. There were more trees than I had expected and I wondered if we could use them to hold off the Germans. It would allow the others the chance to escape but would doom us to a swift death with a bullet in the back of the neck. The Waffen SS did not forgive. It was when we were coming through a tree lined section that I had my idea. I stopped.

"Gordy, keep watch." I took out the parachute and cut two of the cords from it. I broke the porcelain on my last two stick grenades and tied the cord to the arming string. I tied the parachute cords between the trees. The sound of the truck was closer now. It was on the downhill section and was making good time.

"Hurry up Corp!"

I finished tying the cords and I laid the last stick grenade next to the bole of the tree. "Done! Let's run!"

We hurtled down the road after the others. When we reached the houses, which were closest to the headland we saw that the beach was some sixty yards to our right. I risked a glance at my watch and saw that we had just five minutes left. I saw a flash from the sea. The submarine, at least, was there but would the dingy reach us before the Germans did? Would it be big enough for eight of us? I could see the others just reaching Ken and the motorcycle on the sand. Any concerns I might have had ended when there was an explosion behind me. The Germans had tripped my booby trap. I hoped that would end any pursuit.

The Major nodded when we reached him, "Another Harsker booby trap?"

I nodded, barely able to breathe, "Nev taught me well sir." I looked at Harry Greely who nodded. He remembered the Spanish Civil War veteran who had taught us both so much.

"There, I can see it!" Ken's finger pointed beyond the surf.

Then I heard the sound of a vehicle in the distance. "And Jerry isn't far behind. Ken, take out your charge and your timer. Harsker go with him and try to buy some time!"

"Yes sir."

Ken brought his Bergen and followed me. He was opening his bag even as he ran. There was an old pre-war ice cream stand at the head of the beach. We dropped next to it. I knelt and aimed my machine gun ahead. "Set the timer for five minutes and put the charge this side of the hut. It will blow the building in the direction of the road." I peered towards the sound of the vehicle which was approaching from the dark. I could see the glow from the burning German lorry. The two grenades would not have killed many but they would be on foot and disorientated. It was the second vehicle which was the greatest danger.

"Done!"

"Let's get the hell out of here!"

We ran the hundred and fifty yards to the surf. The rubber dingy was there. The sailor said, "Sorry lads, I'll have to make two trips."

The Major nodded. Daddy said, "You go with the dingy, sir. I'll stay here with Gordy and Harsker. We'll get the next boat." The Major hesitated, "Sir, you have the information."

The Major nodded and clambered into the boat. It disappeared into the darkness. Daddy said, "Lie down in the water. We will be harder to see. Gordy, we rely on you to get the officers and sergeants first."

"Don't worry Sarge, this rifle is a little beauty."

The dimmed headlights of a German truck appeared and we saw men disgorge. Suddenly there was a crack and flare shot into the sky. As it descended it made night day and the German officer pointed a finger at the dinghy. Even as he shouted something Gordy's bullet smacked into him. The Germans dived for cover. I saw three of them setting up a machine gun. Daddy and I fired a burst at them. We missed but their evasive action delayed the setting up of the gun. Gordy fired again and one of the machine gunners fell.

As the flare's light faded then the night became dark once more. "Sarge, let's head back into the sea. The water will give us protection." I had learned, at school that a bullet soon loses its velocity when fired into water. The chatter of the heavy machine gun began. They were firing blind and our movement had confused their aim. They were hitting the edge of the surf, where we had been.

Daddy's voice came from the dark. "Back further into the water. We will stand up while it is still dark." By standing we were able to move quicker and we walked back until the water was up to our necks. The waves kept splashing over our heads but I hoped that it would hide us. The second flare put an end to that.

Behind us I heard a voice, "Hang on lads! We are on our way back for you!"

Two things happened at once. A fusillade of bullets flew across the sea and I heard a shout as Daddy was hit. Then the TNT went up. It was spectacular and lit the whole of the beach up. Behind me I heard the sailor's voice, "Bugger me!" I saw Germans thrown to the ground. The crew of the machine gun were scythed in two by the fragments of the hut. I waded through the water to Daddy.

"Where are you hit?"

"Shoulder and arm." He grinned weakly and nodded towards the inferno on the beach. "Nice explosion, Curtis."

The rubber dinghy nudged into the back of my head. "The Sergeant is wounded. Here Gordy, give me a hand!" Between us we pushed Daddy so that he could be hauled aboard. I knew that I would not make it with the Bergen and so I took off my pack and put that in the dingy before hauling myself onboard. It was hard for my clothes were sodden and I was exhausted. I flopped in the boat as the sailors paddled back to the submarine.

The Germans had advanced to the water's edge but the sea was dark and their shots were blind. When we bumped into the steel hull of the submarine I knew that we would make it.

Chapter 11

I had never been in a submarine before and I didn't realise how cramped they were. We were taken down the forward hatch. The leading seaman said, "Wounded man, sir."

I heard a cultured voice say, "Take him to the sick bay attendant. Get a move on chaps, let's not over stay our welcome eh?"

There was a dim red light when we entered the Stygian depths of the torpedo room. The dinghy was manhandled into the sub and then the hatch was closed.

"Hatch secure."

A voice came through the internal tannoy. "Diving!"

There was no sound of an engine but I was aware that we were moving. One of the sailors handed me a blanket, "Here you are Army. We'll have some cocoa once we get under way." He nodded to the red light. "That will change to white soon enough. It looks like a brothel in Lime Street like this don't it?"

The cheerful sailor wandered off. I looked around for Daddy and saw that he had been whisked off. There was just Gordy and me. The other sailor who remained was deflating the dinghy. "Where are the others?"

"They have been taken to the mess. I'll take you once the captain gives the all clear." He nodded to the ceiling, "It will soon be daylight and I reckon the sea will be swarming with Krauts."

Gordy asked, "How was the Sarge?"

"He was hit twice and there was a ton of blood. Still he will be better off here than on the beach." I tried to sound confident but mum had told me of the effects of a couple of bullets. Uncle Lumpy had lost a forearm and hand because of a German bullet. I prayed that we would have a speedy trip back to Blighty. Daddy needed a hospital.

I put my hands to my ears as we began to descend. They hurt. The seaman said, "Hold your nose, close your mouth and blow hard."

I did as he suggested and the pressure eased slightly. Gordy asked, "How do you cope with being in this steel coffin?"

"You get used to it. I take it you don't like confined spaces?"

Gordy shook his head, "Can't stand them."

"Me, see I was a miner. I could have had exemption, been a Bevin Boy but I wanted to do my bit. My granddad died in the Great War and... well it suits me." He finished tying off the deflated dinghy and said, "Follow me and watch your heads."

He led us through the narrow boat. It was so tight that you could not pass someone coming the other way. One of you had to duck into a side cabin. When we reached the mess the seaman said, "There you are. Door to door service eh?"

Major Foster pushed over two mugs of cocoa. "You two did well. Shame about the Sergeant."

"How is he sir?"

The Major shook his head, "I am not sure. The SBA has stopped the bleeding and given him something for the pain. He is sedated but he needs a doctor. The Captain is heading for the nearest port rather than taking us to Weymouth." I nodded. It was not the best news but it was not the worst. "However, I am not certain he can continue in the Commandos." He shrugged, "We will have to see."

Poor Daddy would be mortified if he had to leave.

I realised, as the Major turned to speak with Sergeant Greely, that they had been in the middle of a debrief. "So, when you were cut off you headed for Calais."

"Yes sir. There were about thirty of us left and we heard that they were getting them off from there but we got there too late. We joined up with the Highland Division. When they were surrounded about two hundred of us broke out and headed towards the Loire. Another rumour said there was going to be a landing there. We got as far as Brest and we were trapped. We had no food; the ammo had all gone and some of the lads were in a bad way."

"How did you end up at St. Nazaire?"

"One day some lorries arrived, Waffen SS and they took us to that camp you saw. We have been building submarine pens." I saw the Major start. That was as important a piece of intelligence as anything else we had gathered.

"Was there any damage to either the dock or the basin after the bombing?"

Harry shook his head, "A bit of cosmetic damage that was all. The concrete is thick." He looked at the Major, "Was that what you were doing? Thinking about blowing it up?"

"No Sergeant but we had to find out if the new German battleships could use it to repair. They obviously can."

"I don't think there is a bomb big enough to blow it up, sir and those pens are impregnable. They have been pouring concrete for weeks."

"Why the trouble today, sergeant?"

"Last week we had a new colonel arrive. The other one was a bastard but this new one, Colonel Erhart, had a murderous streak." He shook his head and looked to the other two for confirmation.

One of them said, "Some of the lads were, well a bit careless with their work. It was our way of still doing our bit. The old Colonel had the lads beaten. This one had the man shot and the two who were working near him. We had to stop our sloppy work. Then he began beatings if he thought we weren't working hard enough. Fifteen men have died in the last six days. Some of the boys decided to make a break for it this morning. They thought they had nothing to lose. The four of them were shot and then the Colonel had the other men from their hut shot too. We had had enough."

Sergeant Greely took up the story. "We were already planning on breaking out but when you lads shot the guards at the gate and blew up the house every goon in the camp ran to see what was going on. It was too good an opportunity and we jumped the goons in our hut and legged it. There were ten of us started out. The others were either shot or captured. Then we found you."

"And I am glad you did. I shall write this down before I forget it." he began to write out what Harry had told him.

I put down my empty cup and Harry said, "What happened to you?" I told him the story including Nev's death and the SS we had met. He nodded, "I reckon the only good German is a dead German. From now on I shoot every bastard first and ask questions later!" The war did that. It made mild mannered, reasonable men into killers who hated. I suppose I was in that category. I had slit enough throats and shot enough Germans now to be labelled as a cold-blooded killer.

It took most of the day to sneak across the sea. We surfaced just off Southsea and sailed into Portsmouth. The captain had radioed ahead and there was an ambulance waiting to take Daddy off to hospital. As I stepped ashore I viewed the sailors on the submarine with a new-found respect. I could never do what they had done. We had had a reasonably incident free voyage and yet I had been wringing with sweat the whole way; it had been fear for I had been truly terrified.

Harry and his two companions were whisked away. I gave Harry my parent's address. He wanted to keep in touch. We had both lost so many comrades that we clung on to those we still had. Writing to me at the base would be hard. We moved around too much. It was midnight before Sergeant Major Dean arrived with a lorry. I sat in the back with Gordy and Ken. When we were alone we spoke of the mission. We had come closer to death more times than in any other raid and yet all of us were still excited about what we did. I think that was what made us Commandos.

"Who do you reckon will replace Daddy?"

"Who says he has to be replaced? He has a wound that is all." I did not want to contemplate my friend being out of the war.

"But Corp, did you not hear the Major? He reckoned he wouldn't be able to continue. I mean his arm and his shoulder were a mess. Suppose he is holding a rope with you on the end of it; would you trust his shoulder to hold?"

I had had the same doubts myself but I owed Daddy a great deal. "Let's just wait and see. I will run the section until he gets back."

"Unless they stick someone else in charge." Gordy's cheery thought kept us silent all the way back to Weymouth. The other two actually fell asleep but I had too much racing through my mind.

Reg Dean came around to the back and lifted the flap. He shook his head, "A pair of sleeping beauties eh Corporal?" He gestured with his thumb. "I can drop you here at your digs. You can leave your guns in the lorry. I will see to them for you."

I jumped down with my Bergen. "Thanks, Sarn't Major."

He nodded, "And don't worry about Grant. Even if he can't fight there will always be a place for him in the Commandos. I reckon you will be in charge until someone makes a decision." He tied the flap in place. "And well done, son. From what Major Foster told me you saved the mission more than once." He nodded, "See you at noon eh? The Major wants a debrief."

Such praise was better than a medal and I walked up to my room with a spring in my step. The rest of the lads were asleep and there was no hot water for a bath and so I stripped and rolled into my bed. Despite my exhaustion sleep would not come. Sergeant Greely's reappearance had set me thinking about dad. Mum was right; Randolph Marshall would have told mum if he had been wounded or was busy or whatever. The silence meant he was hiding something. Was he missing in action? Had he been sent behind the enemy lines and disappeared? He had done that sort of thing after the Great War but then he was much younger. I must have fallen asleep eventually but my dreams were filled with haunting images of my dad being shot by Waffen SS.

Mrs Burgess, who ran the boarding house, had heard me come in and, when I awoke, she greeted me with the news that there was hot water for a bath. She had forbidden anyone else from taking it. She said that I would need it. Mr Burgess ruled the guest house with an iron hand. The rest of my section might be in the dark about my whereabouts. The other sections would not have a clue where we had been sent. I might have been behind enemy lines but Mrs Burgess knew I had been in danger and she watched out for me. A hot bath was a luxury she would ensure I enjoyed.

I reached the troop headquarters at eleven. I picked up my guns from the armoury and went to clean them. I still had the Luger I had taken from the Feldwebel. I had not needed it but it would come in handy someday. I also retained the German fatigue cap. One never knew when one would need it. It was eleven forty-five when I was satisfied with my weapons and I returned the Colt and the machine gun to the armoury. I headed for the office.

Gordy and Ken ran to catch up with me. "I slept the sleep of the dead last night."

"Me too Gordy. Hey do you think that we had too much carbon dioxide on that sub?"

I looked at Ken, "I don't think so. They have filters and gauges. The sailors survive, don't they?"

"I suppose. I would rather jump out of an aeroplane any day."

Gordy shook his head, "The Corporal here nearly bought it, remember? He barely got out of that Whitley."

Ken was a fatalist, "If your time is up then there you go."

I shook my head, "You don't give up. Even if you think your number is up you keep fighting. Daddy is still fighting, isn't he?"

"I dunno. Have you heard owt?"

Shaking my head, I said, "The Sergeant Major will keep us up to speed."

Major Foster was already there along with the Lieutenant Commander and Reg Dean. For the life of me I couldn't remember the officer's name. He looked to be a happy chap.

"Well done you fellows! You exceeded our expectations! That news about the submarine pens was top drawer stuff."

The Major shook his head, "Right lads. I will go through my draft report. If I miss anything out just shout out. Don't be shy!"

When he had finished he said, "Well?"

The other two shook their heads. I said, "There is that information that the prisoners of war gave us. That we don't have a bomb big enough to blow it up."

The Lieutenant Commander said, "I wouldn't say that. The boffins are working on some extraordinary stuff you know."

Ignoring his fatuous comment, I added, "I think the weak point for both the basin and the dock is the gates. If you damaged the basin gates then submarines couldn't get out and if you destroyed the dock gates then they couldn't use it as a dry dock. The gates have to be made of wood and metal and have a mechanism. That would be how I would attack it. Less loss of life that way."

The Lieutenant Commander stood, "Thank you for your comments, Corporal, but I am sure that the powers that be will have whole panels of great minds working on the solution to this problem." His patronising tone really annoyed me. It was the fact that I was not an officer which coloured his judgement about my comments. The Major was not like that and he valued comments from all of his men, regardless of rank.

As he shook Major Foster's hand Sergeant Major Dean said, to no one in particular, "The difference is that those great minds are sat on their arses in an office somewhere sipping tea. They haven't actually seen the place like these lads."

Major Foster said, "Sergeant Major!"

"Just passing a comment sir." He smiled at the naval officer, "I'll just get your driver eh sir?"

The two of them left and Major Foster said, "I agree with you Corporal Harsker. I will be sending a report to Lord Lovat and another to Combined Operations Headquarters. I will add that piece of information. Someone might take notice. Right you two lads cut along and find the rest of your section. I believe they are on the range. I want a word with Corporal Harsker here."

When they had gone the Major reached into his desk and took out an envelope. "This arrived the day after we left. Congratulations, Tom, you have been awarded the Military Medal."

The Sergeant Major returned and he shook my hand, "You deserve it laddie. Well done."

"Thank you, sir, but I didn't do anything special."

"Don't be modest. You behaved impeccably. To be honest you deserve a medal for this last little jaunt too. You are supposed to go to London to receive it next month. However, our schedule means that you may not actually make that date."

"It doesn't matter sir. I am just grateful for the honour."

"And now, Sergeant Major?"

Sergeant Major Dean went to his drawer and took out a pair of sergeant's stripes, "Congratulations Corporal Harsker. You are now Sergeant Harsker. You take over Sergeant Grant's section until he is fit to return to duty."

"Thank you both. I don't know what to say."

"I do. When you were in St. Nazaire you made some confident decisions. To be frank, Tom, I don't know why you aren't an officer. You are a born leader. I saw that in Belgium and I have not changed my mind since then. If you don't end the war as an officer then I will eat my hat." Major Foster stood and held his hand out. "I daresay you will want to go and sort out your section. I know Jack Johnson will have done his best but they are your lads now."

I went to the range where, rather than firing, Gordy and Ken were telling both sections about our adventures. They all looked at me as I approached. It was the kind of look that says they had been talking about me. Jack said, "Don't worry about Daddy, Tom. He's a tough customer. He'll pull through."

"I know."

"And I take it they are leaving the section with you?"

"They are," I held up the sergeant's stripes, "Sorry Corporal Higgins; you are still playing catch up!"

To be fair to Sean he was delighted, "I am dead pleased for you Tom, er Sergeant. And from what the lads have been telling us you fully deserve it."

I nodded, "And now, with your permission, Sergeant Johnson, I will take my section for a five-mile run." I turned, "Right, you shower, full kit and meet me at headquarters. You have five minutes!"

They had not lost their edge and the run went well. I felt proud of them as they stood smartly to attention at the end of it. For the next five days, I worked them as hard as I could and I never saw the slightest dissension nor heard a single grumble. On the sixth day, we were at the firing range where we were taking it in turns to shoot with Gordy's newly acquired rifle. Sergeant Major Dean walked over.

"Right lads, gather around. This concerns all of you. Sergeant Grant is being discharged from hospital." Everyone cheered. Sergeant Major Dean held up his hands, "However he will have to have some rehabilitation and physiotherapy." I sensed he had not brought us good news. "The MO has said that he will never be fit enough to be able to operate as a fighting Commando." It felt like the heart had been ripped from us all. "However, there is good news. The Quarter Master Sergeant, as you all know, operated his own little systems. He thought he had a cushy little number. Major Foster has returned him to his regiment and, when he is fit, Sergeant Grant will be the new Quarter Master Sergeant. Major Foster spoke to him personally and he is happy with the appointment." He glowered at everyone, "So no sulking!" He turned to me, "Sergeant, a word if you please."

I wandered back towards the Headquarters. "You will need a new Corporal. Who do you have in mind?" He held up a warning finger, "Bearing in mind that I have an idea in my head and that agrees with the idea in Major Foster's. So, with that in mind who would you pick?"

Without hesitation I said, "No argument. Private Barker. He is a natural leader; the men like him and he doesn't panic. "

The grin told me I had chosen correctly. "Then you can tell him." He handed me the stripes. "You will get a replacement for Barker by the end of the month."

I went back to the others. I decided to just tell Gordy simply, "Here you are Corporal Barker, your new stripes! You can buy me a pint tonight to celebrate!"

That evening as I was walking to the pub to meet the other sergeants I stopped at a red telephone box. I had written a letter to mum telling her of my promotion and the medal but I needed to speak with her. I wanted to ask her about dad and I couldn't wait for a letter to reach her and then return. One perk of dad's job was that the Air Ministry had had a telephone put into our home. It was a luxury and I would take advantage of it.

Mum's voice was full of worry when I rang. It told me that she had not yet received my letter, "What's wrong, Tom!"

"Nothing Mum, can't I ring home now and then?"

"As this is the first time since you left University that you have just rung to chat I will let that pass. It is good to hear from you. You weren't in Portsmouth the other day when they had that awful air raid were you?"

"No mum, nowhere near. I have some news. I am now a sergeant and they have awarded me the Military Medal."

She let out a squeal of joy, "How wonderful! I can't wait to tell your father."

My heart skipped a beat, "Have you heard from him then?"

There was a pause, "No I forgot for the moment but I am certain that he will be home soon."

"Any more news from Uncle Randolph?"

"No and I was told that he had moved departments."

That sounded ominous and I could hear, in mum's voice, that she was getting upset. I changed the subject and asked about Mary and Aunty Alice. By the time my money had run out she appeared a little more cheerful. I, on the other hand, was not. However, I remembered dad telling me, once, that you left your personal feelings and worries behind when you took command. I vowed to do the same and, as I bounced into the pub I was a different man. My smile did not reflect the fears I felt.

Chapter 12

The south coast was both wet and cold that January. We still trained every day but, after a five or ten-mile morning run in full kit, we arrived back wet and cold. The rock climbing was even worse for slippery ropes can be deadly. It was fortunate we lost no men. Some other sections had injuries but we were lucky. With just one troop at Weymouth we often found ourselves training alone. Its advantage was that it brought my section closer together. In many ways, it forged us into a hard and tough weapon. We had been under fire before now and knew how each of us reacted. The cold and the wet allied to the repetitious nature of our training was a different kind of adversity and we learned more about each other.

Gordy proved to be a perfect choice for Corporal. He was totally different to me. I think he was a better Corporal than I had ever been. He used humour to chivvy the men along and the section responded well to him. He could talk their language far easier than I could. No matter how much I tried I still sounded a little too posh. His skill with a rifle also gave him an edge. It had been his shots, in St. Nazaire, which had cleared the guards from the camp and enabled the prisoners to escape.

Ken Curtis had become the number three in the section. He had taken over from me as the bomber and demolitions expert. He had learned, again from me, how to improvise booby traps. As sergeant, I now had other responsibilities and problems. Ken was also the signaller. I knew that I should have given that task to another but Ken could do both jobs really well.

Norm Ford was now the oldest member of the section. It made him a little grumpier at times but it also made him the one that the younger lads would go to with their problems. Perhaps I was too distant. I know that some of the section thought I was a different class to them; whatever that meant. I don't think they resented my background but it made them a little wary of talking to me about problems in their lives. Dad had not had that problem in the Great War; his background was the same as the men I now led.

Polly Poulson, despite the newer members of the section, always felt like everyone's kid brother. He was shy but he was also the most of loyal of Commandos. Everyone knew that Polly would never let them down. He was reliable.

Bill Becket had been wounded. It had changed him but in a good way. In our off-duty moments, he would find out all that he could about first aid and medicine. He hounded anyone who could teach him how to tend to the wounded. He was our first aider. Gordy and Ken referred to him as Doc. I think he enjoyed the accolade.

John Connor had also been wounded. In his case it made him enjoy life more. He was the one most likely to be off chasing skirts when we were off duty. He became something of a Don Juan. He had had a brush with death and it made him relish life even more. He was an even better Commando than he had been before his wound for he left Don Juan at home and focussed on being alive at the end of each mission.

Harry Gowland and George Lowe were both new. They fitted in well and they were reliable. Both had married at the outset of the war and, although neither was a dad yet their young wives and the letters they exchanged filled their off-duty hours. As yet neither had a particular skill although both had shown themselves to be handy with ropes. The problem with the Commandos was that you never knew what skill you might need. You had to think on your feet. The important thing about our newest Commandos was that they fitted in and there was no friction.

Daddy Grant returned towards the end of that cold wet month. Reg Dean had warned me of his imminent arrival and the whole section was waiting for him when he arrived from the station. He looked thinner and he favoured his right side rather than the weaker left. Otherwise he was the same. His pipe jutted from battle dress pocket and he had a big smile for us all.

"You didn't think a couple of German bullets would keep me away did you? I might be a cripple but I reckon I can still run the Quarter Master's stores and keep an eye on you!"

Everyone bombarded him with questions. He fended them all well. Then he looked at Gordy, "Well done, Gordy. I am pleased for you." Then he turned to me, "And you Tom, Sergeant and the Military Medal!"

Gordy and the others turned, their jaws dropping. "You got the MM! Why didn't you say anything Sarge?"

I had not told anyone in the troop. The Major and Reg Dean knew. If I had said anything it would have sounded like boasting. I shrugged, "It is just a bit of fruit salad. You should all have one."

Gordy shook his head, "We are the only section to have someone who has won the Military Medal! It is not just about of fruit salad!"

When Daddy and I finally dragged ourselves away from them I said, "We kept your room at the digs."

"I know. I dropped my stuff off before I came here."

"Are you all right, I mean," I tapped my head, "in here."

Daddy and I had trained together and faced bullies and thugs together. We could talk this way. We understood the problems that the mind could create.

He nodded, "I realise that I am just lucky. The arm and the shoulder just ache now and then; especially in the wet. And this has been a cold couple of weeks. The doc wanted to give me another month off but, you know me, I couldn't sit on my arse doing nowt. Besides it's not as though I will be exerting myself issuing clean underwear to Commandos is it. Another thing is that our lass is made up that I am not in danger anymore." He tapped me in the chest. "You stop worrying about me! Worry about yourself. You are a good lad but you take too many chances. You have a future."

"What do you mean?"

"It's as plain as the nose on your face; you are a leader. I saw it when you were making decisions that Major Foster should have made. The brass aren't totally stupid. One day someone will realise that and you will be an officer."

"I am not sure."

He smiled, "Yes you do Tom Harsker so no bull between old mates eh? And now I had better get to the stores; see what kind of mess it is in!"

As he walked away I wondered if he was right. The Major and Reg Dean had said something similar. I had not joined the RAF because I did not want to be compared with my dad. If I was an officer then I would be.

We had no specific officer assigned to train with us. Sometimes it would be Major Foster, sometimes Captain Leigh. More often than not it would be Lieutenant Marsden. He was a likeable young officer. The greenness had begun to wear off him. He had a raid under his belt and I knew, from his questions, that he envied the experiences of me and my section. That was perhaps his weakness. He might, under fire, defer to the sergeant. Dad had told me that a leader led.

Our new recruit, Alan Moore, arrived and boosted our numbers. He was young. Polly was no longer the baby. He came from London and had that cheeky arrogance and confidence which seemed to be imbued into every Londoner. He told us he could not wait to get at Jerry and pay them all back for bombing his beloved city. As most of the section were northerners that arrogance grated a little but Gordy's humour diluted Moore's comments and made them seem harmless. I exchanged a look with my Corporal. Gordy would gradually modify the behaviour of Moore if only to retain the harmony of the section.

By the end of the week our newest member had found his feet. When the lads went to the pub he strutted and was not shy of telling the others how he would sort the Germans out *good and proper* when he got the chance. It was Ken who put him in his place. His next whinge was about the lack of action. When the rest of the section turned on him he realised that he was outnumbered. I was not there when these events happened, neither was Gordy. The section had their own code; Ken told us about them and how the section had dealt with him. They had told him in no uncertain terms that he was lucky to be in the best section in the whole of the Troop and that, until he had earned the right to be called a Commando, he should keep his mouth shut.

I spoke to Daddy about it as we walked back to the digs. "We were lucky with the section Tom we were given when we were first promoted. They were all good lads. We trained them. This is a new boy and he is different. You will have to work on him."

Events transpired to delay that work. The new recruits were sent, at the start of the next week, to Ringway to complete the parachute training. They went with the other sections who had not received it. Moore went with them and just two sections were left at Weymouth. Ken was quite happy to have Moore away for a couple of weeks. "No more 'cheeky chappy' and Cockney wisecracks! If I hear *'up the apples and pears'* one more time I will smack him one!"

Polly said, in all seriousness, "I don't think he is a Cockney, Ken!"

"All Londoners are Cockneys. They all think they are Max Miller. Now George Formby he can make me laugh."

"I prefer Stan Laurel."

"There you are, two northern comics, proper comics!"

The debate, such as it was, went from Moore's deficiencies to the merits of comedians. Harmony was restored.

Things had shown signs of going well in the Middle East. The Italians had all but been defeated and then Churchill had sent some of the better troops to Greece to help them. We had heard that the Germans were now in North Africa and that they were pushing us back. We read about this in the newspapers and it caused much argument. Some thought Churchill was wrong and that we should fight one enemy at a time. Others would not hear a word said against our charismatic leader. I said little; Dad had been in the Middle East and no one had heard from him for months.

The rest of the troop arrived back at the beginning of the month at the same time that we heard of the success of the rest of the Battalion. Lord Lovat had landed on the Lofoten Islands and many German prisoners had been taken as well as destroying much of the seal oil used to produce glycerine. Their aeroplanes would suffer as a result. It was a vital part of the cooling systems of the fighters. It was a boost akin to winning the FA Cup. We had not been with Lord Lovat but we had trained with these men and they were like our brothers. Their victory was our victory.

Even as we were celebrating Quarter Master Sergeant Grant gave me a warning, "We just received some new equipment, Tom; shorts and lightweight summer gear. Some poor sods are going to get their knees brown."

He was proved right. I was summoned, along with Gordy, to a meeting in the Headquarters building. This time there was no one else but the Sergeant Major present. "Take a seat lads, Major Foster and Lieutenant Marsden will be along in a moment."

"What's it about Sergeant Major?"

He shook his head, "I thought you knew me better than that Sergeant Harsker. All in good time. What I will say is that you and your section were asked for. It seems that your name is becoming known in Whitehall." He straightened his blotter a fraction. "And I think you will miss your meeting with the King too." He smiled enigmatically.

The door opened and the two officers entered laden with papers and maps. We jumped to our feet. "Sit down chaps. We have a great deal to get through."

Lieutenant Marsden began to pin a map up. He was doing it badly. Sergeant Major Dean tutted and said, "Let me sir!"

I saw that it was a map of the Mediterranean. That explained the desert clothing and equipment which were now in the stores.

The Major smiled, "Smoke if you wish." Gordy was the only smoker and he lit up. "As you may know General O'Connor had almost defeated the Italians in Libya when the Greek thing started. He was sent back to Cairo before the job could be finished. Herr Hitler sent troops to Tunisia and Libya. They have pushed us back to here." He pointed to a line about seventy miles from the Egyptian border. "It is called the Gazala line. General Auchinleck thinks he can hold the Germans there until we can send more tanks, fighters, and men to him. The Germans are also short of tanks. Now, ordinarily this would not be of any concern to us save that the Germans have captured some of our senior officers who were in the forward areas when the German advance began. General Carter and two of his staff officers are being held in German Headquarters at El Agheila." He pointed to a coastal town some hundred miles behind the German front lines. "The town was in our hands just before the attack. It was considered captured." He sat down, "Your job is to go and get them out."

This was Gordy's first such meeting and I could see that he wanted to say something but felt out of his depth. I asked for him, "Sir, by the time we get to Africa they could have been moved; sent back to Germany, anything."

"If you were going by sea then that would be true but you are leaving tonight, by air. At Gibraltar, you will transfer to a modified bomber. You will go in by parachute. By this time tomorrow you will be there. If they have been moved it will be damned unlucky. I know it is a tall order but you were asked for as a section. Lieutenant Marsden will be the officer who will lead."

I turned and saw the eager look on the Lieutenant's face. "I am sure we can do it, Sergeant."

"How do we get out, sir? As we have found out before getting in is easy but getting our can be a trifle difficult."

I saw the Major take a deep breath. "You will need to steal a vehicle. You are to drive out across the desert. Your skills as a sailor and a pilot will help you, Tom, and Lieutenant Marsden has done desert training. The hard part is stealing a vehicle." He smiled, "We did it in France and it worked out well eh?"

I didn't point out that it had been an accident. We would have to find and steal one without being detected.

"Sir?"

"Yes Corporal?"

"Won't there be guards and such?"

"The Headquarters is in an old colonial hotel, the *'Antiqua Roma'*. It is on the outskirts of the town. The RAF flew over it and they say there are about twenty people there. That includes clerks as well as soldiers. They have vehicles there too." He added as though it would be simplicity itself to steal one.

I stood and went to the maps. One showed the building the prisoners were being held in while the other showed the route to safety. "Sir, do we have to stick to this route back to our own lines?"

"Well no, Sergeant, but this is a route which has been produced by great minds and it will be Lieutenant Marsden's decision to deviate."

"Sir, with respect, I am not certain what a bunch of officers with a little bit of red around their collar tucked away in London know about sneaking around behind enemy lines. We both know that you have to be flexible."

Lieutenant Marsden said, "It sounds like you have got cold feet, Sergeant Harsker. Don't you want to go?"

"It is not up to me is it sir? But I want a chance to get out of this alive rather than being a glorious gesture. I have a good section and it would be stupid to throw it away because of a decision made in London. All I want to know is do we have flexibility? Suppose we find a boat we can steal? Would that be an option? What if it is close to an airfield and we can steal an aeroplane? All I am saying is that this road is the only one, apart from the coast road and it may well be swarming with Germans and Italians. If it is we would have to go a different way."

I had stunned the two officers although I saw a wry smile on the Sergeant Major's face. Lieutenant Marsden reddened, "Well I am a little disappointed, Harsker. I thought this would have been right up your street. Isn't this how you got your medal?"

That was it! The Lieutenant was glory hunting. "Sir, I got my medal by doing my job. I didn't set out to win one. As far as I am concerned I don't need medals to do the job I do."

The silence in the room made everyone but the Sergeant Major uncomfortable. He still had a smile upon his face. That surprised me for my attitude was not, necessarily, what they had all expected. Major Foster broke the silence. "Your section has the best chance of succeeding Sergeant Harsker. If it were otherwise I would send another section. If you have to deviate then that will be Lieutenant Marsden's decision. Is that clear?"

I stood, "Of course sir and if that is all the men need preparing and I daresay we have new equipment and ammunition waiting for us."

The Major nodded and Sergeant Major Dean said, "Sergeant Grant has it waiting for you. Report back here when you and your section are equipped."

As we left Gordy said, "That wasn't like you Sarge. What is the problem?"

"You mean apart from the fact that we have to break into German Headquarters, rescue high ranking prisoners, steal a vehicle, and then make our way across the desert?"

"Put together that does sound a tough one. But we can do it."

"Of course, we can. But we need to be flexible and I am not certain that Lieutenant Marsden has enough experience yet. We have not fought with him up to now. I think he has only been on one raid. If it was Major Foster then I would be more than happy. He has a cool head under pressure." I shrugged, "We follow orders and do as we are told. Go and fetch the lads. I will be at the QM stores."

What had really made me so irritable was that the Lieutenant suddenly looked and sounded like the Hooray Henrys who had been at the Officer Training Course in Manchester. What would he be like under pressure? I put that to the back of my mind as I entered the stores. "You were right Daddy. We are the lucky boys who are off to sunnier climes."

He nodded, "I knew before. I have packed a bag for each of you lads to make it easier. There are extra canteens too and dried rations. You have enough for a week. There is twice as much ammo and grenades for you." He shook his head. "I wouldn't like to carry that lot around with me in heat."

"Luckily we don't have too much walking to do."

"And there are spare canteens and salt tablets in every pack. You will need those. I stuck a couple of little petrol stoves in too. They are light and all you need is to steal some petrol."

"Stealing petrol is the least of our worries, Daddy."

"You don't seem happy about this Tom."

"You know me; for King and Country and all that. It's just that we have an unknown quantity with us this time; Lieutenant Marsden."

"We had the same problem with Lieutenant Reed and he proved to be a good 'un."

"You might be right. We will have to see."

There was a noise outside as the section came in. "What's up Sarge? Gordy told us bugger all!"

"And I will tell you precisely the same Private Curtis. Pick up a bag each, get your weapons from the armoury and meet me at the headquarters."

Private Moore asked, "Where are we off to?"

"When we are in the lorry I will tell you Private now cut along will you?"

The Major and Lieutenant Marsden walked in after the section had left. Daddy said, "Here you are, sir. Everything that you will need."

He grabbed his bag and left without a word. He was tight lipped. I hefted my Bergen as Major Foster said, "Give us a moment eh, Sergeant Grant." Daddy nodded and, taking his pipe went out of the back door. "Look, Tom I know what it is. You are worried about the Lieutenant but I can assure you he has received top marks in everything."

I nodded, "I think he will be a great officer sir but for this one I would have hoped for someone with more experience." I hesitated, "Like you."

"Thank you for that compliment. I would love to be there but I have to prepare the rest of the troop for another big raid. We are stretched at the minute."

"I see sir. Well in that case I am sorry for my attitude back there." I tapped the stripes, "Perhaps you ought to take these sir. Maybe I'm not cut out for this."

"You are and all that you said was understandable. I am relying on you to guide the Lieutenant. You will be a fine team. He is new but he is bright as they come and he will adapt. I did. Lieutenant Reed did. You are the most experienced sergeant we have and that is why you were chosen for this. If anyone can get them out it is your section." He looked at his watch. "You had better push off now."

The rest of the section was in the lorry as I arrived with my guns and Bergen. The Lieutenant was seated in the front with the driver. Sergeant Major Dean nodded, "You look after them, Sergeant. All of them!" he nodded towards the cab.

"Will do Sergeant Major."

I dumped my bag in the bottom of the lorry and took a seat at the back close to the tailgate. It was the least smoky part of the lorry. I took off my beret; I would be leaving that with the rest of my kit. "Right lads, we are moving now so I can brief you. We are going to Africa."

I let that settle in. There was a buzz of conversation. I saw money changing hands. They had been gambling. "This will not be easy so pay attention. We are going to fly to Gib and change aircraft. We are going to parachute behind enemy lines and rescue some high-ranking officers from German Headquarters. Then we steal a vehicle and drive over four hundred miles through the desert to reach British lines."

I let that sink in. Private Moore broke the silence, "You are having a laugh ain't you, Sarge?"

Gordy shook his head, "No me old cock! He is not."

"There will be guards there, that is obvious and I daresay we will be extremely lucky if we are able to avoid having to use our guns but I want us as silent as we can be and delay the inevitable. Curtis, we have no explosives to worry about but I know that we can improvise some booby traps when we are there. The biggest problem, as I see it, is stealing the vehicle."

George Lowe said slowly, "If it is any help, sir I was four years into a mechanic's apprenticeship before the war. I can fix most vehicles."

I clapped him on the back. "That is the best news I have had all day. As of now, Lowe, you are in charge of all things mechanical!" The young man beamed.

Bill Becket said, "What is going to be a problem sir is the water. Or should I say lack of it as well as dehydration."

"We have salt tablets in the packs and we need to conserve water whenever we can."

"We will spend the time in Gib going over the maps. Aeroplanes are a bit noisy and, besides, I think we all need to try to get some sleep if we can."

We pulled up less than ten minutes after I had finished speaking. The flap opened and a seaman said, "Right this way gents." I saw that we were not at an airbase but by the sea. We were going in a seaplane. I saw the huge Short Sunderland bobbing up and down on the water. I worked out that we must be in Southampton Water.

"Quick as you can, sir. The pilot wants to get off as soon as he can." The airman pointed to a Nissen hut. "You can change into your gear over there if you like. We have been ordered to send your kit back to your base in the lorry."

We went into the hut and all began to strip off and put on the shorts and tropical gear. It was chilly but when we reached North Africa then the temperature would soar. I was pleased to see that the Lieutenant was not self-conscious about changing with us.

I used one of the spare bags and held it open. "Right lads, letters, documents and anything incriminating in here. If we are caught it is name rank and serial number." They all deposited their items in the bag. I handed it to the airman. "Make sure this is safe eh?"

"Will do Sergeant. Right lads time to board."

We waited for the Lieutenant to lead us aboard. The young lieutenant who was the pilot greeted us cheerily. "Good show! Cloak and Dagger eh? Makes a change from stooging around looking for damned U-Boats. Get aboard and next stop Gibraltar. It should take eight hours or so. You have time for a sleep and my chaps will have some hot food for you too. We have beds and a galley! First class service!"

His crew were equally cheerful. The interior of the huge aeroplane actually had a couple of bunks. It would certainly be more comfortable than a Whitley. The Short Sunderland was positively luxurious compared with the Whitley and was much quieter. The take-off was barely noticeable. We saw little of the crew for the first few hours. The gunners were all in their turrets for we were flying, in daylight, close to the coast of France.

Soon after we had taken off Lieutenant Marsden waved for me to join him. Some of the men were asleep in the bunks whilst a card school was the focus of the rest. "I thought we should chat, Sergeant. I think we got off to a bad start."

"Yes, sir. Sorry sir."

"No, it was my fault. I was so gung ho and enthusiastic. Too much so I am afraid. You were right to be cautious. The problem is,

Sergeant, that you and your section have become so successful that I think I assumed it would be a breeze. The major had a chat to me. I now see what you meant."

"I didn't mean any disrespect, sir."

"I know and I will be relying on you heavily. I know the theory but the one raid I was on was led by the Major. Like you he is something of a legend."

"I have known the Major for some time sir. He is solid and dependable."

"I want you to feel free to offer an opinion. I know that this is foreign territory, quite literally for me."

I patted my bare legs. "Well sir, this is a first for all of us. Northern France is quite familiar but the desert? I can foresee problems that we don't even know will be problems."

He nodded, "Well Sergeant, I am glad we had this little chat. I wanted the air clear between us."

"Yes sir and don't worry about my feelings. I have thick skin and I always prefer the truth."

I left him and went to a quiet corner near to the starboard side blister to study the maps. I knew the value of having the maps in my head. I spent half an hour studying the various routes we might take. What worried me was that some of them were just dotted lines which told me they were tracks. I had never been to the desert but I knew about shifting sand. My compass might be our salvation yet.

A shadow approached and I looked up. It was young Moore. I looked beyond him to the card game which was still in progress. "You had enough of cards?"

He shook his head and sat down next to me. "They were taking the micky out of the way I speak. I don't think they like me."

I put down the map. "Listen Alan what you have to know about these lads is that they have been together a long time. They know each other. You, well, you come over a bit strong and cocky." I held up my hand, "I am not saying you are but to them you sound cocky. You know what I am saying?"

He smiled, "I suppose you are right. The trouble is me old man legged it when I was a nipper. Mum brought me up on her own and she worked every hour God sent to keep a roof over our head and food on the table. I grew up on me own. I had to be cocky to survive." He held out his fists. "I used these a lot and when they didn't work I tried to be a funny bugger. It's why I joined the Commandos. They seemed like me, tough and able to look after themselves."

"And they are but there is something else; we look after each other. You don't need to prove yourself to these lads. They will take you for what you are. Look on them like your mum. Your mum always wanted you to do well didn't she?"

"I'll say. She was as proud as punch when I went home in my uniform."

"Those lads feel the same. They want you to be the best Commando you can be for if you are then they have more chance of surviving. You are the new boy so just be a bit quieter and listen a bit more. Gordy was like you when he started. He has learned not to be so, well, full of himself." I smiled, "I'm not having a go at you here Alan. This is just advice. I joined up when I was younger than you. I learned to listen more especially to lads like Gordy, Norm, and Ken who have been around the block a couple of times."

He nodded, "Thanks Sarge and I won't let you down."

"I never thought for one moment that you would. And listen if you get a bit scared when we go into action don't let it worry you. We all do. You just don't let it overpower you. Use the fear. It will keep you sharp."

As he returned to the others I berated myself. I should have had the chat in Blighty and not while we were ten thousand feet above the Bay of Biscay. I was responsible for that young lad. I was pleased I had had the talk for it now gave me an insight into him.

Once we neared the northern coast of Spain they went to the galley and made us corned beef hash and cocoa. The Royal Navy liked its cocoa. We got on really well with the crew. They were intrigued by us for they had not transported Commandos before and my section was fascinated by this huge flying boat. It seemed all too soon that we were descending into the black pool that was the Mediterranean. The pilot taxied us over to a floating jetty where a Royal Air Force officer awaited us. We gave a cheery farewell to the Coastal Command crew who had looked after us so well. We were now as far away from home as I had ever been. As we followed the airman, laden with our belongings I could even smell the difference. There was an exotic warmth and fragrance to the air. A lorry waited for us at the road and, once again we were whisked into the night.

Chapter 13

The journey to our next aircraft was even shorter than the one in the Flying Boat. We drove directly into a hangar. There a Captain of Intelligence waited for us. He held his hand out to Lieutenant Marsden, "You must be Lieutenant Marsden. I am Captain Lloyd." He waved his hand around the hangar. "Sorry about this but there are German spies in Algeciras. If they saw a bunch of Commandos on the airfield then they would put two and two together and know something was up. Your chutes are over there. Have you eaten?"

"We had something on the Sunderland."

"We have some tea brewed ready for you. I am afraid we will be taking off fairly sharpish. We had hoped you could get here a little sooner. It would be better if you jumped in the middle of the night. Still, you chaps know your business eh?"

Lieutenant Marsden nodded, "Sergeant, have the men get their chutes and grab a mug of tea. We are taking off sooner rather than later."

"Right sir." I turned to Gordy, "You heard the Lieutenant; and bring my chute over and a mug of tea."

As if on cue the pilot wandered over from the waiting Whitley. "Whenever you chaps are ready."

"Two ticks and we'll be there." I was pleased that the Lieutenant appeared to be taking charge. "Any more intel on the targets Captain?"

"As far as we know the prisoners are still in the Headquarters building. We send a Hurricane over every couple of days to take photographs. There are the same number of cars and lorries in the vicinity and the same number of guards." He shrugged apologetically, "That's all we know."

Gordy helped me put my parachute on. He handed me a cup of tea and Ken gave one to the Lieutenant. He wrinkled his nose as he drank it. I suspect Curtis had put his normal four sugars in it. "Sir, do we know what vehicles they have there?"

The Captain looked at me as though I had risen out of the ground and appeared magically, "Vehicles?"

"Yes sir you said the vehicles hadn't changed. What are they? Lorries? Tanks? Armoured cars? Half-tracks?"

"Oh, I see. Well there are a couple of nice Mercedes staff cars. Four or five Kübelwagens. Two lorries and an armoured car."

"Thank you, sir, that helps."

I began to work out the best vehicles for our escape with the hostages. I figured on taking two. We would need a lorry; that was obvious but we needed a second one and if they had a Kübelwagen with a machine gun then that would be perfect. The half-track would be good in the desert but the Lieutenant had told me he planned on using the road. We had discovered, while on the Sunderland, that there were three west to east roads. One went by the coast and would be out of the question. There was a second further south and that looked to be the most direct route. The last one went perilously close to the Great Sand Sea. If we were taking that route then the half-track would be best.

The Lieutenant handed the half-drunk mug of tea to Ken Curtis. "Right chaps. Get on board."

The pilot waited for us. "I have checked the aerial photographs. I will drop you south and west of the Headquarters. It means that the German road blocks are to the east of you. There is nothing between you and the target." He grinned, "Of course I have no idea how you jokers are going to get out of there but I am just the delivery boy."

"What is the landing site like? Any trees?"

"This is North Africa, Sergeant, trees are as common as rocking horse droppings around here. It is just scrubland. Tell your lads to watch out for snakes and camel shit."

With that happy thought, we boarded the Flying Coffin. I wished it was a Sunderland.

It was too noisy to speak and so we all checked our equipment. After our last jump the Major and I had decided that it was better to attach our Bergens to our bodies by means of a tether. If we had had explosives then we would have worn them but this way it meant we had a clearer view of the ground. We each tied our Bergen to our waists. We would still hold the Bergen until the last minute. We had contemplated tying the machine gun to it too but that was just too risky.

This time I would jump first and Gordy last. The Lieutenant had never jumped under combat conditions. We put the three of us with experience at the front and the back. I put Norm behind the Lieutenant. I told him to give the officer a shove if he hesitated. Ken would do the same for Alan.

I knew that the pilot was getting every rev he could from the ageing bomber. The last thing he wanted was to be caught in daylight. With just machine guns at the nose and at the tail the Whitley was a sitting duck for any fighter, even the ones used by the Italian Air Force. The pilot took us well south, over the desert, and then headed up to the coast and our drop zone. We would be dropping to the west of the town and, even if the sky was becoming lighter, we would be hidden in darkness.

The navigator came aft. "Five minutes to the drop. Better get ready." I clipped my chute to the cable running the length of the empty bomb bay. Bill, behind, checked me and then tapped my shoulder. There was a sudden rush of air as the door in the floor was opened. The noise intensified. The navigator walked down the stick checking the cables and he came back. A moment later the co-pilot stuck his thumb out and the navigator tapped me on the shoulder. I dropped my Bergen through the hole as I jumped. The jerk on my shoulders as the parachute deployed was reassuring. I looked down and saw just blackness. This was not Europe. We were landing in featureless desert devoid of buildings. The others would have to follow me and it would be my task to find the safest place to land. I peered down between my legs to try to spy somewhere flat and rock free. It was strange to be wearing shorts. The air whistled over them. The last time I had worn shorts had been on holiday in France before the war. This was no holiday.

As my eyes adjusted to the night I saw an open and reasonably flat patch of land to the south of me. I tugged on one side of the chute and I veered towards it. The sound of my Bergen hitting the dirt was enough warning to enable me to brace myself. I landed standing up. I quickly gathered the parachute and rolled it up as I walked. I glanced to my right and saw Bill and the others landing. They were some forty yards from me. I took off my parachute pack. Untying my Bergen, I jammed the chute into it. As soon as my pack was back on my back I cocked the Thompson and peered around for danger. The sky in the east was becoming lighter but there was no noise save the distant sound of sheep or goats. I was no countryman and could not discern the difference.

I ran back towards Bill and the others. Bill was just cocking his gun. He nodded and followed me. The others were all in the process of removing their chutes and preparing to move. I watched Gordy as he came in to land. We had all made it. The quiet was eerie. While the Lieutenant and the others readied themselves, I turned through a full circle checking for danger. As I listened I thought I heard the sound of a diesel engine in the distance. I dropped to one knee and peered north. It was barely visible but I saw a shadow moving from west to east. There appeared to be two very dim lights. It was a truck and that meant we were close to the coastal highway.

The Lieutenant appeared at my shoulder. "What is it Sergeant?"

I pointed north, "I think the coast road is there."

He nodded. "That makes sense. We'll head in that direction. We need somewhere to lie up during the day. You and Becket take the point." He turned, "Corporal Barker, rear guard."

Bill and I moved off. It was not sand we were crossing but poor dirt and scrubby, weedy growth. The ground began to descend towards the road and, I hoped, the hotel. I had studied the aerial photographs and maps on the Sunderland. The hotel we were seeking stood alone at the western end of the town. I think the Germans had picked it for its isolation and, I daresay, the quality of the accommodation. It had been a five-star hotel before the war. I did not expect, therefore, to see any buildings in front of us.

I heard an engine and, raising my hand I dropped to one knee. Bill did the same. This time I knew what I was looking for and I saw the German lorry trundling along the coast road from west to east. Its dimmed lights gave me an idea of distance. It looked to me to be about a mile away. This time I followed the lorry as it headed east. I heard the driver change gear as he slowed down. You only did that when you came to a junction or other traffic. I said to Bill, "We'll head further east."

The going was now more difficult. It was uneven. We passed scrubby trees and bushes as we neared the road. I noticed that there was even some scrubby grass. We were closer to the sea and moisture. I used time to estimate distance. When I judged we had travelled half a mile I halted and scanned ahead. The sky to the east was lighter and I could see more. I could just make out a large building in the distance; there were the tiny dots of light which showed it was inhabited. It seemed to be about a mile or a mile and half away; it was hard to judge at night. "Bill, do you reckon that is the hotel?"

He nodded, "Makes sense, Sarge."

"Then we look for shelter."

"I have seen bugger all yet. Not even a hollow."

We moved forward more slowly now. If this was the hotel then we had almost reached our objective. Care was needed. I saw a pile of stones just a hundred yards or so ahead of us. They were too regular to be natural. I went to them. It was an ancient mud hut. The roof had long collapsed, the walls had gradually eroded but, in places, about four feet remained. Bill and I skirted the outside and then waved the others forward. It would be a perfect place to observe. It looked to be about a thousand yards or so away.

"This looks like shelter, sir." I pointed to the north east. "I think the hotel is over there."

"Think Sergeant?" It was a straightforward question. I don't think the Lieutenant was trying to be funny.

"Becket and I will go and check, sir."

We dropped our Bergens in the old hut and then began to run across the scrubland towards the distant hotel. I noticed that there were more signs of humans all around us. There were pieces of broken vehicles; exhaust pipes, pieces of tubing and patches of oil. I guessed that, before the war locals had brought old cars here to either repair or to cannibalise. I doubted that the Germans would allow them to continue such actions this close to their headquarters. The closer we came to the large building the bigger it looked. When we were four hundred yards from it I waved Bill to the ground. I saw lights on the lower floor. They were dim but then there was a sudden splash of light as a door was opened. I heard the sound of voices. Two locals carried a pan of something which they hurled towards the ground before us. It was close enough for us to see them. They could not see us for we were in the darkness yet. They went back inside and there was just the glow of light from the ground floor. For me that confirmed this was the hotel and I studied it to see if it fitted the building I had seen in the photographs.

If the men had brought something from the kitchen then the vehicle park was to the east. As I looked in that direction I saw a wire fence. It was barely visible in the dark; it helped that I was looking for it. That would be the vehicle park. I was about to order Bill back when I caught a distant red glow. There was a sentry by the car park and he was having a cigarette. I tapped Bill on the shoulder and pointed. He nodded. We would wait until he moved off. Having seen his cigarette, we saw his shadow. We waited and I heard the hum of a generator. That was where they got their power. That might prove useful for without power their radio would not work.

As we watched a movement caught my eye. Something scurried across the ground towards the spot the kitchen staff had hurled their refuse. It was a rat or some such creature. Soon it was a writhing mass of vermin as they fought for the scraps. That, too, was useful. If we had to do a closer reconnaissance then the animals would disguise our tracks. All we needed to do was to leave food for them. The sky was definitely becoming lighter. It was with some relief that I saw the sentry move. We turned and ran, crouching, back to the others.

There was relief on the Lieutenant's face when we arrived in the derelict hut, "You had us worried, Sergeant."

"Sorry sir. It is the hotel. There was a sentry on the vehicle park and we had to wait until he moved. It looks like that is the only place they have a fence. When it is daylight we should be able to see it clearly from here."

"Right we will have to wait here until this evening now. Sergeant, organise the watches."

"Right sir. Bill and I will take the first stag. Norm and George will be next followed by Ken and Alan, Connor and Polly, Gordy and Harry and then back to us. We just do an hour each. That way we all get some decent shuteye."

"What about me?" The Lieutenant looked upset I had not included him.

"Do you want the watch with Connor and Poulson sir?"

"Yes, that will be fine. I am one of this section too you know."

I grinned, "Yes sir, I know."

The hut was crowded when they all lay down. Bill and I had to find perches in the two corners which remained. I opened my Bergen and repacked it while I watched. I put the parachute in the bottom. I took out the piece of camouflage netting. I had a swallow of water from my spare canteen and then repacked the Bergen. I put the camouflage netting over me. It disguised my shape. Bill saw what I had done and he did the same. Half of us had the netting. It was not desert camouflage but it was better than nothing. We now had bare white legs. They looked quite stark. I wondered if we would be here long enough to get them brown!

Dawn broke and the hotel was clearly visible. It was a large building. It could have held far more than the twenty odd men that the Hurricane pilot had seen. I did not use the binoculars for fear of giving away our position. I saw that the Germans were not wearing grey but a sand coloured uniform. There was more movement around the hotel and we heard the sound of engines being started. There was also increased traffic on the road. Some vehicles came from the east and stopped at the hotel. I saw a petrol tanker come from the west and pull in. I worked out that there must be a port to the west which was supplying the Germans. It made sense that they landed during the dark and used the night time to send lorries and trucks to deliver the supplies. The RAF would be hunting such targets.

We woke Norm and George. I gave my camouflage netting to George. "Here you can borrow this sheet; Norm has one of his own. It will help hide you."

"Thanks, Sarge."

"See if you can work out which vehicles would be the best to steal. You can just see them through the wire and they started them a while ago."

I curled up in the warm spot vacated by Norm Ford and was asleep in minutes. Gordy and Harry woke me. I saw that George had put the netting over me like a blanket. "Anything?"

"We saw some British uniforms about an hour ago. Jerry brought them out and marched them around. There weren't three prisoners though there were six. "

"All staff?"

He shook his head, "No, a couple wearing RAF blue, and a naval officer."

"Thanks." He sat in the corner. "Not getting any sleep, Sarge?"

"No, I had a good long one. Besides we are a bit close to the Krauts for me to be happy sleeping during daylight."

I wet my finger and held it up. The wind was blowing from the north. "We could risk the little stoves if you lads fancied a brew."

"No petrol yet, Sarge. Still at least we can talk without Jerry hearing us."

"Tell you what, have the lads cut some of the cords from the parachutes. They might come in handy."

I went to my corner and covered myself in the net. I studied the hotel. The problem I foresaw was getting from the hotel to the middle road across the desert. We had no idea if there was a roadblock to the east. I had heard lorries changing gear and stopping during the night. It suggested a road block. We definitely needed two vehicles; especially if there were six prisoners to be rescued. When George woke I would ask him about the vehicles. I saw one Kübelwagen as it was driven out of the compound. I saw that it was open and had a machine gun on the passenger side. That was a good thing. I saw that, strapped to the back were jerry cans. They could have contained water or petrol or both. We would need to carry plenty for our long journey.

I watched as some Arab boys sneaked up to the vehicle compound. They crawled like Commandos. One sprang to his feet and tried the gate. I had seen the German lock it when the Kübelwagen had left. I smiled to myself. I knew why the Germans had a fence and a guard. Anything not nailed down would be stolen. What it did tell me was that the ground was not mined. The German sentry came out and shouted at them. He waved his gun and they ran away laughing. They were opportunists.

A couple of the others chose to go back to bed once they were awake. I was ready for action and I could not go back to sleep. All of used the south side of the hut for our ablutions. The wind from the north took the smell away from us. We were neat campers. The other advantage was that there was a dip there and we were hidden from all sides. Being Commandos, we were used to deciding when we ate. We needed no orders. As we all carried our own rations it was our responsibility to eat sparingly. The lads ate either individually or in pairs, sharing their rations.

When I woke the Lieutenant, he nodded towards the camouflage net. "Where did you get that Sergeant?"

"The old Quarter Master Sergeant might have been corrupt but he was handy to get stuff like this. Me and some of the lads bought it. It is very useful." He nodded. I could see he was envious. "There are six officers to be rescued sir. There are two RAF types and a sailor."

"We will definitely need two vehicles. I have spotted a Kübelwagen with a machine gun. If we could get that and a lorry then we would be all right." The sun had now risen and it was hot. I pointed up to it. "We will need plenty of water and petrol if we are to make the four hundred miles through the desert."

"I know and what will we find on the other side of the hotel?"

"We have the town to go through…"

Just then Polly said, "Aeroplane, to the east!"

"Cover! Here, Lieutenant, under this netting with me." It was a cosy fit but we managed to snuggle beneath the netting. I saw the spotter aeroplane as it passed overhead. I hoped that the netting would have hidden us. If it came back then we would be in trouble. After what seemed an age but could only have been moments I heard it recede as it continued west.

"All clear."

"Thanks, Sergeant. That came in handy."

As the afternoon wore on we prepared for action. While Gordy kept watch the Lieutenant briefed the men. We had spent some time discussing what to do now that we had seen the actual building.

"We will split into three groups. Lowe and Curtis will break into the vehicle compound and deal with the guards. We leave our Bergens with them. Sergeant Harsker will take Poulson, Moore, and Connor. They will enter the hotel by the front. I will take the rest through the kitchen at the rear. We use knives. If we have to then we use our Colts. I do not want machine gun bullets flying around. We have six officers to rescue. Whoever achieves their objective first secures that entrance and then seeks the prisoners. We have to be quick as well as silent. We leave at seven. It will not be totally dark but we will need to take that risk. I want Lowe and Curtis to be able to have as much time as possible to steal the vehicles." He looked to me.

I added, "I want the other vehicles disabling or destroying. You need to take every drop of fuel and water that you can. It will be a long journey home. Any weapons and grenades, as well as supplies will come in handy."

Chapter 14

The waiting had been necessary. A good Commando did not rush into a situation. We had to make sure that we had our exits and our entrances worked out. Had we rushed in as soon as we had landed then we might have been spotted by the guard hidden in the compound. While we waited for the off I gathered my men around me. "Polly, you will be tail end Charlie. John, you and Alan tuck in behind me and watch my back. We have the hard job. The main entrance will be guarded. We use the shadows. Remember knives only. Alan, you haven't been in action before; when you strike with the knife do not hold back and you must kill silently. Any sound could spell disaster." He nodded, nervously. He was not as cocky now as he had been. I was pleased that I had spoken with him. I took the Luger from my Bergen and tucked it in my belt.

"What's that, Sarge?"

"A German weapon. If I have to fire I will use this. It might confuse them for a second or two. The crack of a Colt is unmistakeable."

As it became slightly darker the Lieutenant looked at me. I saw that the sky had clouded over a little and it would soon be dark. Here it went from daylight to dark almost instantly. It was a risk but we had to take some chances. I nodded. He waved us forward. I had my Thompson over my back and I carried my Bergen. We kept low as we covered the four hundred yards which took us to the scrubby bushes Bill and I had used that morning for cover. We dropped to our knees as Ken led George to the compound. This would be the tricky part. We had no idea where the Germans would be within the wire. Ken had his wire cutters. We had seen that the gate was operated by a bolt from within. By cutting the wire Ken could put his hand through and slide the bolt open. The danger was the noise of the snap of the cutters. When I saw his hand open the gate I knew that the obstacle had been overcome. Lowe and Curtis slipped inside the compound. We trusted them to their job and we would do ours.

The Lieutenant waved us forward. We ran to the wire and dropped our Bergens. I led my men to the left, around the side of the building. We would be operating blindly now. We would not know what had happened to the others. In the time it had taken us to close with the hotel and for the gate to be breached, darkness had fallen. We moved along the side of the old hotel. I could hear the murmur of voices from within and the smell of food being cooked. The rattle of cutlery and the buzz of conversation told me that we were passing the dining room. Perhaps any officers would be at dinner. I hoped so.

As we neared the corner of the building I held up my hand and, drawing my dagger slithered forward. I could see, across the road, a heavy machine gun with two men behind the sandbags. I peered to my right and saw, by the front entrance, a guard leaning against the portico. I glanced at the machine gun. The men had their backs to me. I drew my Luger and held it in my left hand. I returned to the other three. I mimed that I would kill the guard to the right. They nodded. I led them to the corner and pointed to the machine gun. I made the sign to kill. I pointed to Polly and then my stripes. He would be in charge. He nodded. I slipped around the front of the building. I felt almost naked. If the sentry turned he would see me. I had to force myself to make small movements. I smelled the smoke from his cigarette. His night vision would be impaired as there was a light just above his head. The fact that he was smoking also told me that he knew no superior would come his way. I edged closer. He was wearing a field cap as were the machine gunners. He wore no helmet to cause me problems when I struck him. I was just four feet from him when something made him turn. I jumped at him and punched him in the mouth with my Luger. I heard his teeth as they broke. I ripped my dagger across his throat and he slid to the ground.

I turned and looked at the machine gun. My three men were creeping towards it. They pounced. One of the gunners gave a small cry as he was struck. Had my sentry not been dead then the alarm would have been given but he lay dead. No one came running out. We had succeeded… so far. I turned and climbed the steps to the entrance. I peered over the half glass door. The interior was well lit. That would be the generator we had seen; they had their own power. Behind the desk I saw, not an Arab but a German. There was also a guard with a machine gun across his lap. He was seated close to a fountain in the lobby. There were many potted palms and plants dotted around. Were it not for the swastika flying from the roof it could have been any hotel, anywhere.

The other three joined me. Our objective had been the front entrance. We had achieved that. Now we had the tricky task of taking out a guard. As far as I could see there were just the two men in the lobby. When I saw the guard stretch and then stand I took my chance. I slipped through the door and dropped behind a large potted palm. I held up my hand to halt the others. It was unbearably hot inside the lobby. I heard the German sentry say, "Where is that Arab who is supposed to operate the fan? It is hotter than hell in here tonight."

The one behind the counter did not look up from the newspaper he was reading. "A couple of them ran off yesterday. I don't think they have been replaced."

The guard turned to face the man behind the desk and I waved the other three to join me.

"They are untrustworthy bastards anyway but they are handy for pulling the fan." The others had joined me as he looked up at the ceiling and said, "You think they could fit a motor to it."

This was our chance. I waved them forward and I took four strides and put my Luger into the German sentry's back. I hissed, in German, "One sound and you are dead." Polly had his Colt aimed at the second German.

"Moore, Connor, use the parachute cords to tie them up."

My German chose that moment to be the hero. He turned and tried to ram his gun into my stomach. I punched him with my hand which held my dagger and then brought the barrel of the Luger across the side of his head. He fell to the ground, dazed. I switched the Luger to my right hand and hit him on the back of the head with the butt. This time he stayed still. I glared at the second German who raised his hands even higher.

I put the Luger back in my belt and took my Thompson from my back. The next part would not require silence. While the two men were being tied up I waved Polly forward. I could hear the sound of cutlery again. There was a door to my right. I peered around the side. This looked to be the place the Germans were using as a dining hall. I glanced quickly in and then jerked my head back. I counted fifteen men. There looked to be a table made up of officers.

Just at that moment, as Connor and Moore joined me, I heard the crack of a Colt and then the sound of a machine gun. There was no time to lose. I leapt into the dining hall with my Thompson levelled and shouted, in German, "Hands up!"

There were four Thompsons aimed at them and they should have known better. The furthest point of the room was just forty feet away and I knew we could not miss. I think the enlisted men and the sergeants would have surrendered but I saw an officer reach for a gun.

I shouted, "Don't!" He continued and that made the others reach for theirs. I pulled the trigger and swept the machine gun across the officers' table. The other three guns joined in and cleared the room. "Moore, check they are all dead. You two come with me." We ran back to the lobby. "Connor, watch the entrance. Polly, upstairs. Use your Colt." We were now looking for the captured officers and accuracy with our weapons would be more important than firepower.

There was a central stairway and we both ran up. We reached the landing. Two guards raced from a corridor to our right. We both fired from the hip as we rolled to the ground. They were still trying to bring their rifles to bear when the .45 bullets tore into them. I heard steps behind us. I turned with a levelled gun.

Gordy held up his hands. "The Lieutenant sent me. He hasn't found the prisoners yet."

I pointed to the right. "These guards came from down this corridor. We will try there."

We stepped into the corridor and a fusillade of shots greeted us. As the plaster from above our heads shattered us Polly and I dived to the ground and we emptied our Colts at the two Germans. I drew my Luger and sent two more bullets towards their bodies. We sprang to our feet. Polly holstered his Colt and cocked his machine gun. "Be careful with that." As I glanced up above I saw a sign. It was in English as well as Italian. I recognised the English word, '*Ballroom*'. I waved Polly to the other side of the door. Gordy stood to my left. I kicked the door open and we raced in. There was an officer and he held the General before him with a Mauser to his head. The other prisoners had their backs to us and a guard was covering them with his machine gun.

"Drop your weapons or I shoot the General!" I raised my Luger and pointed it at him. "I am not, as you English say, bluffing. I will shoot him."

Gordy was to my left and he had a better shot. I nodded and murmured, "Take the shot!" As I squeezed my trigger his Colt barked. My three shots obliterated the German guard's head and the officer fell backwards, shot in the left eye by Gordy.

General Carter said, "Damn fine shot, Private."

I said, "Well done Gordy."

"If I can't hit a target four feet away then I need my eyes testing."

"Are you gentlemen hurt?"

The five of them stood. One of those in an RAF uniform turned and said, "I am fine, son. Thank you for coming for me."

"Dad!"

The General's mouth opened and closed and he said, "Is this the fella you have been talking about Group Captain Harsker?"

"Yes sir, it is my son."

"Sorry Dad we have no time to catch up. Grab your stuff and follow Poulson. Polly, take them to Curtis."

"Right, Sarge."

"Gordy, search the officer in case he has any papers."

Dad and the other officers did not have much to take and they were soon out of the room. Gordy pocketed the officer's Mauser and handed me his wallet and papers. I stuffed them in my battledress. I would read them later. On the way down stairs I spied the radio room. I smashed it up with the stock of my gun.

By the time we reached the rear of the hotel the others were all there. Lowe was behind the wheel of the Kübelwagen while Harry Gowland was behind the wheel of a large German lorry. I saw Bill tending to the Lieutenant and Norm Ford. Norm looked to have a wound to his hand but Bill was bandaging the Lieutenant's leg. That looked to be a more serious wound.

"How is it Bill?"

"Not good, Sarge. I have stopped the bleeding and I think it went through but I have no idea what sort of damage has been done."

The Lieutenant smiled weakly. "I am fine, Sergeant."

"Put him in the lorry. Polly, you and Connor get in the Kübelwagen. Ken how is the demolition coming along?"

"All set Sarge."

"Right, Harry, get the truck on the main road. George, wait over there with the Kübelwagen."

Gordy asked, "What do you want to do about the prisoners Lieutenant? Shoot them?"

The Lieutenant was in pain but he shook his head, "We would gain nothing by that. Leave them!"

We all helped to carry the two wounded men and carried them to the truck. We passed the dead German sentry. We laid the two wounded men in the vehicle and then the officers climbed in. "Gowland drive and wait down the road. We won't be long."

When the vehicles had left the compound, Ken took a stick grenade out. He grinned. "I went for simplicity. We punctured the fuel tanks. When this goes up it will be like Blackpool Illuminations. I'd stand back, Sarge."

We had planned this fireworks show to draw the Germans here. By using German vehicles, we hoped to slip by them unnoticed in the chaos. I ran to the Kübelwagen. Ken hurled the grenade and then ran to me. There was a crump and then the petrol ignited. It was like a wall of fire. "Jump in the back with the other two."

As soon as we were aboard I said, "Right Lowe, drive. Overtake the lorry. We are the lead vehicle." I handed the map from the front of the Kübelwagen to Ken. As we came around the corner I said, "Stop!"

I jumped out and ran to the machine gun emplacement. I grabbed some of the ammunition, the stick grenades, and the two field caps. I climbed aboard, "Drive." I passed the ammunition and grenades back to Ken. I took off my comforter and put on the field cap. I did the same for George. "It might fool a roadblock for a few seconds; that is all that we might need." I saw the lorry up ahead. "Come on George, put your foot down."

He jammed down on the accelerator and we sped past the slower lorry.

"Keep your foot down. I want to eliminate any trouble before the lorry reaches it. That has the wounded in it and the General!"

I knew from the map that the hotel was only a couple of miles from the town. Poulson shouted, "Sarge, Germans coming the other way!"

"Slow down, Lowe. You lads in the back get ready with the grenades. Wait for my command."

It was a German armoured car which was coming towards us. If he fired then it would be the shortest escape in history. Thankfully he slowed too. He saw what he expected to see, a German vehicle with Germans driving it. The hatch opened as he drew level with us. I smiled as his head appeared. I was leaning nonchalantly on the machine gun; the barrel just happened to be facing the armoured car. Behind him I saw a lorry filled with troops.

The officer had doubt written all over his face as he said, "We heard gunfire."

I waved him to put his face closer to our vehicle. I said, "False alarm." Then in English I shouted, "Now!"

The truck filled with German troops had closed with us and had stopped. I cocked the machine gun and raked the side of the truck and the cab. I was so close that I could not miss. "Drive!"

Lowe put his foot down not a moment too soon. The three stick grenades demolished the armoured car. It was a blazing wreck. I kept firing as we passed the German truck until I had no bullets left. I had no idea how many we killed but I know that I had hit the driver for the vehicle had swerved savagely to the left and smashed into one of the mud houses which lined this suburb. "Is Harry still behind us?"

"Yes, Sarge!" Ken's voice sounded calm and in control.

"Lowe, take the next right and then the first left. I want to get off this main road."

"But Sarge it will slow us down."

"Every Kraut worth his salt will be racing down this main road. We can't be lucky twice."

The roads we travelled did indeed narrow. Ken shouted, at one point, "The lorry has lost his mirrors!" We could live without mirrors.

I was aware of signs pointing to the left. I did not recognise the words but I did the picture of a ship. The port was to our left. If we continued down this road then we would soon be beyond the town. The locals shook their fists at us as we screamed down roads more used to camels and donkeys than trucks and Kübelwagens.

The road ahead stopped. It was a dead end. "Reverse and take the next left."

Harry almost slammed into the back of us as we reversed down the road. We rejoined the main road but we were in a quieter section. I reloaded the machine gun with a new drum. As we headed towards the shanty side of town I began to believe we had made it.

"Sarge! Ahead, a road block."

"Slow down as though you are going to stop but keep going. No matter what happens don't stop. Any grenades left?"

"Two. The rest are in our Bergens on the lorry."

"They will have to do. Have your guns ready. This looks like a bigger detachment than the one at the hotel."

I could see guns levelled as we approached them. They were suspicious. I stood and leaned against the gun again. I had my right hand on the Luger. "Have you seen the Arab terrorists?"

When the guns lowered just a little I knew they were buying our story. It was too dark to see the colour of our uniforms and the hats showed us to be Germans.

"Arabs? No! Where are you going?"

All the time he was talking Lowe was edging closer to him. "We have been ordered to clear the coast road."

Just then a sharp eyed Feldwebel saw something awry. "Englanders!"

I pulled my Luger and fired at the Feldwebel and the men manning the machine gun. The three grenades sailed high into the air and then the other three all let loose with their Thompsons. Lowe had done as I asked and he was moving forward slowly. "Floor it!"

He stamped down and we leapt forward. The second machine gun had managed to fire and it hit the space we had occupied. Then the grenades went off and the four men manning it were thrown high into the air as the grenades exploded. I turned the German heavy machine gun and raked the tents to my left. And then we were through and driving into the darkness. The lorry behind had given us enough space to clear the road and they missed the blast from the grenades. Harry Gowland was proving to be a cool customer or perhaps Gordy was giving him orders.

Ahead there was nothing for almost a hundred miles until we reached Aidabiya. When we reached that town there were three routes we could take. We now had a lead and, if we kept going at full speed we should be able to outrun anything which followed us. During the day, they could send up air patrols but, at night, we had the darkness in which to hide. I had no idea what we would meet at Aidabiya. With luck, no one was left alive to tell them that the Kübelwagen and the lorry were being driven by the enemy. I regretted not taking some of the jackets from the dead Germans. It was too late to worry about that now. A hundred miles would take us between two and three hours to cover. It looked, from the map, to be flat and that would help us keep up a steady speed.

"Well done Lowe. That was good driving. Did you manage to get enough fuel and water?"

Ken answered, "Aye we did."

"How is the fuel going?"

George tapped the gauges. "I reckon this one is the fuel. We are just over half full. I doubt we'll make this next town without refilling first though."

I looked at my watch. It was gone midnight. We would need to hide up somewhere but I wanted to make that after we had negotiated Aidabiya. "Let me know when you need to stop."

Now that I knew which gauge it was I watched it. Alarmingly it began to go down quickly. I realised that it had a short range; either that or the tank had a leak. I checked my watch again. It was two. We would have to stop. "You had better pull over and refill with petrol. How are you three doing in the back?"

"It is a bit cramped, Sarge."

"Connor, you go in the lorry when we stop. We are probably a bit overcrowded and that will drink the juice."

As soon as we stopped I leapt out and ran to the back of the lorry while Polly and George grabbed a couple of jerry cans and Ken went to fetch more grenades from the Bergens. The flap at the back of the lorry opened, "How is the Lieutenant?"

"Sleeping Sarge."

"Good. That will probably do him more good than anything else. This will be the only stop we make before daylight. We will lie up of the day then."

The General said, "You did damn well back there. Mind you all that we could hear was the guns and the bombs. It was when we passed through that we saw what you had done."

"We aren't out of the woods yet, General. We have another town just ahead. There we have to decide which road to take. I have no doubt that there will be a roadblock. Jetty will have radioed ahead. We may have to go across country."

George came back. "All tanked up now sir and we filled up the lorry too. We are good for a couple of hundred miles now."

"Right. See you chaps later."

Dad waved and gave me thumbs up as I left.

The next town, Aidabiya, was not on the coast. There looked, from the map, to be some sort of swamp close to the coast. "We don't need to rush any more, Lowe. If we hit trouble then take us off into the scrub. Make sure, if we do, that you head to the right. I don't want to get trapped in the swamp."

We hit houses soon after we had stopped. There were no Germans but it was a warning for us. The road climbed, "Slow down when you reach the crest. Turn out your lights."

"It's bad enough with them dimmed as they are, Sarge."

"There is a town ahead. Just take it slowly. I will stand and keep watch for you." I used the machine gun to keep me upright. "Stop!" He stopped so sharply that I nearly plunged over the top. I jumped out of the Kübelwagen and bellied up to the rise. There was a roadblock and it was four hundred yards down the road. They had a small half-track and a machine gun. It looked to be manned by about ten men.

I ran back to the vehicles. "Turn off your engines. Gordy bring grenades. Moore, you come with us. Connor, you too." The captured officers looked down at me, concern on their faces. "There is a road block and a half track. It is blocking our way into the town. We will have to eliminate it. Then I intend to cut across country. We are going to take the southern road. Harry, George, as soon as we come back I am going to head due east. Go on foot and find the best place to leave the road. It will be daylight soon."

"Yes Sarge."

Dad's voice came out of the dark, "Take care, Tom."

"Will do, Dad."

I led the handful of men back to the Kübelwagen. "Gordy take half and make your way down the side of the road. I will do the same on the left. When you are close enough use your grenades and then machine guns."

I saw that he had left me with Curtis and Moore. We left the road and walked as quickly as we could on the uneven ground to the left. I hoped that the attention of the Germans would be on the road. They looked to have five men on watch. The rest were resting. Our rubber soled shoes helped us to make a silent approach. When we were thirty feet from them I took out a grenade. The others did the same. We all pulled the pins. I threw and a heartbeat later so did they. We flung ourselves to the ground. There were three loud cracks and then screams as men were hit. Three more explosions told me that Gordy's men had thrown theirs. We leapt to our feet. I had my Colt in my hand. A

German staggered towards me with a rifle in his hands. He was disorientated but he was a good soldier and going to the danger. I shot him in the chest and he was thrown to the ground. We moved amongst them shooting any who looked to be a threat. "Find stick grenades. Ken, I want this half-track blowing up and then a couple of booby traps leaving."

I ran back up the road. "Start your engines. Which way, George?"

He pointed to a spot some thirty yards ahead. "It looks to be a track of some sort there. The ground is hard enough."

Gordy led the rest of the men back. "Get aboard."

There was a sudden explosion and the half-track rose and then fell. It would need a low loader to take it away for repair. I walked to the gap that my men had found and waved the two vehicles forward. After they had driven into the scrub I got on my hands and knees and used a broken branch to sweep dirt and sand across it. It was not a perfect job but it would delay the pursuit. I jumped back into the passenger seat and we began our journey across the sand. I had thrown the dice. I hoped for a double six and not snake eyes!

Chapter 15

By the time dawn broke we were twenty miles beyond Aidabiya. I took out the German map we had found. I could see, ahead, the sandy trail that was the poorly made road we had to follow. "Join the trail."

We headed east and were making good time. In ten miles, the trail would bend north. According to the German map there was a dotted line which continued east. Eventually it joined a solid line. I hoped that this meant a track. I would risk the track. The sun began to beat down on us. We could have rotated the drivers and kept going but I knew there would be an air search. I saw the camel prints and knew we had found the right place. "Take that track."

Once again, I stopped the Kübelwagen and jumped down. Polly joined me and we made a much better job of disguising our route than the hurried one the night before. "You lads drive on but slowly. Polly and I will disguise our tracks." Where we had left the road and joined the sandy track it was soft earth and sand. The tyre tracks we had made were fresh. We swept them away, then we walked backwards for a hundred yards until we found ourselves on a rocky surface which did not show the tracks of the two vehicles.

We remounted and soon were travelling at a healthy twenty miles an hour It was faster than I would have thought we would have been able to do on the sand. "Keep your eyes open for shelter."

Ten minutes late Ken shouted, "There to the right."

I looked where he was pointing. There were a number of huge rocks just fifty yards from the road. Two of them were bigger than the lorry. "Perfect. Head there but go slowly. Ken, you and Polly disguise our tracks."

They jumped from the slow moving Kübelwagen. The land began to slip away. We drove down a long shallow incline towards the large rocks. We stopped the two vehicles close to the massive blocks of stone. One overhung us and, when I looked back, I saw that we were below the level of the road. I went to the back of the lorry. "Everyone off. We are here. Gordy, use the camouflage nets to hide as much of the two vehicles as you can."

He said, "Sarge there is a big camouflage net here. It is a proper desert one. It will hide the whole lorry!"

"Perfect."

"Bill, break out the stoves. We might as well have a hot brew."

I ran back to the road and helped Ken and Polly disguise our tracks. As we descended to the camp I felt satisfied. When I was at the roadside I could not see the vehicles at all. We had got further with fewer casualties than I had expected and we had somewhere to hide. We had no sooner rigged the nets when Connor shouted, "Aeroplane!"

"Everyone down!"

It happened that I was able to lie at an angle and could view the sky without looking up into the sky. It was a Storch. They were a slow-moving spotter aircraft and had a limited range but they had good visibility. He was flying to the north of the track we had been on. He disappeared and his engine faded. "Keep still. He is coming back!"

Sure enough the noise of his engine increased. This time, when he passed us I saw him heading north east. When I was satisfied that he had gone I rose. "You can all get up now."

Gordy came up to me. "Do you think he saw us?"

"We will find out in about an hour. If he did then the Germans will either send fighters or, more likely, troops. We can do little more. If we move they will see us. We sit tight. Have a cup of tea and some food and get some shut eye."

I was shattered. But before I could sleep I would need to speak with the Lieutenant. He was awake and Bill was checking his dressing. "I'm sorry about this, Sergeant. Damned inconvenient catching one like this."

"Don't worry, sir. The lads have all rallied around. We have done all right. Only you and Norm with wounds. Doc reckons Norm is not that bad. It is you we are worried about. To be honest I didn't think we would get this far. I should apologise for my outburst in the office."

He shook his head, "No, Sergeant, you were right. I was, am, too inexperienced. I will be better the next time out. If there is a next time. How do things look?"

"Surprisingly good. We are taking the desert route. Unless Jerry comes knocking in the next hour or so then his spotter didn't see us. I intend to push on as soon as it is dark and try and reach the British lines before dawn." I paused, "If you are happy with that, sir?"

"That is fine. Carry on, Sergeant."

"You get some rest, sir. I'll just go and check the sentries."

I found Gordy. "Have you arranged a rota?"

"Aye Sarge. The lads know what they are doing."

"When am I on?"

Gordy shook his head, "You should be letting the young lads do the duty." I just stared at him. "How about last stag, before dark." I nodded. "Sometimes, Sarge, I reckon for a bright lad you are a bit soft in the head."

I saw steam coming from the pan of water and I headed over to it. Dad cut me off. "You sit down, son and I will make you a brew. I have been watching you. You have never stopped. "I hesitated. "Sit!"

I laughed and did as he asked, "Sir! Yes sir!"

He wandered over to the stove and then returned with a mug of tea. He shook his head. "You make me tired just watching you."

I shrugged, "I am sure you were the same when you were my age, dad."

He sat next to me on the rock and sipped the tea. "Perhaps. It is a hard task you have ahead of you."

"I know but I have found that if you focus on the next part and don't worry about the end result then the job is less daunting."

"And of course, you found more men to rescue than you were told."

I nodded, "Twice as many actually but it doesn't change the nature of the job, does it?" Dad shook his head, "So how did you end up a prisoner?"

"I was a prisoner before the General arrived. I suspect that if you hadn't been sent for General Carter then I would be a prisoner yet.

Lieutenant Commander Graham and I were flying along the coast looking for suitable bases for our ships and our aeroplanes. That was back when we were chasing the Italians. We were advancing so quickly that it was hard to resupply the forward troops. We wanted to see what sort of fields and ports the Italians had. Our pilot," he gestured to the young lieutenant, "is a good lad but he took us too low. I think he was trying to impress a British ace. We were hit and had to crash land. He did well to bring us down in one piece. The gunners and the rest of the crew were sent to a POW and we were taken to the hotel where you found us. It was the Italian Headquarters. They were going to send us to Rome and then the Germans took over. The German general is a General Rommel. He went on the offensive as soon as he arrived. The hotel you found us in had been almost the front line. Jerry advanced and captured a couple more towns east of us. They captured General Carter a week or so ago and then you came." He nodded, "And just in time too. The Colonel, the chap your corporal shot, had just enjoyed telling us that the SS were coming to question us."

"Mum was worried. She got no joy from the Ministry when she tried to find out where you were."

He smiled, "I bet she rang Randy." I nodded. "He is in Intelligence now and he knew that we were missing. I spoke to him the night before we took off. Don't blame him. He couldn't tell your mum anything. He probably thought I would escape and arrive back in Cairo."

"I am surprised that you didn't."

"I'm not as young as I used to be and ... well to be frank the other two seemed quite happy to be prisoners. It isn't in my nature to leave someone behind and so I stayed. Then the General arrived and I knew he was far more important than me. He has secrets in his head which the Germans would love to pry loose."

Gordy came over, "Sarge, you need to get your head down." He flashed a look of irritation at my dad.

I held up the mug of tea, "Just as soon as I have finished this, mother!"

He went off shaking his head.

"I remember when my men treated me like that. I didn't know it at the time but it is a mark of the respect they have for you. Your boys would follow you to the ends of the earth and beyond you know. I heard them talking about you when we were in the lorry. Every time there was a problem they knew that you would find a way to get them out of it. But he is right." He took the mug from me. "Give me your cup. Get a couple of hours sleep. I don't envy you getting us a safe route home. You have the Sand Sea to one side and German and Italians to the other."

I lay down next to the Kübelwagen beneath the shelter of the netting. It would be cooler in the heat of the day. It actually took me a few minutes to get to sleep as I ran through the momentous events of that day. Having my father in my care scared me more than the prospect of the sand or the SS. If I allowed anything to happen to Dad how could I face Mum and Mary?

I awoke naturally in the middle of the afternoon. I had had more than enough sleep. I rolled out from under the netting. There was no sign of anyone. I smiled. I had told them to keep hidden and they had done just that. I went to the back of the lorry. The General and the others were there. I took the top from the jerry can and sniffed it. It was water. I filled my canteen and then the empty mug I saw there.

"Everyone all right?"

The General nodded, "The lieutenant here was telling us of some of your exploits young man. I can see why they chose you for this mission. I am grateful."

"How is he?"

Bill lifted his head and rubbed his eyes, "He is much better, Sarge. I have been keeping him asleep and the wound well cleaned. He won't be running a five-mile run in full kit any time soon but I reckon he could walk in four or five days."

Dad was leaning against the back of the lorry smoking his pipe. Ken had salvaged some tobacco from the dead Germans at the hotel. He gestured to the skies with the stem. "Jerry has had aeroplanes up all day. I am guessing they haven't seen us. That is a good thing. It means they have to widen their search. It gives us a chance."

"We have three hundred miles to go. I think we will be lucky to make thirty miles an hour over this terrain. The odds are we will be crossing the front lines just after dawn. There will be no hiding place then."

The General nodded, "And the front line is such an imprecise thing. It ebbs and flows."

"Well I will go and check the vehicles."

George Lowe was awake and busy under the bonnet of the truck. "They are good machines these, Sarge. Solid."

"Make sure they both get as much water as they need. We can always go on short rations if we have to. Are they all full of fuel?"

"Yes Sarge. How far do we have to go tonight?"

"Three hundred miles."

"Then we will need to stop at least once."

"Make it twice. When we get close to the front line I want to be able to keep going."

"Good idea sir and that will be better for the engines."

Gordy appeared behind me with a mug of tea. "Well Sarge, it is going better than we thought."

"We have a long way to go but I am hopeful that they will be too busy up north to have this little road either patrolled or with a road block. They might be looking for us but their priority must be driving our lads back to Egypt. My biggest worry is that our troops have begun to retreat. That would be a disaster. We would be playing catch up."

As the afternoon wore on the wind velocity increased. It whipped the sand from the south. Our location afforded us protection but it made the sand begin to build up on the road. The good news was that it stopped any German aeroplanes from flying over our position and even if they had flown over they would have seen nothing such was the size of the sandstorm.

The wind abated towards dusk. We left as soon as it was dark. Things began to go wrong from the start. We had driven no more than forty miles when Ken said, "Sarge, we have lost the lorry."

We reversed two hundred yards down the road. The heavy vehicle had become bogged down in soft sand. Gowland said, "Sorry Sarge, that was my fault. I should have taken it slower but I was trying to keep up with you."

"Then I should have realised that you are heavier than we are. Are there any sand tracks?"

Gordy said, "No Sarge. That was the first thing we looked for. There are shovels."

"Then we dig."

It took twenty minutes but eventually, with much pushing and shoving from everyone but the two wounded men we managed to get going once more.

"We will drive slower from now on Lowe."

As we drove at a ridiculously slow speed I realised that we would not make our lines before dawn. Could we risk another day hiding beneath nets? We might not find such a good spot the next time? Would we be as lucky a second time? I was also aware that we would be closer to the front lines. Even with the slower speed the lorry became bogged down on two further occasions. We used the opportunity to fill up the two vehicles each time we stopped. We would not need a fuel stop.

Disaster struck again just before dawn. I had been using the odometer to estimate how far we had to go. I reckoned we were just twenty miles from the front line. Sporadic flashes of gunfire to the north confirmed this. The lorry stopped again. When we returned Harry had the bonnet open. "It's not the sand this time Sarge. There seems to be a blockage. The engine was hunting."

Lowe looked inside. How he could see anything I had no idea. He nodded as though he knew what it was. Striding to the tool box he returned with a couple of spanners. "It is a blocked fuel line. The German fuel has not been filtered. It is either that or sand got in when we filled from the jerry cans."

It took him an hour to clean the blocked line by which time it was dawn. "Keep your eyes peeled for aircraft. We are like sitting ducks here."

Sure enough our Storch returned. This time there was no doubt that he had seen us for he high tailed it north quickly.

"Get a move on Lowe, or Jerry will be on us."

"Almost done sir. Two minutes." He tightened something and said, "Turn her over Harry."

The engine spluttered a couple of times and then banged into life. "Well done." There was a hatch in the cab of the lorry. "Ford, take the spare German machine gun and brace it on the cab. If Jerry sends aeroplanes you are our first line of defence." Norm might be wounded but he would not have to move and I wanted the rest of my men ready to fire their own weapons and to move quickly if we had to.

"Righto Sarge."

The one benefit of daylight was that we could see the sand. It meant Lowe could slow us, and therefore the lorry, down when we came to larger drifts. He could also take us over the more solid rock. We managed to get through the sand drifts, albeit slowly. Ten miles down the road we hit more sand and this time the lorry did become bogged down once more.

As we got out the shovels dad said, "Just a thought but if we put the canvas from the lorry in front of the lorry it would be like a carpet. It would be quicker and we would get better traction."

Anything which would speed things up suited me. "Right lads, get the canvas off."

It came off far faster than I had expected although it took everyone but the wounded to do so. We had just laid it in front of the front wheels when we heard the sound of aero engines. Ford shouted, "To the west! Stukas. Three of them!"

"Get everything off the lorry. Get the Lieutenant to safety, Doc. Harry, as soon as we are empty move forward slowly. Everybody, if you wait until the Stukas are close and all fire at once you have the best chance of bringing them down. General, go and shelter behind the Kübelwagen. It will be safer there." He and his two staff officers left.

Dad said, "Have you a spare gun?"

Norm threw down his Thompson, "Here you are sir, use mine!"

Even Lieutenant Marsden propped himself against a rock and pointed his gun at the skies. The German lorry moved inexorably slowly. It was a race against time. Would the dive bombers reach us before the lorry managed to get a grip on the canvas? As the first Stuka peeled off I realised this was one battle we would lose.

He screamed down. The moment we fired had to be carefully judged. There was little point in wasting bullets. It was a split-second decision. The retreat to Dunkirk had taught me the right time to open fire. "Now!"

Every gun opened up at the same time as the German fired. Lieutenant Graham collapsed in a bloody heap as the two German machine guns ripped him in two. A heartbeat later the wall of fire we had sent up tore through the engine and the Stuka hit the ground just a hundred yards from us. The explosion knocked us all to the ground.

Norm Ford shouted, "Sarge, Harry has been knocked out."

"Doc, get him out of there. Lowe, as soon as the Stukas have made their run get behind the wheel."

The next two Stukas decided to attack together. They would divide our fire.

"You lads on the far side take the left-hand Stuka. Norm, you take the left-hand Stuka. The rest, we have the other one."

The death of the RAF pilot had made everyone find somewhere to shelter. The naval officer and one of the General's aides cowered beneath the lorry while the other one was close to the Kübelwagen. My men were using their Bergens and rocks as cover. Ford took a bead on the leading Stuka. He opened fire first and I saw his bullets strike home. The Stuka juddered.

"Fire!"

Our fire was not as effective as it had been. We had to divide our bullets between the two targets. Even so one of them began to smoke and then their bombs dropped.

"Cover!"

I buried my head beneath my Bergen as the bombs both struck on the far side of the lorry. The concussion totally disorientated me. It rushed over me like a wall of heat. I forced myself to struggle to my feet. The lorry was on its side. Beneath it lay the bodies of the Commander, Lieutenant Graham and one of the general's aides. I had not even had time to find out his name. I just knew that he was a major. Poor Norm Ford had been cut in two as the lorry had been blown over.

I saw the two Stukas limping home. Both of them had smoke pouring from them and one looked to be descending. Norm had had his revenge.

"Anyone else hurt!"

Gordy said, "Just Norm and the three captives. We didn't do them much good did we, Sarge?"

"This is no time to feel sorry for ourselves. Jerry will be back. Put the Lieutenant in the Kübelwagen."

"I am still giving orders, Harsker!" Lieutenant Marsden tried to struggle to his feet.

"Yes sir I know but we have one vehicle. We are going to have to run the last fifteen miles to our lines. Do you think you can manage that, sir?"

I saw a smile cross dad's face. The Lieutenant shook his head, "You are right, Sergeant Harsker."

"Dad can you drive?"

"Of course."

"You have a full tank. We will bury these poor sods and then follow on foot." He nodded, "If you could send some help for us when you reach Torbruk then it would be handy."

Dad climbed into the driver's seat. He gestured to the passenger side, "Right General, do you want to operate the machine gun?"

"Damned right I do. I am fed up of being shot at!" He settled himself in the seat and began to examine the German machine gun.

Lieutenant Marsden said, "I promise I will send help as soon as we reach Torbruk or our lines."

I turned to my men. We had to move but we could not leave the dead to be ravaged by wild animals. They deserved more than that.

"Gordy, get four graves dug. Ken, scavenge anything we can save from the German lorry."

I went to the bodies and took their identity tags and the papers from their pockets. I had no time to examine them in detail. That would come later but I would not leave it for the Germans. I suspected they were letters home. The Royal Navy Commander had a watched inscribed, *'To my darling, Come home safe'*. The watch might help some young lady in England. It was a grim task but I had to do it. The burial was a hurried affair. I mumbled some words. They did not do them justice but I now owed a duty to the living.

I tightened the straps on my Bergen and hung my Thompson around my neck. With the extra ammunition and weapons, we had taken from the lorry and the dead we were well laden down. The Germans knew where we were and they would be coming down the road as quickly as they could. They would be delayed when they reached the lorry for it blocked the road and there was shifting sand on both sides. If they had half-tracks or tanks then we were dead men walking!

"Right lads we are going to have to move. We run for half a mile and then walk half a mile. Gordy, you lead. Ken and I will bring up the rear. And just before we go I have to tell you that no other section could have done what you have done. I am proud of each and every one of you. Now let's show these Krauts how Commandos can move!"

Chapter 16

As we ran east along the sand covered road I contemplated singing as we had done when I had first become a Corporal. It was not the time with Norm so recently buried. My words must have had an effect for I had to shout to tell them to walk. They would have kept on running otherwise. It was now a case of counting the miles. The map had indicated roughly fifteen miles to safety but I knew not where the front lines were. All I knew was that when we began running again we were a mile closer to safety. I counted each step as we walked and then as we ran.

In front of me Moore began to slow a little as we ran. "Come on Moore. Pick up the pace."

"I'm sorry Sarge but another fourteen bleedin' miles will kill me!"

"It isn't fourteen miles. You only have to run for half a mile. You can do that can't you? Imagine you are running to the pub before last orders!"

"Now you are talking Sarge. Running down to the Griffin for a pint of Watneys. Lovely!"

"I like a nice pint of mild myself. Lovely and refreshing."

"That's a northern drink Sarge. We don't have that in London."

Ken snorted, "Flat warm beer in London! Give me a pint of Theakstons from Yorkshire any day of the week."

"Walk!" I winked at Ken who grinned back at me. "There you are Moore. You don't need to run again for at least half a mile!"

We managed another two miles before we heard the sound of an aeroplane. "Cover!" We dived to the side of the road and swung our Bergens in front of us. There was no cover and we would have been spotted. The Bergens gave us the illusion of protection. We were perilously short of ammunition. Firing at the aeroplanes had eaten into our supplies. I had half a magazine and one spare. "Don't waste your ammo on the aeroplane. He is spotting anyway."

The 109 opened fire but the bullets just splattered into the sand and he banked away. He made a couple of circles and then headed west. His presence and the circling meant that mobile infantry were coming. As his engine receded I stood and, taking out the binoculars, I peered down the road. I saw, in the distance, sand from someone following us. I focussed and saw the two German half-tracks. They looked to be more than two miles away but they would be upon us within ten minutes. I looked east. If we were going to fight then we needed a better position. Less than half a mile away a ragged mound of rocks rose from the desert. They looked like we could hide there. If we could make them then we would stand a chance. It was far enough from the road that we would be able to create a killing ground.

"Gordy, take the section to those rocks and set up a defensive perimeter."

"You heard the Sergeant, move yourselves!"

"Curtis, take out the last of the stick grenades. We will make a booby trap here. There is a dip in the road and we are hidden from view. They will come over the top and not see it... I hope."

I took some more of the parachute cord and tied it to the grenade. Ken piled as many small stones around the grenade as he could. It would hide it and it would add to the effect when the tiny stones were hurled through the air. We tied the other end to a small scrubby bush. We strung the cord across the road and tied it to another bush. We had four grenades and we spread them out in the hope that one would work. We had just finished and I saw the half-tracks were less than a mile away. "Let's run!" It was the first time I had had a foot race with a vehicle. This was not a gentle jog; this was a full-blown sprint with a heavy pack on my back. I found myself trying to suck in air. When I got the stitch, I had to ignore it and run through. Gordy waved us into the safety of the rocks and I collapsed.

Gordy opened his canteen. "You are a mad bugger Sarge! Drink this!"

The warm stale water tasted like Champagne. "Here they come, Sarge!"

Polly's finger pointed to the spot we had just vacated. There were two half-tracks and soldiers marching along the side. With the crew in the vehicle we were outnumbered by four to one at least. I was wondering if they had avoided the grenades when there was a sudden crack and four men fell to the ground clutching their wounds. Another two cracks on the far side told me that at least three grenades had worked. The half-tracks stopped and men jumped out. As they did so the last grenade exploded. I caught the glint of light on glass as the officer scanned the road ahead.

Ken said, "That has eased the odds, Sarge."

"Don't forget we are almost out of ammo. I would pray for dark but it is too far off." I suppose we could have tried to run further away but the half-tracks would have caught us. We had one chance, hold them off until dark, and then sneak away in the night. It was a long shot but it was hope at least. "Conserve your water and your ammo."

Gordy said, "I have plenty of .303 Sarge and I have the scope."

"Can you hit them from here?"

"They will fire accurately up to three thousand yards, Sarge but the effective range is just six hundred yards."

"All you have to do is hit the half-track. Any kind of ricochet will cause damage. Give it a go!"

He leaned the rifle on a rock and took aim. I used my binoculars to see the effect. There was a crack. The soldier on the machine gun next to the officer suddenly disappeared. The red explosion of flesh told me that Gordy had hit him.

"Well done!"

As soon as the bullet hit the German, soldiers all piled back into the half-tracks and every head disappeared. I saw then that there were six bodies. Our grenades had done their work. I watched as the half-tracks began to move and then one stopped. As two men jumped out Gordy's gun cracked again. We heard the ping as it hit the half-track and the two men dived for cover. I focussed on the half-track which had stopped. The grenade or the stones had thrown a track. The second one came forward down the road. The odds had been halved.

As soon as it neared us Gordy had more chance of hitting something. He fired a couple more shots and hit the vehicle. On the third shot he shouted, "Got you, you bugger!"

I could not see what he had hit, "What were you firing at?"

"I was aiming for the flap the driver uses to see. I hit inside. That bullet will have rattled around in that tin box."

As if to prove his success the half-track veered to the right so that Gordy could not hit that spot again. He began to fire from his elevated position into the back of the half-track. The effect was the same. The bullet pinged off the metal and I saw an arm flung in the air as he hit one of the occupants.

The damaged half-track had disgorged its men and they were running to follow the half-track.

"Gordy!"

He switched targets and brought down another two before they made the safety of the half-track. We had an impasse. If they turned to approach from head on then Gordy would continue to cause casualties. We, on the other hand, could not move. We were both stuck. The German Commander had had enough of taking punishment and there was a sudden fusillade as the Germans opened fire. It was long range for a rifle without a scope. We ducked back behind our stone defences. It would take a really lucky shot to hit us and I hoped that they did not have a sniper with them.

The day wore on. Polly had sharper ears than the rest and he said, "Sarge. I can hear lorries. They are coming from the west."

Sure enough there were. I took the binoculars and scanned the horizon. There were two trucks of Italians. They were being reinforced. Gordy took out another clip of ammunition. "Do you think they will send anyone to help us?"

"I don't know, Gordy. We have no idea what problems there are or how long it will take them to reach our lines. Let's just say we have to rely on our own resources and get ourselves out of this fix." I pointed to the Italians who had pulled up next to the half-track. "I think you will need to discourage these Eyeties too."

He nodded and snuggled into the stock of his rifle once more. The Italians and the Germans began to move forward using whatever cover they had to hand. "Hold your fire lads. Let Gordy thin them out a bit. Have your grenades ready. We hold them until dark and then head back across the desert."

There was a crack as Gordy fired his first shot. The officer waving the Italians forward fell. The others went to ground. I saw a German officer urging them to advance. He fell to Gordy's next shot. I think they realised, at that point, that we only had one rifle. They rose as a line and began to run towards us.

Ken murmured, "That's put the cat amongst the pigeons."

Gordy did his best and every bullet found a target but they were closing with us. Moore said, "Now, Sarge?"

"Hold your fire. And use short bursts. We have no spare ammo."

The Germans and the Italians were firing wildly as they ran. I did not mind. They were wasting ammunition and were in no danger of hitting us. They gained in confidence when we did not fire. I think they thought we had run out of bullets. When they reached the road, less than eighty yards from us, I shouted, "Fire!"

Eight Thompsons opened up. The first ten Germans and Italians fell and the rest dived to the ground. They had learned that we still had bullets. They began to slither back.

"Hold your fire."

They were harder to hit and we could not afford to waste bullets. My aim was to stop them advancing and wait until dark. We held the advantage at night. They pulled back behind their vehicles once more taking their wounded with them. Ten dead bodies lay between us. Another fourteen or so had crawled and limped back to the security of their vehicles.

I studied the lorries through my binoculars. "Gordy, can you try to hit the petrol tank on one of those Italian trucks?"

"I'll have a look." He peered through his telescopic sight. "It's possible."

"Just try three bullets. It might worry them."

What worried me was the prospect of either more aeroplanes or more trucks. We were holding the thirty or so who remained before us but any more and we would be in serious trouble. Gordy hit the petrol tank with the first bullet but nothing happened. "I hope it isn't a diesel!"

I looked at the tank through my glasses. Petrol was pouring out. If nothing else we were emptying the tank. "Try another." I was staring at the petrol when Gordy fired his second shot. The explosion was so bright in my binoculars that it made me pull my head back. Within a minute the truck was a blazing inferno and they had to move the second Italian vehicle to prevent it being burned as well. That cost them one man when Gordy sent a bullet into him.

Then someone behind the vehicles took charge. I saw the enemy split into two and move to encircle us. Gordy could only fire at one group and they were at extreme range.

"Ken, take half of the men and position yourselves to the east. They are going to try to flank us."

"Poulson, Connor, Moore, with me!"

"The rest of you find a better position to the west. Gordy keep sniping."

I took out my Luger. I now had almost as much ammunition for that as I did for the Colt and the Thompson. I laid four hand grenades before me. I had one more swig of water and then I watched.

Once they had divided our firepower they began to move forward. They kept large spaces between them and that lessened the advantage of the machine gun. This time, when they fired they did so in a measured manner. They kept our heads down. I heard Harry Gowland cry out.

Are you hit Harry?"

"A bit of rock hit my face. I'll be fine. I saw the bastard who did it. He is a dead man!"

Gordy said, "That's it Sarge. I am out of ammo." He took out his Colt.

When they were fifty yards away and advancing more confidently towards the lower rocks I shouted, "Let them have it!" I squeezed off two bullets at one man who ducked down and then I waited for him to pop his head up. He obliged and I sent three bullets towards him. One of them must have hit him for he fell back.

I heard a shout and Harry said, "George has been hit."

"Doc, go and see to him." I took the pin from a grenade, released the lever and hurled it high into the air. "Grenade!"

We were in as much danger as the enemy from our grenades and all of us buried ourselves into the rocks. The grenade exploded in the air sending shrapnel into the enemy ranks. On the other side I heard Ken shout, "Grenades!" as he and his three men hurled their grenades at the same time. There were four ragged explosions and then screams.

Gordy and Connor shouted, "Grenades!" as they both launched their bombs. I stayed hunkered down as the concussion from two bombs sent shock waves towards us. When the smoke cleared I raised my Thompson. The enemy were falling back. I fired a short burst. We watched as they ran back to their vehicles to lick their wounds.

"How is Lowe?"

"He has been hit in the arm. He will live."

"And I can still fight, Sarge!"

"Gordy, you and Connor get down and see if there are any weapons we can get. I will see Ken." I moved carefully through the rocks. "How are things over here?"

"Polly was hit in the hand. It is not serious. They fell back when we used the grenades."

I looked at my watch and then the sky. "It will begin to get dark in an hour. We move out then."

"Isn't that a risk, Sarge?"

I pointed to the north. "We go across the sand. They have one half track and we can hear that coming. If they follow then we ambush them." I shrugged, "It's not much of a plan but if we stay here then they will bring more men and we will be prisoners."

Gordy had found a machine gun and three rifles. Connor had five cartridge pouches and half a dozen stick grenades. I nodded. "That is better. Right lads. As soon as it is dark we leave here quietly and head north across the sand. Have a good drink now and get some food inside you. I don't think they will come soon. They will probably wait until dark. Use your parachute cords and the stick grenades to booby trap the rocks. Doc, take George and go to Polly. He is wounded. I want the three of you on the north side. While it is still light look for markers to help us in the dark."

"Right, Sarge!"

I had my Silva compass and we had a torch we had found in the Kübelwagen but I did not want to show the enemy where we were. I tried to guess what my opponent would be doing. He would not want to signal his intent of attacking me in the dark. He would wait. We had a small window of opportunity to slip away before they had begun to cover the killing ground before us. I needed to buy my men some time. Our two wounded would slow us down somewhat.

Gordy slithered next to me. "Booby traps all in place."

"Good. Give me one of those captured rifles."

He handed me one. "Have you something in mind?"

"Just a little idea. Listen I want you to go to Ken. Have him take his men to join the Doc. I don't want the enemy to see us. When you come back let them see you moving toward me but don't get shot."

I could see he was intrigued but he just nodded. "Right Sarge." He paused, "That leaves just you here."

"I know. Tell Ken that I want him to start north east as soon as it is dark. He is to ignore whatever happens here."

As Gordy slipped away to the left I raised my head and moved to my right. As I had expected there was a flurry of bullets. I ducked down and moved down towards the dead Germans and Italians. Looking east I could see the sky becoming slightly darker. It would not be long now. I saw the nearest dead Italian. I darted forward as though I was trying to get something from him and more bullets came my way. I had been moving back before the first bullet struck and I made my way, unseen back to my original hiding place. I heard bullets striking the rocks to my left and knew that Gordy was on his way back.

"They are on their way. What have you planned then, Sarge?"

"I reckon they will come over as soon as it is dark. I want to confuse them. I am going to fire my Luger and my Italian rifle. You do the same with your weapon. I will shout in German and you shout, 'We are surrounded. We surrender.' Then we pull out in the dark."

"What do you think that will achieve? I can't see it myself."

"If we were attacking Germans and we heard British weapons and then the Germans saying that they surrendered what would you think was happening?"

He nodded, "That some of our lads had come to our aid."

"And they will come over expecting the position to be safe. I want them to walk into the booby traps. We need to delay them long enough so that they lose us in the dark. Now move to your left and let them see you. I will do the same to my right." I took off my comforter and, raising my head moved eight feet to the right. Another fusillade rattled amongst the rocks sending small slivers of stone flying. One scored my cheek. I put my hand there and felt blood.

When I got back Gordy said, "Have you been hit, Sarge?"

"Just a scratch." I looked at the sky. "Not long now. Get ready." I was becoming used to these African sunsets. An English one could sometimes take almost an hour. Here you were lucky if they lasted ten minutes. Once it was dark I was certain that I heard movement. "Ready?"

"Yes Sarge."

I pulled the trigger on my Luger and shouted, in German, "Now! Attack." I fired my rifle and Gordy did the same.

Gordy shouted, "We surrender! We surrender!"

"Let's go!"

Having scouted our escape route, we moved quickly around the rocks. Gordy led. He knew where Ken and the others had been. Behind me I heard orders being shouted in Italian and German. We had just reached the bottom of the rocks when I heard the first booby trap go up. There was a rattle of gun fire as they fired into the dark. Gordy pointed to the north east. I nodded and, using the stock of my rifle wiped our prints away as I walked backwards. In daylight, they would be easy to spot but I hoped, in the dark, that the enemy would be confused. There was another volley and a scream. They were hitting each other. Confusion reigned. After twenty feet or so I turned around and we began to jog. There was a second explosion and then a third.

The sky behind was suddenly lit up as a flare was launched. Gordy and I threw ourselves to the ground and did not move. It seemed to take an age for the night to become dark again. As we had had our faces in the sand our night vision had not been affected. I knew that the Germans and Italians would have none. They did not try a second flare and I hoped that we had lost them. I rose and tapped Gordy on the shoulder. Ten minutes later I heard a hissed, "Over here, Sarge."

I headed in the direction of Ken's voice. I whispered, "Everyone safe?"

"Yes Sarge but you had us worried."

"Do you have a line in mind?"

"Yes Sarge."

"Then we keep going for an hour. Doc, you determine the pace. You have the two wounded and you know the pace they can maintain."

I heard George whisper, "We are fine Sarge."

"Go."

Night is never truly black and we were able to walk quite quickly. I remained at the rear and I looked at the footprints I passed to make sure we were not deviating from a line. Every now and then I stopped and listened. I could hear in the distance the sound of engines. That was good. If they were using their vehicles then the odds where they were on the road and we were getting further away. Ken stopped after an hour.

"Get some water."

I took out the compass. "Gordy, get your body here in front of me." I put my Bergen to the side and, kneeling down shone the torch on the compass. I could see that we had been going east north east. I mentally corrected the line. Switching off the torch I said, "Gordy, you bring up the rear. I reckon we can make three miles an hour. We stop every hour or so to check we are on course. We should reach the front lines in about six hours. We might have to wait until dawn to cross over. Our lads might have itchy trigger fingers."

I led with Lowe close by. "You let me know if you can't keep up."

"It's just my arm Sarge. I can still walk."

Bill Becket's voice warned, "You have lost blood. Let me know if you feel dizzy eh? Don't be the hero!"

Each time we stopped I used the torch to check that we were still heading in the right direction. We had been travelling for four hours when Lowe collapsed. Doc cursed, "I told him to tell me. Sarge, have you the torch?"

He shone the torch on the wound. It had opened. He looked at me. "I'll rebind the wound. We'll have to carry him."

"Get your parachute out. We'll use that for a litter. Harry, empty Lowe's Bergen and share it out with everyone else. Moore, you take his guns." As they did as ordered I peered to the south. There appeared to be no pursuit. By dawn they would have a spotter aircraft looking for us. As far as they knew the General was still with us. That would keep them looking for us. We could do without this delay. I reckoned we were two thirds of the way home but carrying Lowe would slow us down.

"Gordy take the rear. I will take the point. We swap over with two of you every ten minutes. Let's go."

George Lowe was a muscular man and he was heavy. Our speed was cut dramatically. After an hour, we had all had a turn with the wounded man. He had woken and told Doc he was fit enough to walk. "You are fit enough when I say so, Lowe. Lie back and enjoy the ride."

The sky in the east began to lighten. We stopped to change carriers and I looked at the map. The terrain was largely featureless but I detected to the north east a cluster of buildings. Was it British held? It was still too dark to tell. "We head for the buildings ahead. When we get close I will go with Ken and have a look see."

As we neared the buildings I smelled smoke. They were inhabited. The dawn was definitely breaking. I waved for the section to lower Lowe to the ground and, slipping off my Bergen, I waved Ken forward. There were a few scattered rocks and scrubby bushes and we used them for cover. I heard voices. They were too indistinct to make out the nationality. I cocked my Thompson. I had about eight bullets left. I waved Ken to the right and we approached the low wall which surrounded the mud huts.

I listened carefully. I heard a door creak open on the other side of the wall. I dared not lift my head. Then I heard, "Get that kettle on while I have a pee!"

I grinned and stood. "I hope you have spare mugs because I am gagging for a brew!"

Chapter 17

When the Corporal had recovered his composure, I discovered that we had stumbled upon a British outpost. It was a company of the Green Howards. They were dug in and guarding the road. While Gordy went to fetch the rest of the section I was taken to Captain Troughton who commanded the depleted company. "Where in God's name have you come from, Sergeant?"

I pointed south, "We lost our vehicles twenty miles south west of here."

"But that is the desert and, the last time I heard, the Italians still held it."

"They do sir. We were dropped behind enemy lines at El Agheila."

"Good God, that is four hundred miles away!"

"Something like that."

The Corporal handed me a mug of tea, "There you are Sarge. You fair put the willies up me back there."

"Sorry, Corporal, but we have spent the last few days dodging Germans and Italians. We did not know where the front line was."

The Captain nodded, "It is here. We are at the very southern edge of the British lines. Our job is to guard this crossroads. This is the back way to the coast. All of the action is going on north of us. General Wavell is in command."

Just then my men came in with the wounded Lowe. "Have you a doctor, sir? We have wounded men."

"Of course. Corporal, take the wounded men to the Doc." He looked at me. I will radio Headquarters and tell them about you. Who are you?"

"Sergeant Harsker Number Four Commando."

He nodded, "Well you are just in time for breakfast. I am guessing that you have been on short rations."

"You could say that, sir."

"What the hell were you doing four hundred miles behind enemy lines?"

"Rescuing a general the Eyeties had captured."

"Where is he?"

"We sent him in our one remaining vehicle. Hopefully he will be in Torbruk by now."

He disappeared shaking his head. Polly handed me my Bergen. A Sergeant appeared. "Right lads, if you come with me I'll take you to the mess tent." As we went he looked at my shoulder badge. "Commandos eh?"

"Yes Sergeant."

"It's Company Sergeant Graham Latimer and I am guessing you have seen more action than we have. All we have done for the past few weeks is chase the Eyeties west. Some of the lads are desperate for a bit of action."

I nodded, "It is highly overrated."

"So is watching a crossroads in the middle of this shit hole!"

The rest of the Green Howards were already at breakfast and the sight of my unshaven, unkempt section drew the gaze of everyone. The Sergeant growled, "Get back to your breakfast. These are proper soldiers!"

We sat down and enjoyed hot food for the first time since the brew up in the desert. That seemed a lifetime ago. The lads who smoked enjoyed their first cigarette since then too. I could not really believe that we had extricated ourselves from such a perilous position.

The Captain returned fifteen minutes later. He shook his head, "You are a modest fellow aren't you Sergeant?" I shrugged. "These lads, Sergeant Latimer, dropped behind enemy lines and rescued General Carter and some other important officers and brought them all the way across the desert." He shook his head, "Amazing. The general could not speak highly enough of you. They are sending transport. If all goes well it should be here by this evening."

I nodded, "Thank you, sir. If you don't mind, the lads and I need a bit of shut eye. It is two days since we slept."

"Quite. Sergeant Latimer?"

"Right, follow me. We have one of the huts we cleared out. It will be cooler than a tent." He looked at my battledress. "Paratrooper eh? You have to be mad as a fish to jump out of an aeroplane."

I laughed, "Actually Sergeant you have to be mad, full stop, to be in the Commandos."

We walked across the camp. They had the mess tents and the other tents behind the mud huts and, in front of the mud huts, we saw slit trenches, sand bags and machine gun emplacements.

He was right, the interior of the hut was cool. As I lay down to sleep Gordy said, "If the General was so pleased with us why did he not send a lorry for us?"

"We were behind enemy lines. Perhaps he was arranging it. It turned out well didn't it?"

"Aye, Sarge, but only just!"

I have no idea how long we had been asleep but we were woken by the sound of gunfire. I was awake and had grabbed my gun in an instant. "Outside lads. This does not sound good."

The Corporal we had frightened when we arrived ran up. "Sergeant, the Captain sent me to wake you. We are being attacked by Italians. They have tanks and infantry."

"Right lads. Grab your weapons. Leave your Bergens here."

"We are short of ammo, Sarge and these lads only have .303."

"Then we use the captured weapons and grenades. Gordy go and see if you can get yourself more ammo and some more grenades for us."

The Howards all had their hard hats on. I could see a defensive line with sandbags. The tents were behind the huts and there was a dry river bed to the north. It obviously only filled in times of the rare heavy rain. Captain Troughton had a Bren gun there. He had four Vickers in the centre of his defences and I could see another four Bren guns being deployed. The four mortars also added their fire. Sergeant Latimer ran up to me. "Can your lads fight?"

I laughed, "Try and stop them. We are short of ammo but we have grenades. Where do you want us?"

He pointed to the two centre Vickers, "If you support the two Vickers there that would be handy."

I led my men towards the two guns. I heard the sound of the Italian guns. They were not large calibre guns. It sounded to me like twenty-millimetre cannon and machine guns. As we dripped behind the sandbags and into the shallow trenches I wondered if the company had any anti-tank guns. If not then it was an error of judgment on someone's part.

Gordy ran up. He had a box of grenades in his hands. "I have ammo for my rifle and I have twenty grenades here."

With our wounded in the sick bay there were just seven of us remaining. I distributed the grenades. Ken said, "I have the ammo from the other two." He shared out the bullets and I filled one magazine in my Thompson. I also refilled the clip on my Colt. It was better than nothing and I still had my Luger and plenty of ammunition for that one.

Suddenly the two Vickers on either side of us began to fire. "Gordy, try and pick off the officers. The rest of you hold your fire until they are close enough to hit."

I counted four tanks. Only half had cannons but that was enough. Even as Gordy shot an officer urging his men on the two cannons fired at the nearest Vickers. Although the shell struck the sandbags the force punched a hole in them and the machine gun from a second one tore through the crew. The machine guns raked the mortar crews.

"Moore, with me!"

I rolled behind the sandbags. The crew were dead. I pushed them so that they filled the gap where the sandbags had been damaged. It was harsh but they could continue to fight even though they were dead. Their bodies would absorb the bullets meant for us. "You feed the gun." I took the helmet from one of the dead gunners. "Here put this on."

I aimed the Vickers not at the tanks but the infantry to the side. Machine gun bullets punched into the two dead Howards as I opened fire on the infantry. The Vickers is a powerful weapon and it scythed through them. It has an incredibly good rate of fire as they discovered in the Great War. More importantly it rarely jammed. The Italians concentrated their fire on us. Miraculously when the bullets hit they struck not flesh but the Vickers. Moore and I were thrown to the ground as the machine gun was destroyed. I saw that Moore's cheek was cut open.

"You are wounded."

He put his hand to his face. "It's nothing Sarge."

I rolled out of the emplacement as the leading tanks, now just a hundred yards away concentrated their fire on the gun. The other two were firing at the second Vickers. Its crew and the gun suffered the same fate. Gordy was picking off as many as he could but it was like spitting in the wind.

"Right lads. Open fire!"

The range was a little far and the smoke from the guns was obscuring the targets but we fired anyway. My Thompson clicked on empty. It was a waste of time to use my Colt. That would be a last resort. The tanks were now just sixty yards away. They had shifted their fire from the now defunct Vickers to the tents and buildings behind. Perhaps they thought that, with so little gunfire coming from our position, we were dead. I stuffed two grenades into my battle dress and holding another in each hand I rolled over the front of the sandbags and lay there. I expected bullets to thud into me but I must have been too low for the gunners to see or perhaps they could not depress the gun low enough. I rolled forward towards the advancing tanks. It might have looked dangerous but the tanks were moving at walking pace only. I pulled the pins out with my teeth and then threw the grenades just in front of the leading tank. I leapt back over the sandbags shouting. "Grenade!"

The gunner saw me then but by the time he had fired his machine gun I was behind the bodies and the sandbags. The grenades went off under the tracks of the tank and it ground to a halt. It was less than twenty yards from us and its gun could not target us. The tank itself stopped the troops behind from firing. I took out another of the grenades and sprinted to the front of the tank. There was a flap through which the driver looked. I pulled the pin on a grenade and after releasing the lever dropped it through the gap. I barely made it to the sandbags when there was a dull crump and smoke began to pour from the stricken tank. It began to burn and when the crew tried to leave my men cut them down.

Emboldened by my action the Green Howards began to hurl grenades at the tanks. When a second had its tracks damaged they began to back away, firing as they went. I lay in the charnel house that was the Vickers emplacement and sucked in air. That had been a close thing.

I heard the Captain shout, "Cease fire! Stretcher bearers!"

The Howards had suffered badly. Three Vickers had been destroyed along with their crew. I counted at least twenty corpses but we had held. Gordy and the others joined me. "Well done lads. Good shooting, Gordy."

He shook his head, "It is a good job they weren't German tanks. We would be dead now."

Captain Troughton and Sergeant Latimer came over and surveyed the wrecked positions. "Well done Sergeant Harsker. Sergeant Latimer, get some men to rebuild this emplacement and bring one of the flank Vickers and crew here."

I said, "What you need is an anti-tank gun."

Sergeant Latimer said, "The grenade rifle! The way those tracks came off means we have a chance."

I stood, "Do you think they will come back, sir?"

"I don't know. We were told that the Italians were trying to flank us. There is a battle going on up north. The Germans are trying to regain the ground we captured. They have to capture this outpost. It guards the road to Torbruk from the south. I think we surprised them but they will be back." He smiled, "I don't think your lorry will be here anytime soon." He pointed to the machine gun emplacements. "Get those sand bags refilled!"

"Come on lads. There are enough rocks around here. We can put them in front of the sandbags. I reckon we need more protection. Moore, you keep a good watch on the Eyeties."

"Sarge, it's just a scratch."

"I know but I need someone to watch the enemy and you are it!"

The Italians had retreated beyond the range of our machine guns. I wondered what their next move would be. It was obvious that we could not be reinforced. I wondered if those who had been chasing us would be called in. Perhaps they would try a night attack although that was always risky. Sergeant Latimer joined me. He had a crew for the rifle grenade. It, effectively, lobbed a grenade more than a hundred yards. It couldn't hurt a tank but it could damage the tracks. It was why the Italians had retreated. Our grenades were making their tanks vulnerable. The Germans would have persevered. I had fought German tanks before.

We completed our defences and the cooks brought us hot soup and stale bread. It went down well. Suddenly Moore shouted out, "Sarge! German half-track. It looks like the one that was chasing us the other day and there is an Italian lorry too. And a Kübelwagen. "There was a pause. "They are pulling field guns. They look like three-inch jobs."

Sergeant Latimer said. "That is a problem. They may not be very big but they can blast us out of these holes any time they like."

Captain Troughton joined us. "Well Sergeant Latimer. What do we do?"

"We can't pull out, sir. Those tanks might not be very fast but they could easily catch us. If we stay then they will winkle us out."

"We need the guns destroying."

Sergeant Lambert shook his head. "You'd not get near them, sir."

We all looked west. After a moment or two I said, quietly, "We could."

"What?"

"We could sir, my Commandos. It's what we do."

"But we have no explosives. How would you blow them up?"

"We wouldn't. All we have to do is destroy the wheels. They can't fire if they have no wheels." I pointed to the dead Italian bodies around the destroyed tank. "I am betting they have grenades on them and we can use them. We can use some of the petrol they have for their vehicles and when the grenades go up they will ignite the petrol and the wheels will be destroyed. The explosion will probably damage the barrel too."

"But your men… they must be exhausted."

"I will just take four, sir." I could see the doubt on their faces. "If we do nothing then they will fire in the morning when they are set up. They may even have a pop this afternoon. Sergeant Latimer is right; we can't stand against artillery, tanks, and infantry. We are outnumbered as it is. Our only hope is to do what they don't expect and attack them."

"Anything we can do?"

"Have some men close to those wrecked tanks. If we are followed then we will need some help."

"Right then. You had better select your men."

I whistled and my six men joined me. "Five of us are going over tonight to destroy those Italian guns." It was a measure of their confidence that none of them questioned the suggestion. "Gordy, you and Ken will be with me. Polly and…."

"Can I come, Sarge?"

I looked at Moore. "Connor has more experience."

"I know and I am never going to get it this way, am I? Look I know I came over as a cocky little Cockney but I want to be part of this team. I know you have been looking out for me and giving me safe jobs. Let me do my bit, Sarge. I want to be part of this section. I figure I have earned the right to be treated the same, eh Sarge?""

I saw Gordy and Ken nod. "Right. Becket and Connor, the Sergeant is sending out some men to the tank to cover us when we return. I want you two there with them."

They nodded.

"Now get blacked up. We take Colts and knives. We are going to take hand grenades and we will search the dead, after dark, for their grenades. We will blow the wheels off the guns. Polly will stand guard while Curtis and I set the charges. I want Gordy and Moore here to get some petrol. I want the whole thing to go up like a Roman candle."

We had to remember to black up our legs and arms too. The grenades we carried in haversacks we got from the Howards. I took my Luger as I had more ammunition for that. I gave my spare ammo for the Colt to Gordy. I sharpened my dagger while I could.

There was a sudden double crack and a cloud of smoke as the two guns fired. They had them on a slightly higher piece of ground above their camp. It meant they were protected from a frontal attack by three tanks, a couple of trucks and a half track. We would not be using the front door!

They were ranging the guns. Their first shots were long but after three or four they managed to hit the huts. They were empty. Luckily for us night fell and they stopped firing. I suspect they did not have confidence that they could hit us in the dark or perhaps they were short of ammunition too. I was just grateful that they had stopped. As soon as it was dark we took our leave of the Howards. "Good luck, Sergeant."

Sergeant Latimer shook my hand, "Don't worry. We'll be there waiting. I won't leave you to hang out to dry."

We crawled along the ground towards the burnt-out tank. It was too much to hope that any explosives had survived. We crawled to the bodies. Something scurried away. It was a rat. Our bullet holes made easy entrances to the human body. I found three grenades on the first body but none on the second. By the time I reached the last one I had a total of five. The others headed for me and we crawled north. There was a dry river bed there. It was not deep but it meant we could walk crouched rather than crawling. Had I been the enemy commander I would have had a sentry there. It would not have done them any good for we would have killed him but it showed slackness on their part.

I stopped for I could hear Italian voices to the left. I peered over the top and saw a fire with half a dozen soldiers seated around it. I saw from its glow that the vehicles were just behind them. I slipped back down and continued our journey. When the voices faded I risked another look. We were level with the slight rise and I saw the snouts of the two guns. I climbed up and waved to the other others. Drawing my dagger, we made our way to the guns. The ground was full of small rocks and it rose steadily to the artillery. I heard voices. They had left guards with the two guns. As we waited for our eyes to adjust to the dark I saw the shape of the Kübelwagen. They must have been using it to move the guns. They were only small calibre artillery pieces and the Kübelwagen would easily be able to move them. It was parked close by the two guns. Once we were out of the dry gully we crawled towards the guns. We had learned to make small slow movements. My worry was Private Moore who had not done enough of this. Perhaps I would regret bringing him along. We moved in silence and tried to keep our breathing steady. It was not easy.

I caught the smell of cigarette smoke and pipe tobacco along with the strong smell of salami. There was a slight breeze and it blew the smell towards us. It identified their position. They had a fire. It looked to be made with scraps of wood and petrol. It gave off a blue light and it helped to show us where they were. We crawled further forward and I counted them. There were four as far as I could see. I held up four fingers. I waited a few minutes longer in case one had gone to relieve himself. I drew my finger across my throat and then we rose like wraiths. The four Italians were facing the fire and had no night vision. The first they knew of our presence was when the daggers slid silently across their throats.

I pointed to the Kübelwagen and then at Gordy. He tapped Moore and they went to get some petrol. With Poulson keeping watch I took off my pack. We had various grenades. I put one of the Mills bombs in the barrel and attached a length of parachute cord to the pin. I broke the porcelain on the stick grenades and placed them next to the wheel of the gun. I tied the cords to a single piece of parachute cord. Finally, I put another length of cord through the pins of three Mills bombs and fed it through the wheel. I carefully tied my three cords together. I had tied together six lengths of parachute cord to make a long fuse. I tied it to my three cords and walked backwards. When I was twenty feet from the gun, I stopped.

Ken had done his and I watched as Moore poured, as quietly as possible, half a jerry can of petrol on each gun. Gordy took the filler cap off the Kübelwagen and then walked towards the gun pouring petrol from the last jerry can. He nodded. I waved them back to me. Polly, Gordy and Moore all ran to the dry river bed. Ken and I walked backwards until we had run out of cord. We had to do this together. I held three fingers up, then two and then one. I pulled. The pins came out of the Mills bombs. We had seven seconds. I was no Jesse Owens but I made it to the dry river bed and rolled in closely followed by Curtis. We made it with two seconds to spare. There were a series of explosions. I saw the guns lift into the air. As they came down I saw that the wheels had been broken. Then the flames lit the petrol and there was an almighty whoosh which lit the sky and made it like daylight. When the flames reached the Kübelwagen it was lifted in the air too.

"Run!"

All attention was on the inferno and the devastation we had caused. I hoped we would make it back to the tank before we were seen. The party of Italians spoiled that. The flames shone on us and they opened fire. I drew my Luger and, kneeling carefully, fired eight shots off as calmly as though I was on the firing range. Bullets flew over my head and struck the edge of the bank but I was spared. I shot three of them and the rest of my section got the others. I was about to run when I saw that Private Moore was lying on the ground. The other three were already racing towards the tank some three hundred yards in front of us.

He looked up weakly and tried to smile, "Leave me Sarge."

I picked him up and slung him as gently as I could over my left shoulder. "We never leave a wounded Commando behind. Now you watch my back." I ran.

By now the enemy camp had come to life and although some were dealing with the fire others were firing at the fleeing figures. We were running into the dark and it was hard for them to estimate distance and speed. They largely missed. I saw the other three dive beneath the tank. I still had over a hundred yards to go. Suddenly Moore shouted, "Behind you! Three of them!"

I spun and dropped to my knee. Bullets filled the space above my head. I fired my last three shots. Two of them fell. One clutching his face, he was dead. I was out of bullets. Moore raised his hand and emptied his Colt at the last German who was raising his rifle to shoot me. The German was thrown back by the force of the bullets.

Then I heard Sergeant Latimer's voice as he shouted, "Fire!" I saw the flames from the ends of the guns as a veritable barrage erupted.

I stood and lumbered the last hundred and forty yards. Gordy and Ken came to grab Moore from me. I nodded, "Thanks Sergeant. Now let's get the hell out of here!"

I heard Gordy shout, "Medic! Bill!"

We reached the safety of the sandbags. Moore was lying on his back. Bill was there and I saw a doctor racing with a stretcher. I looked down at Private Moore, "Thanks Alan, you saved my life."

He nodded and tried to smile. I saw a trickle of blood from his mouth. Bill moved him so that he could see the wound. Moore's face was close to mine. "I'm not going to die am I Sarge? I don't want to die! I'm scared!"

I smiled, "You? A Commando scared? I don't believe it."

I saw Bill shake his head. The doctor arrived. Even before he had examined Moore I knew that the boy was going to die. "Sarge, tell my mum..."

He pitched forward and died in my arms. I would never know what he wanted me to tell his mum.

Chapter 18

We did not even have time to mourn as Captain Troughton shouted, "Here they come!"

The Germans and Italians must have been maddened by our attack and they hurled themselves across the open ground before us. The damaged tank worked in their favour now as it blocked the field of fire of the Vickers. I was weapon less. I took the Colt from Moore's dead fingers. I rested the gun against the sandbags. The Vickers were sweeping side to side and hitting targets but some had clambered on top of the wrecked tank. One Vickers' crew were killed before we realised. I took a bead on an Italian and, at eighty yards range the white face disappeared. I moved the Colt a little more and saw a second Italian clutch his arm and fall. I heard Gordy's Lee Enfield as he began to pick them off.

Sergeant Latimer shouted, "Sir I can hear the tanks! Johnson, Drake, get that grenade rifle in action."

It was a desperate defence. We were in the dark and our enemies were advancing in great numbers. When my Colt clicked empty I climbed into the Vickers' pit and pulled the triggers. I managed to fire a dozen shots before I needed to adjust the belt. Bill Becket jumped in and began to feed the ammunition through. I just kept swinging the gun from side to side. I was aware of bullets coming towards me but I forced myself to ignore them. I heard the crump as the grenade rifle lobbed grenade after grenade towards the advancing enemy. The surviving mortars also created a firestorm through which the enemy had to advance. The trouble was that we were firing blind.

I don't know what made me look down but I did and I saw two Germans crawling along the ground. I could not depress the barrel and, when they saw that I had seen them they leapt at me with their bayonets. I heard Bill shout as he was speared. I managed to knock aside the barrel of the German rifle. The German fired and I heard a scream from behind me. The German was a big man and he knocked me over. I reached down for my knife but I could not find it. I did find the Luger and I swung it hard at the side of his head. He rolled from me but his left hand grabbed my battledress. As I fell on him I punched him repeatedly in the face with the butt of the pistol until his face was a bloody mess and he was still.

I wrested the rifle from his dead hands and swung the bayonet down into the back of the second German who was trying to strangle Bill. I pulled his body and shouted, "Medic!" The bayonet had pierced his arm and he was bleeding heavily. I worked the bolt and swung the rifle up just in time to shoot an Italian who was levelling his rifle to shoot me. He was just ten feet away and the force of the shot threw him back.

And then it was over. There were no more men in front of us. Sergeant Latimer shouted, "Cease fire!"

We had held them. I turned and looked at our line. There were entwined bodies of Germans, Italians and English. Captain Troughton was lying clutching his shoulder. He had been shot. I turned to Sergeant Latimer, "The tanks?"

"One has pulled back and there are two still there. I think we hit them but in the dark..."

"Curtis, Barker, grab some grenades and come with me."

I took out my Luger and reloaded it. Picking up two stick grenades from the Germans I had just killed I ran into the dark towards the tanks. A hand reached up and tripped me. As I fell I shot the German between the eyes and then struggled to my feet. I saw one of the tanks. Its cannon had been bent. Suddenly the machine gun fired and I barely had time to dive out of the way. I was fortunate it could not depress to the right. I clambered up on top, opened the hatch and dropped a grenade in. I shut the hatch and dived to the side. Six seconds later a wall of fire and hot air came from the driver's visor.

I saw Gordy and Ken leap on to the second tank and drop grenades inside. "Right lads, back!"

There was just one tank left now and it only had a machine gun. I began to hope we might survive.

We waited for the next attack which never came. Dawn broke and we could see the remains of the battle. A pall of smoke still drifted over the battlefield. On the rise, the wrecked guns and Kübelwagen showed the success of our raid. The enemy had retreated back to the high ground. We had taught them to respect us at least. The khaki bodies lying covered with blankets showed the cost. Sergeant Latimer came over with a mug of tea for each of us.

"Well, Tom, it looks like you and I are in command. The only officer without a wound is the Doctor."

I nodded, "And how many effectives?"

He shook his head, "We just have your lads, four of them, and I have forty-two."

"Any chance of relief?"

"The Captain is staying by the radio chivvying them up but they Germans and the Italians are still attacking up north."

"Then we make it hard for them. We have to make a solid wall around the front. Make them come up that drive river bed. We booby trap that."

"Good idea but what do we use for a wall." He waved an arm around the scrubby piece of land. "There's sod all here to use."

"Fill the old ammunition boxes with sand. They will stop a bullet. Those sandbags stopped the cannon shells. Use rocks." I pointed to the mud huts which had borne the brunt of the shelling. "Use bits of the hut."

He nodded, "Right."

"I'll take my lads and we'll see if we can make the river bed a death trap."

I found the others looking hollow eyed. They too were drinking tea and eating corned beef on days old bread. "Right lads when we have finished breakfast we need to make the dry river bed a dangerous place for the Germans."

Gordy nodded as he picked up his mug. "Aye, now that we have shown them how to use it they will be along soon enough. Any chance of relief, Sarge?"

I shook my head, "The attack further north is as bad as here. They will get here when they get here." I finished my tea and laid it on a rock, "Why are you in a hurry? Have you got a date?"

The others laughed. Ken shook his head, "It was hard last night. I thought they were going to overrun us."

"And tonight, they will come mob handed. They must know how close they came to breaking through. They will bring more guns and next time we won't be able to sneak up on them." I stood. "Still we will do what we can do. Ken, see what explosives you can get." I pointed to the enemy bodies lying just beyond our perimeter. "There may be some left there. Gordy, take Polly and see if there is any spare barbed wire. John, get the last of the parachute cord." I pointed to the Bergens of the wounded. "There may be some left in their bags. Mine is all gone."

While I waited for them I checked my Luger. Thanks to the men we had killed I had plenty of ammunition from their bodies. The rest of the section was now using Lee Enfields. There were plenty left from our dead and wounded. Sergeant Latimer was busy directing his men. I saw that there were just two Vickers left in action and they had had to cannibalise the others to make two of them function. There were three Bren guns and the saviour that was the anti-tank rifle. The mortars were all gone.

I put the Luger in my belt and wandered over to him. "Graham, just a thought, if you half bury the mortar shells you have left then you can fire at them when they advance. If they explode it might make life difficult for them. They are no use, otherwise are they?"

"I'll give it a go." He looked up at the sky which was now cloudless. "I reckon we will have aeroplanes today."

I nodded, "I am surprised they didn't send them yesterday." I saw my men returning. I picked up the entrenching tool. "I'll be off."

Ken had six stick bombs. "There wasn't much left."

"They will have to do." The others followed me to the river bed. "John, give me the cords. Now go ahead of us and keep a look out. I don't want to be surprised." He handed me the cords and ran at the crouch ahead of us. We all kept low. I saw John kneeling behind a bit of scrubby vegetation ahead, "Now we crawl."

The dry bed was some four feet deep. The bottom was largely rock free. We had found it easy to cross in the dark. The enemy would too. "Gordy, I want you to lay the wire just beyond Connor. We need it to reach from bank to bank. It does not matter if it isn't one piece just so that it is an obstacle."

While he and Polly used the bits of wire they had found I led Ken back down the bed. "They will be cautious until they come to the wire. It won't take them long to get through it. I reckon they will check the first few yards for booby traps. That is why we will put them here, thirty paces from the wire. They will have a good chance of tripping them if we put a cord all the way across." I handed him the small spade. "Dig holes for the stick bombs. I'll be back." I used some of the precious parachute cord to make short trip wires. They would find them and expect bombs. These were decoys. I dug holes and buried the cord in them. I used just four short cords at random. They would waste time with them...I hoped.

Gordy and Polly joined me. "Pick up as many small stones as you can."

Ken had finished three holes. "Spread the other three out further down. We are trying to make them slow up." I broke the porcelain on the first of the grenades and took out the arming cord. I laid it down so that the cord hung out. "Now you two fill the hole with small stones. I want to make this into a minefield." I tied a two feet length of cord to the grenade and then laid it out to the side. I used my knife to make a hole. I jammed the end of the cord into the hole and held it there with a stone which I forced into the crevice. I took a handful of sand and small stones and covered the cord.

It took a couple of hours to finish the job to my satisfaction. There were now grenades spread out over a large area. I whistled and Connor came back. As he neared my minefield I said, "Pick your feet up and don't step on any stones."

As we made our way back Gordy said, "I am surprised they haven't come yet."

"Me too. There will be a reason. The Germans are very methodical."

The perimeter looked much sturdier when we returned. The Sergeant had disguised the sand filled boxes with bits of vegetation and more sand. None would stop a tank but they only had one left. Sergeant Latimer nodded as I arrived. "We have a line of mortar shells going to the left and right of the first wrecked tanks. The others were too close to the enemy. We might not even need to use a rifle. One of my corporals thinks that the weight of a foot would set it off. Certainly, a tank will."

Just then a voice from behind shouted, "Aeroplanes! Stukas!"

I shaded my eyes against the bright sky and saw the flight of six Stukas heading from the north. "Take cover!"

We had more cover now but we did not have enough machine guns any more. The Vickers could not fire up and we had to use the three Bren guns. We would not be able to use the wall of fire. I picked up a German rifle and dropped into the slit trench. I leaned the barrel on the sandbags and waited. As they screamed down towards us I realised that I should have taken a tin lid from one of the bodies. It would do them no further good and it might save my life. It was too late for that now. The gull winged beasts became larger as they drew near. Suddenly they dived. I had faced them before but some of these Green Howards knew nothing of them. The screaming sirens seemed to fill the air with a primeval cry.

The Bren guns opened up. I waited. The first Stuka seemed to be diving at a point just in front of me. I saw its bomb fall and then it pulled up. As it became a cross in my German sights, I fired as fast as I could pump fresh bullets. The bomb struck the ground ahead of me. The sand bags protected me. I hit the Stuka. I was certain of that. It began to wobble a little and then, instead of rising for a second run it headed home.

I had little chance for self-congratulation for the next ones screamed down. One kept on going as it was struck by Bren guns. It had two bombs on board and the explosion totally disorientated me. It also put off the aim of the next Stukas.

The remaining four rose to make another attack. Gordy said, "I thought I was the marksman. How in hell did you do that?"

"An aeroplane is complicated and there are controls and wires running all over. I was lucky. I must have severed one."

The Stukas dived again. Having rid ourselves of two the men had more confidence now and a third was hit and flew west, low, smoking. The last three left but they had done enough. The new defences had provided more protection than before but there were still wounded and dying men. Another of the Bren guns had been damaged too. The only good aspect was the fact that there were now seven craters which would be a slight barrier to the tank when it chose to come.

When the enemy had not attacked in force until early afternoon we feared the worst. Captain Troughton asked us to go to him so that we could report. We were now the senior NCOs. Two of the wounded officers had died when a Stuka had machine gunned the medical tents. The Company was now little better than a large platoon.

"They'll be back sir. I reckon tonight."

"Can we hold them, Sergeant?"

Sergeant Latimer looked at the ground. "I don't know, sir. They almost broke through last night. We have fewer men and fewer machine guns now. They only have one tank but that is all that they do need. If the grenade rifle packs in then..."

The Captain nodded, "I have radioed Headquarters in Torbruk. They have promised relief as soon as it can be sent but they have only just seen off another enemy attack."

"Perhaps they will back off here then, sir?"

The Captain shook his head, "We have shown how vital this corner of the desert is. They will want it, if only to deny us its use." He looked despondent, "We have to hold until the last bullet."

Sergeant Latimer stood a little taller, "Don't you worry sir, we will. They don't realise that they have tangled with the Green Howards and the Commandos! That is a combination which cannot fail."

As we left the half-wrecked hut I pointed to the dry river bed. "I think that will need defending too, Sergeant."

He shouted, "Reed, get the Bren and set it up to cover the river bed." Peering down he smiled, "I reckon the barbed wire will slow them down."

"Aye and the Bren will discourage them."

The first sign of an attack was the rapid gunfire from the high ground. Although they were too far away to be accurate they kept the defenders' heads down. I heard the sound of the last Italian tank as it lumbered towards us. The craters meant it could not drive in a straight line. Italians walked behind it and were safe from our shots. Gordy was lying on the half roof which remained on the mud hut. He fired at every piece of flesh that he could see. He was wearing them down slowly. We had no target at which to fire. The tank was impervious to our bullets.

The grenade rifle had but two grenades left. They both hit the tank but neither damaged the track. The crew would have had a headache but still it came on. Our only hope was the buried mortar shells. We could not fire at them until the infantry walked close by them. The tank would be the first to cross our improvised minefield. The half-buried shells were laid out in double lines a hundred and twenty yards from us. I braced myself as the tank drove over the first one. Nothing happened. Perhaps the sand was too soft and the shell had been driven deeper. I regretted not doing the job myself. We knew how to make improvised traps; the Howards did not.

Perhaps the second row of shells was buried better for the tank suddenly lifted with a crump as it drove over one. We knew the tank had been damaged when it slewed around on its broken trap. This was where we needed the grenade rifle and it had no ammunition left. The turret on the tank still worked and it turned its machine gun spraying our defences at point blank range. The sand filled boxes and sand bags stopped the bullets penetrating but they also kept our heads down.

Gordy, who had the best view shouted, "Their infantry are attacking!"

His rifle barked as quickly as he could fire it. Then the machine gun in the tank stopped; perhaps it had jammed or run out of ammunition. Sergeant Latimer shouted, "Open fire!"

Tired of being targets every weapon was fired by someone who wanted to hit back. I levelled my Luger and fired at each enemy in turn. One of them took two bullets to stop. Then they found the mortar shells which had been buried properly. A couple went off.

"Gordy! Hit the shells!"

Soon, it was as though we had a mortar firing as Gordy hit all the shells which the enemy had avoided. They began to pull back. Polly rolled over the sandbags and followed the retreating soldiers. He sprinted to the tank and threw a grenade into the driver's side. Instead of running away he dropped to the ground next to the tank. A sheet of flame leapt out. The driver managed to get half out before Gordy put a bullet in him. Polly raced back and threw himself over the ammunition boxes.

"Well done! That was foolish but brave."

When Gordy reported that the enemy had retreated to the high ground to lick their wounds we left our holes and searched the dead for weapons and ammunition. When the tea came around and the last of the food we devoured them like wild animals. Sergeant Latimer said, "That is the last of the food. The tank managed to hit the store tent. We have water for two more days."

"Ammo?"

"If they come again tonight then we will have five rounds per man tomorrow. We will be forced to use the captured weapons and ammunition and that won't last long. We are down to twenty or so grenades."

I nodded to the pile we had collected, "We got some from the Germans."

"But they won't last."

"Nil desperandum eh Graham?"

"Oh we won't surrender; it isn't in our nature but I reckon we will either be in the bag or dead by this time tomorrow."

As it became dark Gordy came to join the rest of us close to the last to Vickers. Our three wounded comrades also joined us. As Bill said there was little point being in the tent. There was more chance of being killed there than in the line of fire. We gave them hand guns. The Italian and Germans had had a number of them. I sharpened my dagger too. It might come down to that. The German rifle I was using did not have the same ammunition as the Luger. It meant I just had five bullet clips. each with just five bullets, to use. I had spent the quiet time cleaning it and the bolt worked well.

Ken lit a cigarette and lay back. He using the tin helmet he had found as a pillow of sorts. "Rum sort of do, Sarge. I never thought I'd end up dying in a God forsaken hole like this. I mean what has this got to go with my mam and dad in England? They are the reason I am fighting."

"I think it is more complicated than that. The Italians wanted an Empire. Mussolini thinks he is a Roman Emperor. They wanted the oil in the Middle East and there is Suez. If the Eyeties get hold of that then how do we get the Aussies, New Zealanders and Indians to the battle fields? You said yourself, once, that we are on our own. How long do you think we would last without Commonwealth troops?"

"I knew there had to be something. This land isn't worth dying for."

Bill said, "He is right in one respect, Sarge. We should be at home. We can stop Adolf invading England. We need to do that."

"I agree with you. We are the victims of our own success. We would still have been in England with Major Foster raiding the coast of France but they needed a team with the skills to get behind enemy lines and rescue the General. That turned out to be us. It is just bad luck that we are still here. As soon as this is over we'll be flying back."

Gordy laughed, "There you are lads! That is what you need. We should have it issued every morning with our tea."

Polly asked, "What's that?"

"A dose of Sergeant Harsker's optimism. We will get out because the Sergeant believes we will and you know what? I believe him too. You don't stop fighting until you can't fight any more. The Sergeant's mate, Sergeant Greeley said it, *'The only good German is a dead German.'* He was right too."

I smiled. They would fight and they would fight hard.

Late in the afternoon we heard trucks in the distance. As they were from the west we knew that it was reinforcements. I listened carefully but I didn't hear tanks. That was a good thing. When night came it was as though someone had switched out a light.

Sergeant Latimer came over. He took me to one side. "I have everyone who can hold a gun armed and ready. We have a couple of flares left. If we hear anything I will send them up. I want you and your lads to hold this gap between the Vickers. We have a Bren on each flank. They will try to knock out the Vickers first."

I nodded, "And when we have run out of ammo?"

He shrugged, "I don't know. Our lads will fight until they are captured but I suspect you and your boys could escape across the desert."

"We could but we won't. What do you take us for? We don't leave our mates in the lurch. What I will say is that if they overrun us then unless you see our bodies we'll be out there." I pointed to the high ground. "And we have our knives. If you are captured then don't give up. We won't."

He shook my hand. "Never doubted it for a moment. When this is over if you are ever up in the North East look me up. I live in Northallerton."

"I will Sarge and it has been an honour."

Chapter 19

Polly said, "Sarge, I can hear something."

It was midnight and I was beginning to think that they would not come. Polly was right. I could hear them too. The enemy did not wear rubber soled boots as we did. They disturbed stones and sent them skittering across the stony desert floor.

I hissed, "Stand to! You lads on the Vickers ready?"

"Yes Sarge."

This was the hard part. We had crossed this ground going the other way and I could picture them. They had a rough idea of our position but we had no idea of their strength or their route. Suddenly, to our right, there was an explosion and a scream. The Bren gun chattered.

Ken chuckled, "They found the booby traps."

"Keep your heads down."

I buried my face in the sand. Above us the sky was lit by the flare. If we had looked then we would have lost any chance of seeing the enemy well. It burned brightest at first.

After four or five seconds I said, "Right! Pick your targets. Gordy, officers and sergeants first."

I levelled the rifle and squeezed off a shot at the nearest man. He was two hundred yards away. He spun around clutching his shoulder. The gun pulled to the right. I adjusted my aim and the second man fell backwards hit in the stomach. He was not dead, at least not yet. I moved along the line firing at the men who still tried to walk forwards. Then the two Vickers fired and the whole line dropped to the ground.

I heard a series of crumps. A few seconds later the ground behind us erupted as the mortar shells landed. It was harder to hit the enemy now. Gordy was having the most success and then the light from the flare faded. The second one flew high into the air. I heard the crack as it was fired and I covered my eyes once more. When I opened my eyes, I aimed at the German who had raised his head to shout something to the man behind. The bullet smacked into his head and he fell still. The

Germans and the Italians had no trenches in which to hide. While the light held we had the advantage.

Then the mortar shells began to draw closer to us. One landed just forty yards from us and I felt the concussion as it hit. I counted on the fact that the nearer they came to our lines the more likely it was that they would stop firing. The fading flare made it seem like a rapid sunset and then it was pitch dark once more.

"They will come hard. Hold your fire until they are closer. Don't waste bullets."

One wag on the other side of the Vickers said, "It would be nice to have a few bullets to waste."

Sergeant Latimer shouted, from the dark, "Fix bayonets!"

It would be hand to hand before long.

We had to wait until we saw the patches of white that would be their faces. Gordy had the advantage of his telescopic sight and he fired. The falling German and his cry gave us an indication of where they were. The two Vickers lit up the night with their fire. I looked down my barrel and saw a face less than twenty yards away. I fired and missed. I loaded another bullet and, lowering my aim fired again. I hit him less than ten yards away. I worked the bolt as fast as I could. When it clicked empty I loaded my third magazine. I was half way through my ammunition. The Vickers on my left went silent.

"No ammo left Sarge."

"Then use grenades and your rifles."

I kept firing and changed clips. "Grenades!"

We all fell to the floor as the two gunners threw their grenades. I heard the explosions and lifted my head in time to see the Corporal of the machine gun being bayoneted by a German. I lifted my rifle and fired twice from the hip. I was so close that he was thrown back and crashed into another German. Ken shot him.

Connor shouted, "Grenade!"

This time I just lowered my head and when I heard the explosion lifted my head and was firing straight away. I realised that the second

Vickers' gunner was silent. I looked into the pit. He had been shot in the head.

"Lads, into the machine gun pit!"

I rolled in and pushed the now useless weapon over the side. It was another obstacle for the enemy. We had our own little fort. With sandbags all around us, we would defend it to the end. I saw that the two gunners still had a couple of grenades. I gave one to Polly. "Grenades!"

I pulled the pin and let the lever spring away. I counted to two and threw it. I fired three shots with my Luger in case any Germans were advancing. Then I ducked down. The grenades would explode in the air. As soon as the grenades had gone off I rose and fired my rifle. When I put in the last clip I heard Curtis and Connor say. "Out of ammo!"

I gave Ken my rifle and drew my Luger. There were faces advancing towards us and the last Vickers had, ominously, gone silent. I fired at point blank range and an Italian's head disappeared in an explosion of blood and brains. A bayonet came towards my stomach. I grabbed the red-hot barrel in my left hand and pulled. We both tumbled backwards out of the machine gun pit. As he fell on me I jammed the pistol into his side and pulled the trigger. I could smell burning from his jacket and he was thrown from me. As I jumped to my feet two Germans ran at me with bayonets levelled. I knelt and fired at one and then switched to the other. He pulled back the bayonet to end my life and my bullet struck him under the chin and he was thrown backwards.

I rolled away and loaded another magazine. I had one full magazine left. In front of me was an explosion as a grenade was thrown at the machine gun pit. It was silent within. I ran towards it, "Gordy! Ken!" I was greeted by silence. I stood on the top of the sandbags which had been knocked down. Oblivious to the bullets which zipped around me I stood on the sand bags and emptied the pistol into every face I saw. When it clicked empty I took out my last grenade and released the pin. I counted to four and then threw it. I dived into the sandbags. I heard the shrapnel whizzing over my head and then I heard the screams of the Germans and Italians that it struck.

I felt dizzy from the fall but I forced myself to load my last magazine. I might be the last one of my men left alive but they would not get me without a fight. I raised my head and suddenly realised that there was no one left in front of me. For the first time, no one was trying to kill me. I heard a moan from beneath me. One of them was still alive. I lifted a sandbag and heard Gordy say, "Who has their knee in my back?"

I stood and held out my hand and helped him to his feet. He had a bad cut on the side of his head but he was alive. If he had survived then the others might too. "Quick let's get the others out."

We threw the fallen sandbags to the other side of the pit. I saw a head move. It was Ken Curtis. Gordy and I pulled him up. He screamed in pain. My hand was covered in blood. "Medic! Be gentle with him Gordy he is wounded." I put my hands under his armpits and, with Gordy at his feet we lifted him out.

A Medical Orderly, bleeding himself, ran up. "Bloody hell Sarge, we thought you were all dead."

"See to him. We will check the others."

We found another three left alive. The new ones, George and Harry had been knocked unconscious and Polly had a wounded shoulder but Bill Becket, our own doctor, was dead. It had been quick. His head had been taken by a barrage of bullets during that last frenzied attack. John Connor still clutched the bayonet in his stomach. My men had been faithful unto death.

"Tanks!" Polly's ears were as good as ever.

After all the sacrifice, it seemed that we would now be defeated by mechanical beasts. We had nothing left with which to fight. I sank to the ground in resignation and then I listened. The sound was not coming from the west but the north. Had we been surrounded? Then I heard from the right the cheers that told me they were British tanks. Relief had come. My joy was short lived. I looked down and saw the two dead Commandos. The relief had arrived half an hour too late for them.

I went to Ken. "How is he?"

"He'll live. The bullet went clean through. It is just muscle damage." He shrugged, "I have done all that I can and the Doc is dead. Let's hope that they have doctors with this relief column." He moved over to Poulson.

I took my canteen and emptied it. As Wellington once put it, it had been a near run thing. The tanks rumbled west followed by cheerful troops. Perhaps they wondered why we did not cheer. We wanted to; we had been relieved but we were too close to death for such luxuries. As dawn broke we heard the sound of lorries heading towards us. I surveyed the slaughter that had been the centre of our line. In places, the enemy were piled three deep. My own men were the only survivors in the centre section of the battlefield. I wondered how the others had fared.

Graham Latimer limped over to me, his arm in a sling and limping. He saw the blanket covered bodies, "Your lads did it. They held. I knew they would. The lorries are for us. We are being evacuated to Torbruk. We will be sent back to Cairo for a rest and a refit. What about you?"

"I have no idea. I hope home. We were not trained for this desert war. We came here to do a job. We have done it."

"What do you normally do?"

"We raid. We are in and out before anyone knows. Much easier than this."

He shook his head and laughed, "I don't believe that for a moment."

The dead were buried close to where they fell. I gathered the papers from my dead soldiers and their identity disks. I had quite a collection. Captain Troughton spoke over all; Howards and Commandos. They had died as brothers in arms and they would lie together until the last trumpet sounded. He shook my hand. "Thank you for dropping in when you did, Sergeant. I am not certain we would have survived had you not. I have mentioned the courage of you and your men in my despatches."

"That's kind of you, sir. We were just fighting to survive and I am happy that we did."

I had Gordy, who seemed to be indestructible, collect the Bergens and the Tommy guns. I was in no doubt that, back in Blighty, both would be in short supply. My four wounded men were deemed fit enough to travel in the lorry with us rather than the ambulances for the more seriously wounded. We trundled our way north to Torbruk. I was silent. Only Gordy filled the air with inane chatter and crude jokes. Wherever we went he seemed to acquire new ones. Surprisingly the normality of Gordy and his jokes made us all feel better. It was a sign that, no matter what befell us, we were of the same mind. We had been forged in battle as a single weapon. It took us until late afternoon to reach our destination.

Torbruk bore the signs of the recent battle. It looked like the German air force had vented most of its anger on the coastal town. The harbour showed the remains of some of the ships they had sunk. A neat little doctor came to look at everyone when we left the lorries. He checked his clipboard and frowned. He saw the bandages on my men and said, "You four go in the ambulance to the hospital to get checked out."

Ken looked at me, "We are fine, aren't we lads." The other three nodded, "We'll stay with the Sergeant."

The doctor shook his head, "I am sorry, gentlemen, but rules are rules."

He looked to be a fussy little man clutching his lists and his clip board. I was in charge of these men and I would not be dictated to. "And I am sorry doctor but the needs of England are more important than your rules. We have to get these men to England as soon as possible." He hesitated in the face of my confidence. "I am happy to sign a piece of paper saying that I overrode your objections."

His face brightened, "Well in that case." He scribbled something on the sheet with my men's names and held it for me to sign. I took the pen and scrawled, *'Winston Churchill'*. He did not even look at the signature. He turned on his heels and strutted off to the next lorry. It was silly but that childish joke made me feel better or perhaps it was that my men did not want to bunk off at a base hospital. They were Commandos and wanted to fight.

While the Howards were taken east we were driven directly to the harbour where we waited while a small troop ship disgorged fresh soldiers. There were a few others being evacuated to Malta too but the ship was relatively empty. It had been a liner before it had been commandeered for the war and we had the luxury of a hot shower and better food than we had had for some time. There appeared to be no hurry to leave and, as I watched the sun set in the west I asked one of the sailors why.

"It isn't safe to leave during the day." He pointed to the destroyer which was next to us, the '*Kelly*'. "During the day, there are Jerry aeroplanes and at night E-boats and the like. The destroyer can protect us at night. During the day we would be at the bottom of the Med before we got half way."

When dawn broke we saw the island fortress that was Malta. This was in the days before that brave island had to hold out against unbelievable odds. It was a point of transit between east and west. We stood, with our Bergens on the harbour wall, wondering what was in store for us. A Jeep pulled up. A Corporal got out and saluted, "I am here to take you to the airfield Sarge."

I looked at the little Jeep. "Well we won't all fit in there will we?"

He looked at us and our bags and shook his head.

"Gordy, you go first with Lowe and Gowland. I will wait here with Curtis and Poulson."

We sat on a couple of bollards, watching the blue sea warm a little as the sun rose. "I wonder why they only sent a jeep, Sarge?"

"Perhaps they didn't know that we had brought you all with us. That little doctor might not be the only one who doesn't know how tough you lads are."

Ken nodded and threw his cigarette butt into the water, "Norm, Bill, John, and young Alan weren't so tough, were they? Or maybe they weren't lucky enough."

I nodded, "Bonaparte liked lucky men around him. I think we have been lucky. I know we lost four men on this raid but remember Sergeant Johnson's section; only two came back from one raid. If we do what we do then we can expect casualties. We managed to do the job without any losses, didn't we? It was just bad luck that they found us. Maybe it was my fault. If I hadn't taken us down that sandy road then we might not have got bogged down."

Ken laughed, "I reckon the other road would have been much more dangerous Sarge. You made the right decision but you are right, we did have a little bad luck."

George shook his head, "Maybe I am to blame. If I had been a better mechanic..."

"Now stop right there. We are Commandos and we don't blame anyone for what goes wrong. We adapt and we improvise. You are a cracking mechanic and we wouldn't have got as far as we did without you."

The self-doubt and analysis was stopped when the Jeep returned. "All aboard, Sarge."

When we reached the field, I saw that it had been bombed. There was a Blenheim at one end of the field and Hurricanes and a couple of Gloster Gladiators were spread around the sides. We were driven to the Blenheim. It was a small fast aeroplane. Dad had always liked the medium bomber. Lieutenant Marsden, complete with stick was waiting for us. He shook my hand heartily, "Well done Sergeant. Others doubted that you could have survived but I knew you would. Your father believed it too."

"Is he still here, sir?"

"No, he and the General were flown to Cairo yesterday. We are heading for Gib."

The pilot stuck his head from the cockpit. "Could you chaps continue your discussion in the bus? I want to be well clear of here before the one o'clock air raid."

We hurried aboard. Ken and the others had taken the bags and the guns. This was no Sunderland. We sat with our backs braced against the fuselage and the Bergens. Once we were airborne it was possible to talk. The Blenheim was not as noisy as a Whitley. The Lieutenant wanted to know all that he could about what had happened to us.

"I heard the bare bones; how you and the Company of infantry were attacked by armour. Then we were whisked away to Malta and heard nothing."

"Does Dad know I survived? I wouldn't want him worrying over me."

"He knows. The General himself said he wanted to be kept informed. He was much taken by you, Sergeant. Like me he couldn't understand why you weren't an officer. Surprisingly enough your dad wasn't surprised."

"That is because Dad was a Sergeant once himself. He thinks it is a learning process and you become a better officer if you have served in the ranks."

I could see that Lieutenant Marsden had never even considered that. He was what I might have been had I not dropped out of the Officer Training Course and University.

We were two hours into the flight when we were attacked. The gunner came running down from the cockpit to the turret which was in the middle. "Watch out gents. A couple of Eyeties have decided that we look like a tempting target."

We shuffled out of the way to allow him to stand and fire the twin Brownings.

As he cocked his guns I said, "I would hold onto something, sir. The pilot will have to toss and turn otherwise they will get him in his blind spot."

"Where is that?" asked the lieutenant.

The sergeant laughed, "Anywhere my guns aren't aimed at. Unless the dozy buggers are daft enough to fly in front of us."

Suddenly the two guns began to chatter. At the same time, we dived. I gripped the side of the fuselage. Ken rolled and his hand hit the Lieutenant's injured leg. I saw the officer wince but he said nothing. The Italians were persistent. The gunner looked down and said, "Can one of you lads get me another belt of ammo. It's near the tail."

I rose to my knees. "I'll get it."

Half bent I made my way back to the ammunition box and took out another two belts of the .303 ammunition. I had just turned when the pilot began to climb. I was deposited on my backside. As he levelled out I hurried back to the gunner.

He grinned, "Just in time, mate!" He loaded the guns. "It won't be long now. They will run out of ammo soon. Then I daresay they will fly back to Sicily and brag about their attack!" He shook his head as he fired another burst.

Five minutes later and the attack was over. The gunner began to walk back to the cockpit. "Now if they had been Jerries then we would have had no chance. Thank God, they were Eyeties. Gib in a couple of hours!"

Lieutenant Marsden looked in pain. "Are you all right, sir?"

"Sorry sir."

"It was not your fault, Curtis. I don't think I will be in action any time soon."

I sat opposite him, "I'm not certain any of us will be, sir."

"We will have to rebuild again, I think."

We saw a little more of Gibraltar this time. We landed in the late afternoon and were told that our transport would not be leaving until the next morning. The pilot had just landed and brought the mail for the island. We actually slept in the Rock on proper beds. It felt like luxury. The privations of the desert seemed a lifetime ago.

When we finally touched down in England the first thing we noticed was the icy blasts which chilled us to the bone. We were still wearing desert kit. We shivered in the lorry which took us back to Weymouth. We had left a half-deserted camp with barely a dozen men there. Lord Lovat and the rest of Number Four Commando had returned from their raid on the Lofoten Islands. The place was heaving and filled with excited chatter. There was an air of both excitement and ebullience. For me that was tempered by the memory of the men we had left behind us.

Epilogue

My Military Medal was waiting for me in the office. It was pinned to my chest by Lord Lovat. He was not a man who was easily impressed but he spent a good hour talking to me about my time in the Commandos. He was particularly interested in our experiences in the desert. "That is an area we will have to explore Sergeant. I would be grateful if you would write a little report for me. What sort of equipment you might need and so on."

"Will we be going back, sir?"

"Not yet. We still have much to do in Europe and your experiences will come in handy. Keep training your men as well as you have done and be ready to go at a moment's notice. We have proved that we can do the job. People will expect success now all the time. The standard will always go up!"

Reg Dean took me for a pint to celebrate. Jack Johnson joined us. "You two are being sent on a demolition course next week. Your new men won't be here for a while and your corporals can whip them into shape."

Training never stopped.

That evening I used the telephone in the Headquarters Building to ring mum. As soon as I heard her voice I felt happy. She was home; she was one of the reasons we were fighting.

"Hello mum!"

"Tom!"

"I had to ring. Dad is safe!"

"I know he rang the other day and told me." There was a pause. "He told me about you and how proud he was of what you did. He wouldn't tell me exactly what but I am guessing from what your dad said that it was dangerous."

"No more dangerous than living with the fear of bombers day in and day out. Anyway, I am back now and I just rang to tell you that."

"Dad says he will be home by summer. His work there is nearly done. It will be nice if you can come home too. You must be due some leave."

"In the Commandos, mum, you never know when you will get leave but I promise I will try."

As I walked back to the digs I knew that it would be highly unlikely that I would be home for a leave that summer. We were Commandos and we were the ones who could hit back at Hitler and his Fortress Europe. We would raid and raid again. The little pinpricks were all we could do for the moment but I knew that one day we would return to France and it would be Commandos who would lead.

The End

Glossary

Butchers- Look (Cockney slang Butcher's Hook- Look)

Butties- sandwiches (slang)

Chah- tea (slang)

Comforter- the lining for the helmet; a sort of woollen hat

Corned dog- Corned Beef (slang)

Fruit salad- medal ribbons (slang)

Gash- spare (slang)

Gib- Gibraltar (slang)

Goon- Guard in a POW camp (slang)- comes from a 1930s Popeye cartoon

MGB- Motor Gun Boat

MTB- Motor Torpedo Boat

ML- Motor Launch

Oik- worthless person (slang)

Oppo/oppos- pals/comrades (slang)

Killick- leading hand (Navy) (slang)

Potato mashers- German Hand Grenades (slang)

QM- Quarter Master (stores)

Recce- Reconnoitre (slang)

SBA- Sick Bay Attendant

Schnellboote -German for E-boat (literally fast boat)

Scragging - roughing someone up (slang)

Scrumpy- farm cider

squaddy- ordinary soldier (slang)

Stag- sentry duty (slang)

Stand your corner- get a round of drinks in (slang)

Tommy (Atkins)- Ordinary British soldier

Two penn'orth- two pennies worth (slang for opinion)

WVS- Women's Voluntary Service

Maps

Western Desert Battle Area1941 en" by Stephen Kirrage talk - contribs - Own work. Licensed under CC BY-SA 3.0 via Wikimedia Commons - https://commons.wikimedia.org/wiki/File:WesternDesertBattle_Area1941_en.svg#/media/File: WesternDesertBattle_Area1941_en.svg

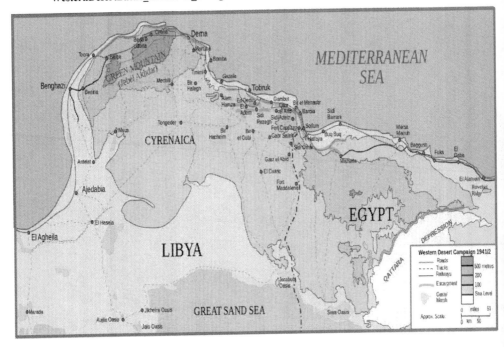

Historical note

The first person I would like to thank for this particular book and series is my dad. He was in the Royal Navy but served in Combined Operations. He was at Dieppe, D-Day and Walcheren. His boat: LCA 523 was the one which took in the French Commandos on D-Day. He was proud that his ships had taken in Bill Millens and Lord Lovat. I wish that, before he died I had learned more in detail about life in Combined Operations but like many heroes he was reluctant to speak of the war. He is the character in the book called Bill Leslie. I went back in 1994, with my dad to Sword beach and he took me through that day on June 6th 1944. We even found the grave of his cousin George Hogan who died on D-Day. As far as I know we were the only members of the family ever to do so. Sadly, that was dad's only visit but we planted forget-me-nots on the grave of George.

I would also like to thank Roger who is my railway expert. The train Tom and the Major catch from Paddington to Oswestry ran until 1961. The details of the livery, the compartments and the engine are all, hopefully accurate. I would certainly not argue with Roger!

I used a number of books in the research. The list is at the end of this historical section. However, the best book, by far, was the actual Commando handbook which was reprinted in 2012. All of the details about hand to hand, explosives, esprit de corps etc were taken directly from it. The advice about salt, oatmeal and water is taken from the book. It even says that taking too much salt is not a bad thing! I shall use the book as a Bible for the rest of the series. The Commandos were expected to find their own accommodation. Some even saved the money for lodgings and slept rough. That did not mean that standards of discipline and presentation were neglected; they were not.

German Panzer Mk. 2 used in the Low Countries. 20 mm gun and machine gun in rotating turret. Photograph courtesy of Wikipedia.

The 1st Loyal Lancashire existed as a regiment. They were in the BEF and they were the rear guard. All the rest is the work of the author's imagination. The use of booby traps using grenades was common. The details of the German potato masher grenade are also accurate. The Germans used the grenade as an early warning system by hanging them from fences so that an intruder would move the grenade and it would explode. The Mills bomb had first been used in the Great War. It threw shrapnel for up to one hundred yards. When thrown the thrower had to take cover too. However, my Uncle Norman, who survived Dunkirk was demonstrating a grenade with an instructor kneeling next to him. It was a faulty grenade and exploded in my uncle's hand. Both he and the Sergeant survived. My uncle just lost his hand. I am guessing that my uncle's hand prevented the grenade fragmenting as much as it was intended. Rifle grenades were used from 1915 onwards and enabled a grenade to be thrown much further than by hand

During the retreat the British tank, the Matilda was superior to the German Panzers. It was slow but it was so heavily armoured that it could only be stopped by using the 88 anti-aircraft guns. Had there been more of them and had they been used in greater numbers then who knows what the outcome might have been. What they did succeed in doing, however, was making the German High Command believe that we had more tanks than they actually encountered. The Germans thought that the 17 Matildas they fought were many times that number. They halted at Arras for reinforcements. That enabled the Navy to take off over 300,000 men from the beaches.

Although we view Dunkirk as a disaster now, at the time it was seen as a setback. An invasion force set off to reinforce the French a week after Dunkirk. It was recalled. Equally there were many units cut off behind enemy lines. The Highland Division was one such force. 10,000 men were captured. The fate of many of those captured in the early days of the war was to be sent to work in factories making weapons which would be used against England.

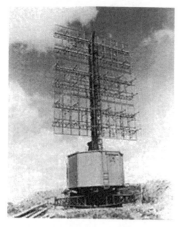

Freya, the German Radar.

Germany had radar stations and they were accurate. They also had large naval guns at Cape Gris Nez as well as railway guns. They made the Channel dangerous although they only actually sank a handful of ships during the whole of the war. They did however make Southend and Kent dangerous places to live.

Commando dagger

The E-Boats were far superior to the early MTBs and Motor Launches. It was not until the Fairmile boats were developed that the tide swung in the favour of the Royal Navy. Some MTBs were fitted with depth charges. Bill's improvisation is the sort of thing Combined Operations did. It could have ended in disaster but in this case, it did not.

The first Commando raids were a shambles. Churchill himself took action and appointed Sir Roger Keyes to bring some order to what the Germans called thugs and killers. Major Foster and his troop reflect that change.

The parachute training for Commandos was taken from this link http://www.bbc.co.uk/history/ww2peopleswar/stories/72/a3530972.shtml . Thank you to Thomas Davies. The Number 2 Commandos were trained as a battalion and became the Airborne Division eventually. The SOE also trained at Ringway but they were secreted away at an Edwardian House, Bowden. As a vaguely related fact 43 out of 57 SOE agents sent to France between June 1942 and Autumn 1943 were captured, 36 were executed!

The details about the Commando equipment are also accurate. They were issued with American weapons although some did use the Lee Enfield. When large numbers attacked the Lofoten Islands they used regular army issue. The Commandos appeared in dribs and drabs but 1940 was the year when they began their training. It was Lord Lovat who gave them a home in Scotland but that was not until 1941. I wanted my hero, Tom, to begin to fight early. His adventures will continue throughout the war.

The raid on German Headquarters is based on an attempt by Number 3 Commando to kill General Erwin Rommel. In a real life version of *'The Eagle Has Landed'* they almost succeeded. They went in by lorry. Commandos were used extensively in the early desert war but, sadly, many of them perished in Greece and Cyprus and Crete. Of 800 sent to Crete only 200 returned to Egypt. Churchill also compounded his mistake of supporting Greece by sending all 300 British tanks to the Western Desert and the Balkans. The map shows the area where Tom and the others fled. The Green Howards were not in that part of the desert at that time. The Germans did begin to reinforce their allies at the start of 1941.

JU 52 Courtesy of Wikipedia

Motor launch Courtesy of Wikipedia

Motor Gun Boat Courtesy of Wikipedia

Short Sunderland
Bunks and galley

Short Sunderland:

Reference Books used

The Commandos Pocket Manual 1949-45- Christopher Westhorp

The Second World War Miscellany- Norman Ferguson

Army Commandos 1940-45- Mike Chappell

Military Slang- Lee Pemberton

World War II- Donald Sommerville

St Nazaire 1942-Ken Ford

Dieppe 1942- Ken Ford

The Historical Atlas of World War II-Swanston and Swanston

The Battle of Britain- Hough and Richards

The Hardest Day- Price

Griff Hosker August 2015

Other books

by

Griff Hosker

If you enjoyed reading this book, then why not read another one by the author?

Ancient History

The Sword of Cartimandua Series (Germania and Britannia 50A.D. – 128 A.D.)

Ulpius Felix- Roman Warrior (prequel)

Book 1 The Sword of Cartimandua

Book 2 The Horse Warriors

Book 3 Invasion Caledonia

Book 4 Roman Retreat

Book 5 Revolt of the Red Witch

Book 6 Druid's Gold

Book 7 Trajan's Hunters

Book 8 The Last Frontier

Book 9 Hero of Rome

Book 10 Roman Hawk

Book 11 Roman Treachery

Book 12 Roman Wall

The Aelfraed Series (Britain and Byzantium 1050 A.D. - 1085 A.D.

Book 1 Housecarl

Book 2 Outlaw

Book 3 Varangian

The Wolf Warrior series (Britain in the late 6th Century)

Book 1 Saxon Dawn

Book 2 Saxon Revenge

Book 3 Saxon England

Book 4 Saxon Blood

Book 5 Saxon Slayer

Book 6 Saxon Slaughter

Book 7 Saxon Bane

Book 8 Saxon Fall: Rise of the Warlord

Book 9 Saxon Throne

The Dragon Heart Series

Book 1 Viking Slave

Book 2 Viking Warrior

Book 3 Viking Jarl

Book 4 Viking Kingdom

Book 5 Viking Wolf

Book 6 Viking War

Book 7 Viking Sword

Book 8 Viking Wrath

Book 9 Viking Raid

Book 10 Viking Legend

Book 11 Viking Vengeance

Book 12 Viking Dragon

Book 13 Viking Treasure

Book 14 Viking Enemy

Book 15 Viking Witch

Bool 16 Viking Blood

Book 17 Viking Weregeld

Book 18 Viking Storm

The Norman Genesis Series

Rolf

Horseman

The Battle for a Home

Revenge of the Franks

The Land of the Northmen

Ragnvald Hrolfsson

The Anarchy Series England 1120-1180

English Knight

Knight of the Empress

Northern Knight

Baron of the North

Earl

King Henry's Champion

The King is Dead

Warlord of the North

Enemy at the Gate

Warlord's War

Kingmaker

Henry II

Crusader

The Welsh Marches

Border Knight 1190-1300
Sword for Hire

Modern History
The Napoleonic Horseman Series
Book 1 Chasseur a Cheval

Book 2 Napoleon's Guard

Book 3 British Light Dragoon

Book 4 Soldier Spy

Book 5 1808: The Road to Corunna

Waterloo

The Lucky Jack American Civil War series
Rebel Raiders

Confederate Rangers

The Road to Gettysburg

The British Ace Series
1914

1915 Fokker Scourge

1916 Angels over the Somme

1917 Eagles Fall

1918 We will remember them

From Arctic Snow to Desert Sand

Combined Operations series 1940-1945

Commando

Raider

Behind Enemy Lines

Dieppe

Toehold in Europe

Sword Beach

Breakout

The Battle for Antwerp

King Tiger

Beyond the Rhine

Other Books

Carnage at Cannes (a thriller)

Great Granny's Ghost (Aimed at 9-14-year-old young people)

Adventure at 63-Backpacking to Istanbul

For more information on all of the books then please visit the author's web site at http://www.griffhosker.com where there is a link to contact him.